THEIR MAGICIAN

and

OTHER STORIES

GLORIA KURIAN BRODER

THEIR MAGICIAN

and

OTHER STORIES

For Diana

with many
many good
wishes

Gloria

HANDSEL BOOKS

an imprint of
Other Press • New York

Permission to reprint from the following is gratefully acknowledged:

"Elena, Unfaithful" originally published in *Harper's Magazine*, 1971; anthologized in *Great American Love Stories*, Little, Brown, Boston, 1988.

"Careers and Marriages" originally published by *Carleton Miscellany*, Northfield, MN, 1980.

"The Intruder" originally published by *Kingfisher*, Berkeley, CA, 1987.

"The Insult" originally published by *Kingfisher*, Berkeley, CA, 1988.

"First Love" originally published by *96, Inc.*, Boston, 1993.

"The Thursday Men's Club" originally published by *Bellevue Literary Review*, New York, 2004.

"The Man Who Loved Detroit" originally published in *Ploughshares*, Cambridge, MA, 1988.

"Staff of Life" originally published by *Kingfisher*, Berkeley, CA, 1989.

"Hero" originally published by *96, Inc.*, Boston, 1994.

"Their Magician" originally published by *Literary Imagination*, Athens, GA, 2005.

"How Lovely Thy Branches" originally published by *Kingfisher*, Berkeley, CA, 1991.

Production Editor: Robert D. Hack
Text design: Natalya Balnova
This book was set in Janson Text by Alpha Graphics of Pittsfield, NH.

10 9 8 7 6 5 4 3 2 1

Library of Congress Cataloging-in-Publication Data

Broder, Gloria Kurian.
  Their magician and other stories / by Gloria Kurian Broder.
      p. cm.
  ISBN 1-59051-166-2 (hardcover : alk. paper)
  I. Title.
  PS3552.R6194T48 2005
  813'.54–dc22

                                    2004018870

For Bill

ACKNOWLEDGMENTS

I'd like to express my deep thanks to Robert Mezey who brought my manuscript to Handsel Books; to my children Tanya and Adam who read the stories and laughed; to Philip Levine who, through the years, improved many pages; and to Nancy Packer for her always valuable suggestions. I am grateful to my editor Harry Thomas of Handsel Books/ Other Press for his kindness and charm and courtly support of the book; and also to the publisher Judith Gurewich and the staff of Other Press whose enthusiasm and spirited efforts carried the stories to publication.

TABLE OF CONTENTS

ELENA, UNFAITHFUL

Alexei Sazevitch leapt out of the barber's chair and looked into the mirror after his haircut, and when he saw that he was exceptionally handsome for his age, he decided to retire. From his office he placed a call to his childhood friend, André, who lived in Paris, and said, "I'm stopping this nonsense, André. From now on I intend to spend all my time with Elena.

"She's getting younger and prettier," he told André, though in fact he thought she was getting older and homelier. After that, he descended a long flight of stairs to the office of a man he knew only slightly, but who was also a Russian by birth and an engineer, and leaning on the man's desk with the palms of his hands, he confided, "Rothkovitch . . . Rothkovitch . . . I have four children—Arianne, Eva, Ilya, and Katya. They are all grown and out of the house now, thank God, and my wife is not growing any younger or thinner; she's not like you and me"—he punched Rothkovitch in the stomach and planted a cigar in Rothkovitch's pocket— "so I've decided to stop all this and retire."

Finally, Alexei gave his secretary a silk scarf, a scarf unusual for being so long. After she had unwound it and wound it up again, Alexei noisily kissed her on the mouth and tossed her in the direction of the radiator. Forcefully he grasped and shook the hands of the rest of his staff and at last went down in the elevator carrying his framed diplomas; a silver plaque for designing the Elgar Bridge; two brass cups for jumping overboard and saving lives at the scene of that bridge; a wedding picture of his mother and father; and a large, embossed, half-eaten box of Ghirardelli chocolates. He put all of these in the back seat of his Bentley and drove through Detroit, cruising one-handedly through streets arched over with dust-laden trees and factory-filtered sunlight, past tight rows of brick-faced houses offering their ancient, cracked, cement porches, out into the raw, bleak avenues of tire and automotive supply stores, and finally beyond, to his own neighborhood of wide and utterly isolated lawns.

"Elena, Elena," he shouted at the front door. And when his wife appeared, he greeted her: "From this moment on, my darling girl, I will spend each and every moment at home with you!"

At these words it seemed to him that Elena's eyes started up and that she turned peculiarly pale. But he was altogether unprepared when, two days later, she took ill and died. The entire family went to the funeral and the priest read a eulogy.

Alexei could not believe anything like this had happened. He caught a cold and felt numb. All the same, grief—which he did not like, which he had always hidden from—threatened to visit him, while terrible questions pushed their way into his clogged mind, such as, had he, during his and Elena's forty-five years together, treated her well enough for a European husband of average morality who was the head of his house and irresistible to women? On her last birthday, had he written a large enough check to Products for the Blind? And why had he gone fishing with his friend, Vassily, and their redheaded, then their brunette, mistresses on the very day that his second daughter, Eva, was born? The following year when Ilya was born? Two mornings after the premature arrival of Katya, and exactly one week later, on the Fourth of July?

Alexei blamed his naïveté most of all. He had thought, initially, that his children would somehow look better. But no, in the early years he had always seemed to come upon them sitting on the linoleum in the pantry in wet snowsuits, holding out their swathed and dripping arms. "Papa, Papa," they would urge, while he would take a few steps back and as a young father observe that they had features he had not wholly counted on, mannerisms he was not prepared for. From the very beginning, Arianne was too awkward, Eva too mean, Ilya too pulling, and Katya unaccountably squashy and low to the ground.

"Think of the poor," Elena sang to them in their cradles, training them for good deeds. "Think of the poor," she warned them, each time he took off for a weekend. Busily, she sent forth baskets of fruit and new shoes, mailed out letters to the city council, and steadily brought in painting after painting of hefty-looking fruit, which she bought from starving artists. Nor was he, Alexei, exempt either, for each time he headed for the door, carrying suitcases, Elena would unlock his fingers, hold both of his hands, gaze into his eyes and say, "Alexei Mihailovitch, think once more about the poor." On these occasions he understood she spoke about herself.

Had it been all his fault then, he wondered. Was there time to start anew? His cold got better, his head cleared, and for a brief time he faced the fact that Elena had died; but he was a man who had always hidden from unhappiness, who now grew aware that a terrible horizon of pain waited in the distance for him like a bank of fog. Massing together, it thickened and inexorably moved closer. In his sleep he moaned; he called out for Elena, and awoke each day feeling drugged and dizzy. Then in the middle of one night Birdie, the old housekeeper, brought him ice water, and after drinking it he fell asleep and dreamed of love, of youth, of bands of handsome, free, unfettered people moving along the banks of a rich, green river. Violets and poppies embroidered the meadows and a scent of lilac inundated the air while he—only he could not be certain it was he—and Elena danced, wandering amidst it all. In the morning he woke up feeling sensual, played upon, vulnerable to desire; and with the idea that something miraculous had happened, he got out of bed, crossed the carpeted bedroom, thrust open the windows, and looking lightheartedly out onto Elena's garden, understood in the sweet, wild, and pungent summer air that Elena Petrovna had not died after all: she had simply run off with another man—very likely with a man who still worked—and she was happy.

Tears of gratitude glistened in Alexei's eyes. A photograph of Elena stood on the dresser. "Look at you!" he exclaimed, pressing the cardboard between his fingers. "Fifty pounds overweight, hair in braids like my great-grandmother, bags under your eyes, forever taking your shoes off and leaving them where I can trip—unable to wear a pair of shoes comfortably for more than five minutes—talking on and on about Congress, the wars, the poor—and yet . . . yet I've misjudged you. I've never fully known what you are!"

He kissed the photograph, leaving wet marks, put it down, opened Elena's closet and looked in. Except for a strange umbrella and a folding chair, it was empty. She had taken all of her clothes, he thought, which was just as well since she did not own very many. His own wardrobe exceeded hers by ten times.

Alexei went to the phone. He wanted to ring up people and tell them his news. He would say to Vassily, "Vassily, just think of it—Elena's going off like that. Isn't it unusual, isn't it ironic!" But as luck would have it, he had recently kicked Vassily out of his house. And then, he debated, if he placed a call to André, there was a good chance André might misjudge his marriage—after all, they had not seen each other in thirty years. As for his children, they doted and depended on their mother much too much: finally he did not wish to cause them any pain.

His hand still on the phone, for a moment Alexei considered telling the lady in the bakery whose blue, fractured eyes already held the knowledge of hundreds, perhaps even thousands, of different lives. Unfortunately, he thought, he did not know that lady. He took the umbrella from Elena's closet and went downstairs, still wearing his robe. Through the double glass doors that led into the living room he saw Birdie dusting the furniture with a feather duster, her hand moving like a pendulum as she mechanically turned here and there, touching the worn, rose-colored satin settee and couches, the samovar on the coffee table, the mended china lamps and clocks. He opened the glass doors and stepped in, then stepped out as a smell of stale oranges and apples rushed at him from the framed pictures of fruit on all the walls. Stepping in again, he shut the glass doors behind him.

"Birdie," he said, thinking perhaps she should be the first to know. After all, she had helped diaper and she had stuck pins, he conjectured, into all four of his children. For that alone she deserved something: should he clap her on the back and shout into her good ear, "Birdie, you old vixen, you demon! Just guess what your mistress has gone and done!" He decided not. She would not believe him; worse still, she might say nothing at all.

"Birdie, whose umbrella is this?"

She took it from him and looked at it for a long time. "It's Arianne. She left it here last week, when it rained." Then she walked past him with the umbrella, which she put in a closet in the front hall.

"Arianne!" he exclaimed; Arianne, he thought. Why hadn't he singled her out from the others? She was his eldest daughter, the only one at whose birth he'd been present, the only child who had grown up as tall as he, with shoulders practically as broad; who beat him at badminton, who was more of a son to him than his other daughters or his son, and who could match him drink for drink at family gatherings until late in the night, when they would smile at one another, clasp their arms about each other's powerful shoulders, and loudly chorus "Auld Lang Syne."

He rushed to the phone in the den, and when she answered in the familiar, hearty voice that cracked in between syllables due to hoarseness and the headlong intensity of her good will, he leaned way back in the swivel chair behind the desk, stretched out his legs, and to the ceiling trilled out, "A–ri–anne, A–ri—anne!"

"Papa, I'm glad you called. I was just about to call and ask you how things are."

"They're wonderful."

"I'm glad to hear that."

"Yes, they're perfect," he offered again, happy with such an exchange. Arianne, he thought, smiling broadly, was always cheerful. Unfortunately this virtue had also become her failing. It even showed on her physically, he allowed, for although up to the neck she stood as proudly as a colt or soldier, her head with its close-cropped, curly, dark hair tended to droop and on her gaunt and pleasant face loomed the resigned and tragic expression of one who can never publicly come up with any but jovial things to say.

"How are your husband and children?" he asked her.

"We're all first-rate."

"Excellent. How is the dog?"

"Getting much better. Thank you very much for asking."

"How is the cat?"

"Papa, uh . . . we don't have a cat."

"Never mind then; forget that I asked you." He leaned into the phone. "Arianne, I have something to tell you." A surge of anticipation welled up inside of him. "Your mother's gone . . . she's gone . . . shopping." His heart sank; he felt that he had failed. He let out his breath.

There was silence for a few moments and then Arianne shouted with no crack in her voice this time, "Papa, what did you say?"

"I said she's gone shopping." The statement sounded plausible enough to him except, of course, that everyone knew Elena never went shopping; it was always he who spent his spare time riding escalators in search of the latest, most elegant accessory from Italy or France.

"Papa, what did you say?"

"She's gone . . ." unsuccessfully, he tried again, "she's gone shopping."

"Listen, Papa, don't think about it. You have a point. Don't think about it and I'll come see you at two this afternoon. You have a point. There are good sales all over town. There are excellent sales in all the shopping centers." She hung up.

Downcast, Alexei remained seated at the desk, thinking that if only he had been able to tell Arianne the truth about her mother, he might have been able to tell her more—such as the differences between some of his competitors' work on bridges and his own work; and how Vassily, after marrying a dreadful woman too late in his life, had forgotten the names of all their mistresses. Subsequently he and Vassily had had nothing to talk about; they'd quarreled over cards; at last Alexei threw him out of the door.

Brooding stonily in the swivel chair, Alexei turned prey to old irritations. Why, he wondered—as he had often wondered—why had Arianne, on the morning before her marriage, jumped into her mother's lap and remained there for half an hour when she was twice the size of Elena and might just as easily have jumped into his? Rehearsing these tales, Alexei's eyes began to flicker, his fingers to touch and move an ashtray, a letter opener on the desk, until all at once he grew impatient, jumped up and ran into the front hall.

"Breakfast, Birdie," he called, "right after my shower." He climbed the stairs, turned on the water in the bathroom, went into the bedroom and slid open the door of his wall-to-wall beloved closet. At this instant, the phone rang.

"Father?"

"Eva?"

"I hear that mother's gone shopping."

Eva's voice, suspicious and complaining at best, now snapped and accused. Alexei held the receiver a distance from his ear and inured himself by gazing at the orderly array of suits, trousers, jackets, vests, and coats that hung from wall to wall, harmoniously arranged by color. It was a sight he found soothing and peaceful, but which angered Eva, for whenever she visited the house, after she had eaten up all the scraps in the icebox, opened and searched in every drawer for childhood mementos, stormed abstractly through the basement and sniffed into the attic, she invariably ended up by confronting his clothes.

"Fifty-one suits," she would declare, pointing to them with a long, ink-stained, crooked finger. "It's disgusting. Give some to the poor!"

"But they're not for the poor," Alexei would inform her, very simply, "they're for me."

Sometimes Katya would follow her sister to Alexei's closet. Katya was the baby. She was plump, with chubby upper arms Alexei liked to pinch. She had a small, cupid's face with hair planted on top of her head like a robin's nest; she had short legs and wore long dresses with uneven hems; and instead of becoming a ballet dancer, as Alexei had hoped, she had gone petulantly, yet unhesitatingly into social work. Hair pins fell from her head, and like Eva she said, "Give some to the poor."

And on occasion Ilya would wander in and, standing with his nose comfortably inside Alexei's closet and his hands on his hips, would inquire with a show of great kindness and concern, "Papa, what are you trying to prove? Why do you have so many clothes?" Alexei would answer, "Why do you have a moustache? Why, in these ecologically troubled times, do you have nine children? Why do you always only act in plays by Gorki?"—to which Ilya would raise his head high and, with heartfelt sincerity and the voice projection of an actor, solemnly intone, "At least I don't have so many clothes."

"What," Eva now pursued, as she liked her facts to fit, "what did mother go shopping for?"

Alexei frowned into the phone. "For?" An expression of pride—self-loving and stubborn—chiseled itself onto Alexei's face. He lifted his chin and reflected. "For shoes. Stockings. A dress. A purse." He paused. He leaned against the bedroom wall and crossed his ankles. "A hat. Some gloves. A bottle of perfume. You ought to go shopping yourself." He referred, as he knew she understood quite well, to the fact that she always wore an old serape and sandals and drove a camper truck with a broken muffler, and beyond that to the greater facts: that she taught in a ghetto school with hungry, angry dedication; that she stared glassily at him through thick lenses while clutching an enormous guitar; that she was bowlegged, vast-hipped, militant about women's rights, middle-aged, and had never married; and that more than any of the others, she had been influenced by her mother, but did not have her mother's grace.

Yet the tone of her voice suddenly softened. "Listen, Papa, tell me something. Have you been feeling yourself? How have you been feeling? Father . . . Papa, I think I'll come sleep at home tonight. Tell Birdie to put out fresh sheets."

"No, no, no, no!"

"Why not?"

"No, no!"

"I'd like to."

"I think . . . it occurs to me," he recovered from her offer, "there's no need to." He smiled and murmured gallantly into the phone, "After all, my dear, you have your own apartment, your own little kitty cats, your guitar . . ."

"What I think," Eva said, "is that I'll pick Ilya up at the airport at one. That's when his plane comes in."

"Ilya?" For an instant he panicked. "Where's Ilya been?"

"Chicago. Don't you remember? In a play. He's been there for two weeks."

Alexei felt both relief and annoyance. "Gorki again. Why does Ilya only act in plays by old Russians? Why doesn't he act in something modern, up-to-date?"

"Right after that," Eva went on, ignoring him, "I'll stop by for Katya at her work and we'll come to you around two."

"All of you?" Alexei objected.

"All of us," Eva confirmed, and added before hanging up, "Arianne said she'd drive over at the same time."

This plan depressed Alexei. He showered and dressed, thinking that his children were coming to see him. What could he do with them? He came down the stairs, shouting, "Breakfast, Birdie, breakfast!" and went into the living room to wait. Opening the double glass doors, he stepped on figured rugs that lay on top of the heavy carpet. He glanced about. Pictures of glossy fruit—one of peaches and pears, one of plums and pears, one of plums and apples, and one simply of bananas—painted by artists, each one more poor, he guessed, than the others—hung on three thick, ivory walls, while at the windows heavy drapes kept out the light, the air. He had never liked this room. He had often told his family it was too old-fashioned, too Russian, and they had answered that they *were* Russian. Each time he came home from an illicit weekend, he had wanted to tear out walls, put in a bold expanse of vinyl floor and a sleek, white modern couch. But

Elena pleaded that he had his office and his outings and that this was her room. She began to go out less and less. She grew heavier, closer to life, less willing to keep on her shoes. Neighbors, teachers, other Europeans, and her own four children came to see her—brought her their troubles as she sat on the worn, rose-colored settee, listening through long winter afternoons, her shoes paired next to her and two bunions on her toes. While she listened, her fingers peeled and divided an orange, and he remembered that her lips would first purse together as if they could taste each trouble and then grow round as if they were labeling and judging the trouble as "pretty good" or "pretty bad." After that, her manner changed. She gave advice. Handing around sections of the fruit, she tossed her head, her black eyes gleamed like a girl's amidst their bed of wrinkles, a high color rose to her flat cheeks, and even her chins—her grand and battered chins—jumped about with a certain ebullience and style.

Watching her in those last few years, Alexei's throat had closed; he had wanted those bursts of animation for himself. At the same time he eyed her audience, wondering if her opinions had come to be more respected than his own. How could that be? He, after all, had built fifteen bridges and designed six exhibits in the 1939 New York World's Fair where, whenever he turned around, one hundred beautiful women seemed to be concentrating raptly on him. And yet just this past spring, unable to make his presence felt, he had shouted into a group of acquaintances and strangers, "Let me talk, let me talk" and then, overcome with shame, with chagrin, had quit the room, fled up the stairs, and placed a call—for no good reason—to André in Paris.

Alexei gazed at the rose-colored settee. It was empty: Elena was not there; and yet he seemed to hear her say, "Alexei, let's not eat cake, let's eat bread." She said it liltingly, with humor and in the voice of her youth, the same voice that had promised him a sweet, judging, shrewd frivolity forever—and then betrayed him.

At breakfast, Alexei ate in the dining room, alone, his eyes fixed on the buffet opposite him. Lifting his spoon, he reflected that inside those carved and massive drawers, both his and Elena's family silver was stored and lay together, rested side by side—a fact that struck him as so peculiarly intimate and fitting that briefly he faced the idea that Elena had died. But he got up at once and went into the den. Like the other rooms in the downstairs of the house, the den was dark and heavily carpeted. Drapes and venetian blinds hung at the windows. Two brown leather couches, a charcoal drawing of mangoes, and a desk lined the walls. In the center of the desk stood an immense world globe, its roundness and airiness, its light-blue color and the fact that it so easily revolved, making it a focal point in the room. Spinning the globe, Alexei's fingers caught at Rome, St. Tropez, at Venice, and impulsively, as though he were proposing some marvelous vacation by the sea, he urged out loud, "Elena, let's be young again!" The sound of his voice shocked him and he retreated up the stairs.

There, looking out the window over Elena's garden, he again smelled honeysuckle, saw fresh primroses, orchids, and daisies, and was once more reassured that Elena had run off with another man and was happy. He phoned the bakery and requested that they send up a cake. Then he lay down on the bed and fell deeply asleep.

When he awoke, he remembered that his children were coming to see him, and he felt pleased. He changed his shirt and brushed his hair. On the landing he met Birdie as she inched her way up for an afternoon nap, her bald head ringed round with ancient markings. They exchanged awareness of each other but no words and Alexei continued down, saw in the kitchen that his cake had arrived and transferred it to a crystal platter.

At two o'clock he stood outside the front door and heard Eva's broken muffler in the distance. Presently the camper came into view and Eva maneuvered the vehicle up the driveway, her head craned out one window of the cab, Ilya's head protruding out the other window, and Katya in between them, staring straight ahead. A few houses down, Arianne parked her VW by the curb and ran at a gallop until she joined the others. The four of them headed up the path. They called, "Papa . . . Papa."

Eva confronted him first. Clasping her guitar with one hand, she removed her glasses with the other and lunged

at him, timing her kiss so that it landed in the air. At this
she looked wounded and angry, as if it were somehow all
his fault. He gazed closely at her, struck as always by the
beauty, not of her features, which were coarse, but of her
translucent, pearly skin. She had, if nothing else, inherited
his grandmother's complexion. He said to her, "Try
again."

Surprised, Eva obeyed and then stepped back, tripping
on her guitar. Katya took her place. She, too, appeared
surprised by Alexei's order. Katya stood on tiptoe. Delicately she bestowed on her father a sweet and prissy peck,
then turned her head away. As she was still his baby, this
greeting—ambiguous though it was—pleased and undid
him a bit. "Katya," he said. "But why are you so thin?"

"I've lost weight."

"Ah, Katya," he mourned, wondering if her husband
beat her. He felt in his pocket for a piece of candy and at
the same time noticed that her hair had turned entirely
gray. "Ah, Katya, you've lost too much weight. You look
like a cobweb."

"I've lost," she corrected him, proud and plaintive at
once, "the right amount."

"Then never mind," he told her, comforting them
both and dismissing her, for behind Katya, Ilya pushed for
his turn, and behind Ilya he saw his tall and self-effacing
Arianne, a brown paper bag in her hand—doubtless it contained brandy—who registered his awareness of her by
signaling above the heads of the others in a voice that

croaked like a frog's, "It's a most beautiful day, Papa—it's a most beautiful day in summer!"

"Arianne . . . Ilya . . . Katya . . . Eva . . . I'm so happy to see all of you!"

"And we're so happy to see you," said Ilya, stepping forward. He took both of his father's hands in his and stared intently into his father's eyes as if trying to glean from them something vital and unknown. His moustache quivered.

Uncertain as to what Ilya wanted, Alexei said, "Your mother isn't home."

"We understand," said Ilya.

"She'll be back quite late. But what I have for you is . . ."

"We understand," Ilya said. "She's gone shopping."

"She's gone shopping," said Katya.

"She's gone shopping," Arianne confirmed.

Alexei felt uncomfortable, but overcame it. "Come in, come in," he said, holding the door open. "What I have for you is . . . I have some very excellent cake. Birdie didn't make it. Your mother didn't make it either. I got this exceptional cake by ordering it from the bakery." He led them through the front hall, the dining room, and turned to face them by the kitchen. "As you will see, it is chocolate and has icing out of spun sugar and flowers and other such decorations." Flute-like, his fingers gestured in the air to convey the ambience of such a cake: its roses, its sugared avenues and lanes, the possibility of castles. "Now who will help me? Katya, put on coffee. Eva, bring out cups and plates. What else do we need? Napkins. Did I forget napkins? Ilya, see if you can find some napkins."

Alexei carried the cake into the living room, carefully set it down on the dark wood of the inlaid coffee table and sat down in the center of the rose-colored settee in what had always been Elena's place. He bent down to remove his shoes, but straightened up again, feeling foolish. His children arranged themselves in a semicircle around him and appeared fascinated. They had an air of being welcome strangers. Conscious of their mood, Alexei sliced the first piece of cake and meticulously placed it in the perfect center of a plate. He sliced a second, third, and fourth piece and handed these around. He had, he supposed, never served his children before and yet now, in Elena's absence, it seemed absolutely proper and what he wanted.

He watched as they began to eat: Eva avidly gobbled, Katya licked, Arianne chewed awkwardly, getting crumbs caught between her teeth and claiming she had never tasted anything better. As for Ilya, his cake went into his mouth and simply disappeared. Alexei smiled. A sense of satisfaction and fulfillment swept subtly over him. He decided he would call for his children's spouses, even all his grandchildren, despite their bad manners and unkempt hair.

To pave the way he said, "I think . . . it occurs to me . . . I have something to tell you. Your mother's run off . . . with a lover."

"Oh, Papa!" all of them scolded at once and Katya added, "Stop it!"

"Don't worry, Katya. It will be a nice change for her; it will do her good."

Arianne objected, "Papa, she wouldn't do such a thing."

Ilya said, "I thought you told us she went shopping."

Katya cried out indignantly, "Listen to that! Have you ever heard such a thing! It's too much! I can't bear it!"

Through thick glasses Eva eyed him steadily and warned, "You'd better be careful, Father. You'd better stay off that track. Go back to shopping."

"But I don't understand," Alexei told them, shrugging. "You act as if your mother isn't capable of having a lover when, after all, she's like everyone else in this world; she's as capable of carrying on . . . of enjoying herself . . . as you and me."

"No more, no more!" Katya wailed. She stamped her foot. "One more word and I'll scream."

But Alexei could not stop himself. "Most likely this is not her first lover. Indeed, there is good reason to think," he went on, lifting a speculative finger into the air, "that your mother has had many different lovers in the past. Perhaps some of them were social workers, community workers, teachers, even psychologists—yet they were lovers all the same." But even as he said this—even as he recognized its hollow sound—he knew he had gone too far.

Ilya stood up and faced his father. A sound of muffled choking issued from his throat. From his moustache came a whistle like a train's. "Murderer!" he accused. Katya fell out of her chair, sideways, and began to sob. Dragging her guitar behind her, Eva started to pace, agitatedly marching up and down the length of the room and in a cold, even voice summing up: "You never deserved her. You never thought of anyone but yourself!"

Of the four, only Arianne approached her father. She put a long, large-boned arm around him and tried to chuckle. "You're mistaken, Papa. She wouldn't do that, you know. She couldn't do that." But then, as if suddenly overcome, she moved off to a corner behind the fireplace, dropped into an armchair and covered her face with her hands.

Eva continued pacing and narrating, "You never tried to understand her. She was a saint, a free spirit." From the floor, Katya sent up sharp yelps. Eva stepped over her and went on, "You never cared enough for her . . . or for us. You were always too vain, too arrogant, too unfeeling." Ilya, who had remained rooted to the same spot, his face pale, his neck livid, now grabbed hold of the cake knife, brandished it in the air, gnashed his teeth violently and cut himself another piece of cake. He then left the room and went into the den to phone his wife. Katya crawled after him; she phoned her office.

Reentering the living room together, the two of them looked about, preparing to resume their angry postures. But in that dim, enclosed room—crowded with the clocks and china of their childhood, the pictures, upholstery, and samovars of their lives—they could not bear the violence of the fury and the anguish that they felt, so that, with a shriek, Katya opened the double glass doors and tumbled through the back hallway. One by one the others followed after her, squeezing through the narrow door and catapulting out into Elena's garden. And there, surrounded by the green spread of lawn and under the splendor of the sky, they seemed more easily able to breathe. They said, "Ahhhh . . . ahhhh."

Ilya stretched out on a chaise, lifting his face to the sun. Eva uncovered an old guitar behind a rose bush and gently administered to it. On her hands and knees, Katya picked herself a bouquet of small flowers, and Arianne, her mighty shoulders bent, emerged from the garage with the lawnmower. At once she sent the tall weeds flying.

Alexei isolated himself from them. Pulling a chaise a good distance away, he lay down and shut his eyes, his head also seeking the summer sun. Instead, in his mind's eye, he saw the brown, chill winter before snow. He stood on the frozen lawn while his small children ran toward him from the candy store, clasping white paper bags and sticks of licorice in their hands, calling him, while he, aloof and detached, held off until they reached him, before embracing and claiming them for his own.

Now it was all over, he thought. They could have nothing more to do with one another; he had waited too long. For the first time he wondered whom Elena had run off with, and where they'd gone. A powerful jealousy invaded him, and almost vengefully he decided he would phone

Vassily and say, "Vassily, do you remember those wig models we met in New York City, in that restaurant on 57th Street? They were eating cannelloni and had ribbons in their hair?" Vassily's memory, he knew, was worth nothing these days, but he would prod it, stir it up. "Remember, you had veal parmigiana and I had saltimbocca and those girls were done up just like gift packages? Vassily, my friend, let's go to New York and look for them. I'll take the taller of the two and since you're so very much shorter . . ."

But he did not feel like going on. He let his hand drop over the edge of the chaise and picked a blade of grass, which he put to his mouth. Once, at the beginning of his marriage, he had lain in a field with Elena and tasted one of her toes. He had never done that again, not having particularly liked it; yet the memory came back to him in the deep, bitter taste of the grass, this time telling him that what he wanted, more than anything else, was to take Elena from her lover and bring her back—beautiful and black-haired—for himself.

Quickly he went into the house and up the stairs, pulled out two suitcases from a closet and opened them on his bed. He chose underwear, shirts, handkerchiefs, and socks. He planned that he would run into a shop and buy Elena a necklace, a new wedding ring. He would buy himself a tie. From down the corridor he heard a banging and Eva's voice that said, "Wake up, Birdie, wake up. There are a lot of things to do. We're taking inventory and Ilya wants to see you." Alexei glanced at his watch, thinking that Birdie had slept long enough. He went on packing, elaborately folding his clothes, taking fresh pleasure in his skill.

But when he descended the stairs half an hour later, he found his way to the front door barred by a carton of books, a samovar, the world globe from the den, and Arianne's umbrella. Behind these, three large paintings stood lined up against a wall. Setting down his suitcases, he followed voices to the dining room.

There, Katya and Eva leaned over the open drawers of the buffet, Katya with a pad and pencil in her hand. They were counting silver. Above them, where a picture of avocados always hung, was an empty space. Everything, Alexei thought, seemed odd. He sensed something—some strange current in the air, some bewildering change that he could not identify. Fear and suspicion seized him. His pulse began to pound.

"Twelve spoons," Katya said, "leaf pattern."

"No, ten," said Eva.

His two daughters stopped when they noticed him. But Ilya and Birdie, who were playing cards at the dining room table, did not look up even after he had entered and demanded, "What's going on? What's going on?" His fear grew stronger, became a kind of panic. Then suddenly he thought he understood: he had been duped. His children had been in on Elena's plan from the very beginning; all along they'd known where she'd gone off to, and with whom.

A false smile stretched across Alexei's face—a whee-dling, over-intimate expression so alien to him it cut his cheeks. "You might as well tell me. There's no point in hiding it. Where has Elena gone?"

Eva strode over to him. It was then that he started to feel the other fear, the other terror.

Eva lifted her face close to his and, looking down at her, he knew what she was going to say. More than ever before, he was aware of her extraordinary complexion, inherited from his own family. And indeed the skin on her face appeared so milky white, so translucent that for a moment he believed in the possibility of seeing right through her to some preferable object—such as bridges, even trees—but was stopped by the stubborn, owl-like challenge of her nearsighted eyes, by her brooding nose, by her chin as she said, "Mama has not run away. She is dead. She died six weeks ago."

Even as Alexei's head cleared, his mouth opened in a cry of pain. "A—ri—anne!"

Eva told him, "Arianne's busy drinking. She's drink-ing because, on top of other things, the house is too big. It's too big for you alone. We're closing it up."

He found Arianne in the den, sitting in the dim room with a bottle of Scotch, a bottle of bourbon, and an ice bucket at her side. Still disoriented and with no exact mo-tive in mind, he tried out his grotesquely unconnected smile on her, but was relieved when she did not see it in the dark. She said, "Come sit down next to me, Papa, and have a drink. I'm way ahead of you. I've finished the bourbon. It was wonderful bourbon. First rate, really. Let me fix you a Scotch."

He drank from the glass she handed him, taking comfort from it and from her hoarse, warm, cracking voice. "Do you remember, Papa," she asked him, "all those games of badminton we used to play? Do you remember all those nights we ended up drinking brandy in the garden at two o'clock in the morning and singing, 'Oh Tannenbaum' and 'Auld Lang Syne'? Those are first-rate songs. I love those songs." She poured them each another drink.

But he would not touch his. Something was stuck in his mind, in his heart. He fought both to locate and to control it, and presently he said, "Arianne, I think . . . it occurs to me . . . your mother died."

Through the slats in the venetian blinds he could see Eva carrying one of the large paintings down the front path. She loaded it into the cab of her camper. Alexei waited for Arianne to answer. But Arianne, as always unable to think of any but jovial things to say, stared straight ahead in her sorrow.

CAREERS AND MARRIAGES

When Minna Coleman's youngest child turned twenty-one, Mrs. Coleman began to fear none of her children would ever leave home. She began to note and weigh their faults. It bothered her, for example, that her eldest son, Mitchell, who looked like a movie star, could nevertheless neither memorize nor speak out any lines: he had no use for language. As for her daughter Rosamunde—tall, dark, and statuesque, she might have pleased her mother by her beauty, except wherever she went, comic books dangled from her fingertips or fanned bright colors about her in the wind.

Then, enumerated Mrs. Coleman, there was gentle Eli. But Eli lacked his brother's and his sister's outward glamour—his mouth too slack from dawdling over ice cream cones; his eyes, if kind and spiritual, yet somewhat dull. Of all four children only Lottie—the youngest, the smartest, the shortest, the single redhead—reminded Mrs. Coleman of herself. She waited for Lottie to do something with her gifts. But Lottie did nothing. Then Mrs. Coleman took to wondering if Lottie did nothing out of spite.

Some years before—on the profit of a single transaction that had crossed Mr. Coleman's path by error one business noon—the family had moved to a neighborhood of wide lawns, thick bushes, and high trees in which they'd encountered scarcely any people. On summer evenings the four children would stand on their front lawn, gazing up and down the street. If a neighbor strolled past and greeted them first—which rarely happened—their heads shot toward the stranger and they said, "Hello, hello!" they cried out hopefully, "Hello, oh hello!" and then remained standing a few feet apart from one another, until, in front of them, the sun set.

Appalled to witness their aimlessness and isolation, and admitting it was she, after all, who had moved them to this house, Mrs. Coleman sometimes suggested after dinner that they leave all the dishes on the oak table and step outside for a digestive walk. They advanced in twosomes—Mr. Coleman in his shirt sleeves, Mrs. Coleman in her kitchen apron. A short way behind, the two girls waddled, while in the rear, hands in their pockets, strolled Mitchell and Eli. Shortly they reached a neighborhood almost as pretty as theirs but not—so Mrs. Coleman informed them—as aristocratic. You could tell, she told them, because of a red wagon left out on the pavement here and a tricycle blocking the driveway there. Defined in this way, the surroundings made them angry. The boys kicked at stones, Mrs. Coleman muttered, the girls kept their eyes down. Mr. Coleman alone appeared not to notice. He was a tall, not undignified man—outwardly composed but with a jarred and abandoned inner look. He said it was a nice and quiet evening, and as he walked he plucked little round leaves from the bushes and seemed to eat them up.

The Colemans proceeded on until they entered a district with weedy front yards and battered pavement, where groups of people sat inside porches or bunched next to one another on the steps. Through open windows came the sound of television and dishes; rubber balls and dispute filled the air. The Coleman children stared. Their eyes grew wistful. Now they led their parents and circled round and round the block. Mrs. Coleman, fearful of her own emotions, urged them, "Let's go home." But everyone continued trotting round the block. Then Mrs. Coleman said, "What are we doing here? We don't live here anymore. We're doing nothing. We'd best go back." And she herded them home, thinking they needed one more lesson on the subject of success.

Once inside the living room, she announced her topic. At this the children arranged themselves in chairs around her and Mr. Coleman slipped up the stairs to bed. Short, compact, plump, and stolid, Mrs. Coleman stood like a penguin in the center of the room. "It is better," she began, donning blue-rimmed spectacles with rhinestones and dealing out her wisdom to the left and to the right, "it is far, far better to be an old man's sweetheart than a young man's slave."

Waiting for her children to react, she paused. She noted that her statement appeared at once to satisfy and to stun them. But then Lottie, quickly recovering, mimicked, "Hear ye, hear ye, hear ye, it is better to be an old man's sweetheart than a young man's slave." She leapt to the top of the coffee table as though to claim her rightful attention. "Well, I'd rather be a young man's slave."

"That's where you're wrong," said Mrs. Coleman.

"Give me a young man," Lottie spread her arms and legs. "I'll be his slave."

"You would not be doing him a favor," her mother pointed out.

"I would be doing him an honor," Lottie insisted. Rosamunde chortled. "An honor!" Lottie repeated, at which moment Eli stood up, moved by hearing sounds and words. Mitchell, a restless listener but too inarticulate for speech, reached under the chair for his camera and snapped his brother's picture.

"But it's my turn to have my picture taken," Lottie said, and Mrs. Coleman said, "Let's get back to our discussion."

"By your attitude," Lottie jumped down from the coffee table and made her way to the piano—"you force me to play the national anthem." Commencing "The Star Spangled Banner," she proclaimed that if her family were truly patriotic, they would all stand up. At once everyone, including Eli, who had just sat down, stood up. Everyone frowned except for Eli. Zealously Lottie pounded on. She hit a block of wrong notes.

Mrs. Coleman put up her hand. "That's enough, Lottie, you're not being considerate. I'm tired, Rosamunde's tired."

A furry, vindicated moan issued from Rosamunde. Lottie stopped playing. She wailed, "You love Rosamunde more than you love me."

The other children turned toward their mother, their own question mutely in their eyes. Mrs. Coleman merely shrugged. "Listen," she said, "I have five fingers." She held them up. "Now do I love this finger more than I love this one?" She touched her second finger, then her third. "Or this one more than I love that one?" She went on to her fourth and to her fifth. "Do I love one finger more than any other? What do you think?" The room grew suddenly quiet—the outside world forgotten. The children breathed in their happy life.

And so the days went on. Mitchell was the only one who worked. And since he worked for his father in their rarely frequented jewelry store on a side street downtown, he found himself with so few duties that he often took the bus and returned home by noon. In the glider on the veranda, Rosamunde rested her head against a stack of comic books, humming as she rocked to and fro. Eli read travel books on the couch. Lottie chased after her mother— chased her upstairs and down—blocked her, cornered her, and buffeted her about with complaints.

Would they, Mrs. Coleman wondered, would they ever venture out, would they ever leave? Was the world with its untried careers and marriages so uninviting? Was the furniture so comfortable at home? Or was there something in her attitude—untoward, unknown even to herself—that had gradually worked its power to wound them? She searched for something irresponsible she might have said and remembered mentioning long before, while cleaning vegetables by the sink: "If in this life you cannot be perfect,"—she had held a half-scraped carrot like a scepter in her hand—"then do not try to be anything else."

They had taken her at her word. She saw that clearly, for they did not try to be anything or to do anything at all. Instead they spent their days in a state of simple but expectant quiescence, as if anticipating their lives to come and take them out, or as if they were waiting to greet visitors.

And indeed, when the lady who collected for the Heart Fund rang their doorbell, the Coleman children welcomed her in with tender warmth. Mrs. Coleman was happy to see her, too. As one the entire group exclaimed over how pretty the woman was and how stylish. They led her to the most comfortable armchair and pulled up the ottoman for her feet. After she sat down, they made her stand up and turn around. In a low voice Mrs. Coleman admired the woman's dress, her hat and shoes. "Look how well the entire outfit goes together," she pointed out. Eli nodded and said, "Yes, yes," and Lottie explained, "You see, we never expected that anyone soliciting for charity would be as attractive as you." Mrs. Coleman echoed that they'd never expected it and Rosamunde, in order not to be left out, said she'd never expected it either. Then in a further effort to stimulate her children's interest in the workings of the outside world, Mrs. Coleman asked about the organization of the Heart Fund and how much money it managed to collect. Murmuring and nodding, the children gradually grew hushed, as if respectful of the fact they had entered into such great intimacy with the Heart Fund.

At this moment a man selling pots and pans knocked briskly at the door. The Colemans let the Heart Fund lady out and led in the man, who spread his stainless steel ware in a semi-circle on the rug. Immediately the family knelt down and praised the kettles and the casseroles, and Mrs. Coleman urged the man to tell the story of his life. He began speaking. She thought him very eloquent. And when he mentioned traveling through mountain streams to distant towns with bell towers, she waited to see if Eli, who so dearly loved his travel books, might not go up to the man and express some yearning to move about, too. She searched among the other children for signs of sudden ignition. The man spoke on. She hoped. But no one caught fire. The most she read in her children's faces was a certain wary satisfaction at contemplating from such close range a totally alien life. In her disappointment she bought no pots or pans.

She felt, with some degree of bitterness, that her husband did not help—for Mr. Coleman spent little time at home, preferring, when he could, to take his meals in a tearoom downtown. All the same it pleased him, every once in awhile, to have a quick look at his offspring; and then he appeared in the archway of the living room and said, "Well, well, look at all of you. The time'll come when you'll all get married and move away." At this the two girls hung onto him adoringly and shouted, "Daddy, daddy, daddy, give us money!"

"What do you have in your head?" his wife demanded.

"Can't you see? They'll never move away."

"Mitchell!" Mr. Coleman called out desperately. "Let's go to work!" And he left without Mitchell.

Mrs. Coleman followed him as far as the veranda, where she stopped. A moment later, Rosamunde came out to the glider. She nestled into the pile of comic books, starting the glider in motion with her toe. She lifted out a magazine and smiled at her mother. Mrs. Coleman refused to smile back. "Rosamunde," she said sternly, "I wish that you'd go out with boys."

Rosamunde's lips curled with love for herself and affection for her mother. Her long-lashed eyes drooped, expressing drowsiness and a smoldering attachment to her magazines. "Rosamunde," Mrs. Coleman went on, "comic books are not everything in life. When I was your age I went out with boys and had a good time and did everything. Except, of course, I saved one thing for your father."

But she knew that Rosamunde didn't care. Angrily she went into the house and encountered Eli dressed in shorts, his knobby knees crossed, his guileless eyes fixed on a travel book. He sat on the couch. Eli, she thought, was twenty-three years old and had never so much as boarded a train, a motorcycle, a Greyhound bus. In front of the fireplace stood Mitchell. She had always felt proud of Mitchell—so rosy-cheeked and straight backed—but now, in his habitual stance of a tenor about to sing—his feet spread apart, his thumbs hooked into an imaginary vest—it once more occurred to her he was tone deaf, he would never sing, he could scarcely talk. She groaned and looked about her at the roster of photographs of her children—photographs in rompers on the piano, gap-toothed pictures over the couch, likenesses in early adolescence up and down the stairs. But it was the latest group, an aggressive series overlapping each other above the mantle, that stared down at her now and pronounced they would march on top of her shoes and break her toes; they would squeeze out all of her blood and drink it for mineral water; they would follow her forever and do nothing.

All at once she began to shout. "Out, out! I need to be alone! I need to be by myself!" With a sudden resolve she folded her arms. "And Rosamunde," she said, "will be the first to leave."

Just outside the living room Rosamunde heard nothing. But in the basement Lottie, busily ironing sheets, caught the timbre of her mother's voice and rushed at full speed up the stairs. Hopping about, she cheered her mother on as Mrs. Coleman informed Rosamunde she needed to enter a finishing school.

"For a number of reasons," Mrs. Coleman explained. "So that you don't bump into things. So that you learn poise. So that you become more instantly attractive, particularly to men."

"Oh you're lucky," breathed Lottie, elated that some change might possibly soon take place. But Rosamunde, as if prodded in her sleep, uttered a long pained cry.

"Yes," said Mrs. Coleman, "she's lucky"; and she instructed Lottie to write away for school catalogues, preferably in the south.

Within a month Rosamunde was accepted to Briar Heather Sweet in Tennessee and the family took her to the airport. As they crossed the veranda she sat down on the glider, gripped its iron moorings with her fingers, and refused to leave. Mr. and Mrs. Coleman and Mitchell supported and carried her to the car. Lottie carried the suitcases. Mournfully Eli dragged behind them, holding an ice cream cone in front of his eyes.

On the highway Rosamunde sang out, "Why must I go? Why must I leave my home?" And when she exited through the gate to her plane, her farewell whine merged with the acute eeeeouuuu of aircraft taking off. The Colemans' faces turned white. Mr. Coleman took off his hat and placed it against his chest.

"Why are you doing that?" his wife asked crossly.

"She looks so young," he said.

"She's not. She's twenty-four years old." To Rosamunde's plane she urged, "Go, go! Take off!"

At this they heard a furious roar and looked up. American Airlines sped up the runway and Rosamunde flew away.

That night as Eli settled into the sofa, his mother pulled up the ottoman and stationed herself in front of him. "You're my best child, Eli," she began. "You have a better character than any of us and you know that I love you." Peering into his face, she paused. "But Eli," she reproached, and her tone was confidential, "you act like a retired man. You're too young to be retired. Besides, you haven't done anything yet."

Eli was too shy and gentle for so much attention. "You're tired, Mother," he patted her shoulder, trying to shift the focus, "Rosamunde's leaving has worn you out."

"Twenty-three years old and you've already got a paunch. That's much too early, Eli. Either you have to find yourself a job or else go back to school and study for some profession. But your grades, Eli, your grades," she continued without a trace of bitterness or sarcasm in her voice, "they'd never admit you to medical or to law school or dental school—all of them nice professions, of course, but not for you. What does that leave?" She regarded her son. Unable to wait, she supplied the answer. "Optometry."

"Optometry?"

"Optometry, Eli. It's a career that allows you to travel. No matter what country you go to—Israel, China, Honolulu—Eli, all over the world people need glasses."

"Yes they do," said Eli. "Yes," he repeated sadly.

"They need glasses."

"But I'll need time to say good-bye."

Mrs. Coleman allotted him two and a half weeks. During that interval she instructed Lottie to find an optometry school three hundred to a thousand miles away. Then in the numbered days that were left him, Eli reread his travel books on the couch—every once in a while raising himself to tiptoe about the room and touch the objects that he passed—the rubber plants, the damask drapes, the overstuffed armchairs, the china clock, the untuned piano. From upstairs he heard Lottie haranguing his mother and he clung hungrily to the sound. "Mama," he listened to his sister, "I'll never get married and it's all your fault."

"Why?"

"Because you never joined bridge clubs and introduced me to the sons of mothers."

"That's no reason."

"Because you're responsible for my face."

"It's not a bad face, Lottie. It's intelligent. It reminds me of myself."

"But is it a good face? Is it pretty?"

"It's not bad," his mother plodded on. Then all at once, losing patience she cried out, "What do you want? Do you want me to go out on the street and run with a bell: 'Dingalingaling, who'll come and marry my daughter Lottie?'"

Eli kept on listening, but Lottie had ended her fit. In the silence that followed, the rubber plant kept wilting and the china clock ticked on. Desolate and alone, Eli remembered the long summer days on the lawn, winter with snow at the windows, and his brother and sisters, his mother and father eating cereal for breakfast in the spring.

In the evenings, as had been his habit, he strolled to the nearest drugstore and bought himself an ice cream cone. On the last evening he bought himself two. And while the rusted wheels and knobs of his body moved through the tree-lined streets, his kindly eyes, all spirit, sought the sky, his lips the ice cream cones. These floated like torches before him, melting from his tears. At midnight he boarded the train and he said to his family, "I love you; goodbye."

With only two children left at home, Mrs. Coleman decided to find Mitchell a proper mate to marry. She broached this plan to Lottie who whooped and hooted in a superior fashion, buffed her nails on her left shoulder, and disclosed that Mitchell already had a girl, whose name was Ada Lincoln. "She lives," Lottie offered, "on the corner —in the big house by the bus stop."

"Does she live with her parents?"

"She lives alone."

Mrs. Coleman's brain reeled with the sudden suspicion Ada Lincoln had done her parents in. Timidly she inquired what the girl looked like.

"How shall I tell you?" Lottie thought a moment. I'd say she's tall, she's skinny as a chop stick, and she looks old and mean . . . I'd say she's close to fifty."

"Lottie, don't say that."

"Then I'll say forty-five."

"Lottie, go away."

"I can't," Lottie said, moving closer to her mother. "Not until you've done something for me. Mama, you've never done anything for me. Only for the others."

"Then I'll go away." She shook off her daughter and, putting on a sweater, walked to the corner where she knocked on Ada Lincoln's door. Soon a tall, thin, pale figure with a printed bandanna tied over its head opened the door, and Mrs. Coleman acknowledged Lottie had not lied: Ada Lincoln was old and Mrs. Coleman judged she also looked mean. Returning home, she informed Mitchell that Ada Lincoln was not his type. "Where did you find her?" she asked, and she forbid him to see her again.

To her astonishment Mitchell began to mourn. He was a man—the notion amazed Mrs. Coleman—intensely suffering because of love. She had never thought his interests lay that way. But as the months went on she saw there was no discounting the fact he no longer snapped pictures of his surroundings—that he brooded from morning to night in a high-backed hair, an unhappy glaze over his eyes. "Mitchell," she commenced, then waited. She rapped him on the head. "Mitchell." With a sigh she turned to Lottie. "Once I had a handsome son. He had a good appetite and he cared about photography. Now there's not even a person here. It's just a shell."

Through sympathy for Mitchell, envy of Rosamunde, and loneliness for Eli, Lottie took to mourning too. Rosamunde wrote from Briar Heather Sweet she was too busy to fly home for the vacations. She mentioned she was learning to fix plumbing and to float magnolias in a dish. Eli did not write. On Thanksgiving day Mrs. Coleman tried to phone him at the optometry school, but the operator said there was no longer any listing. At this news Lottie, who had been dusting the piano, cast the dust cloth over herself.

Then for weeks nothing but advertisements appeared in the mail. The wind moaned outside the windows, and within the drawn drapes the radiator tapped, the china clock ticked, the rubber plant drooped, the photographs cracked, and Mitchell and Lottie sat suffering in living room chairs.

To escape them Mrs. Coleman resourcefully moved to the dining room. On one side of the oak table she put a bushel basket of socks which she sorted through for pairs. On the other side she placed advertisements in different stacks which she pored through with the idea of keeping up-to-date on modern products. But gradually she read and sorted less and less. She found the atmosphere in her house oppressive. Nothing had turned out as she'd planned. With the departure of each child she had expected to feel younger and more and more liberated. She had imagined she might start studying languages, that she might even enter college. Instead, inexplicably, she felt older than before. In another life she might have been a U.S. congresswoman or a supreme court judge. But in this life, as she gazed out the window, she saw only emptiness in the heavy, black sky. Shutting her eyes, she longed to bring her absent children home.

As if in tune with her mother's mood, Lottie approached —gingerly at first, but then with the loud demand: "Mama, let Mitchell marry his lady. She can't be as bad as we think. Mitchell would shave and be happy; Eli and Rosamunde would come home for the wedding. We'd all be together— we'd even have something to do."

"Do you miss them?" Mrs. Coleman asked.

"I miss Eli."

Mrs. Coleman looked coldly down her nose. She shrugged her shoulders. "Since Mitchell's in love . . . ," she began. Then after a few minutes she said, "Understand, Lottie, I'm doing this for you . . ."

The wedding took place on the corner, in Ada Lincoln's house. Rosamunde was maid of honor, but Eli, the best man, did not show up. Two telegrams had been sent him. They had been marked "unknown" and returned. During the ceremony Mr. and Mrs. Coleman linked arms and stood behind the bride and groom while Lottie, the sole audience, wept. She wept large swollen tears out of joy for Mitchell, out of desire for her own unknown lover, out of grief for her brother Eli's absence.

The morning after, Rosamunde refused to stay on. She packed all her comic books into boxes and phoned the Salvation Army to pick them up. In response to her mother's objections she answered, "I'm not finished yet."

"How long does it take?"

With her newly learned expertise, Rosamunde folded sweaters into her suitcase. She lifted her head. "There's a lot to learn."

Lottie mimicked her, "There's a lot to learn." Then she asked, "Are there a lot of men in your school?"

"Not too many. Not that I've noticed."

"Then I won't go there. I thought I might. I have to go somewhere."

"Listen, Rosamunde," interrupted her mother, "can you give me some idea of how long it'll take? Are you half-finished, a third finished? Give me an idea."

Rosamunde abruptly fastened the suitcase shut and remarked it would take a long, long time.

For the last time, Mr. and Mrs. Coleman drove her to the airport. They chose a bench and sent Lottie off to buy her sister's ticket. Rosamunde placed herself at one side of her parents. Gesturing into the terminal, she explained her course of study. She told her family she was learning to grow an organic garden, to swathe a head in bandages, to play the oud, to build a handmade house from scratch, to save the whales. Gradually an expression of fastidiousness and dismay developed on Mrs. Coleman's face, and she turned her head from Rosamunde and with relief caught sight of Lottie across the corridor. She reflected that Lottie, who was negotiating with a ticket agent, was her child, after all—the youngest, the brightest, the only one who reminded her of herself. Even in the past, she mused, her closeness to Lottie had been so extreme that when Lottie went to her high school prom she'd dressed her in her own pink satin party dress which she'd saved in a closet for almost thirty years. Lottie's classmates had found the dress frayed and out-of-date, but they were wrong, she thought, and it was right that Lottie now—despite all calculations to the contrary—should be the one child to remain with her.

Presently Lottie returned with Rosamunde's airplane ticket. "Mama," she said, "I love that ticket agent."

"What do you mean?"

"I kissed him."

"What are you talking about?"

"I've never met anyone like him. He asked me to live with him."

"Lottie, you always exaggerate."

"Not this time," Lottie assured her. "He asked me to come with him to Copenhagen. The airlines are transferring him there. He even asked me to marry him." She paused, for Rosamunde's flight had just been announced. "Goodbye, Rosamunde," she called out to her sister.

Ruefully Mrs. Coleman gazed after Rosamunde, who was vanishing forever. Then she composed herself to face Lottie. It was true, she reflected—she willingly admitted—that she'd always done less for Lottie than for the others—given Lottie less attention and forced her to help with all the errands—but she had done this out of magnanimity because Lottie was the only one who reminded her of herself. Fixing her daughter with a steadfast eye, she inquired, "Which ticket agent do you have in mind?" And when Lottie pointed him out, she went on, "He has an intelligent face. But do you really want to leave your parents and live with him?" And then, since she already knew the answer, without waiting for Lottie's response she declared, "If you've fallen in love, I give you my blessing."

At the end of the summer, Lottie was married. The day after, Rosamunde wrote Mrs. Coleman she had learned the world was filled with tragedy and sin. From Copenhagen Lottie wrote that Tivoli Gardens was beautiful at night and she was sorry not to have noticed that towards the end she had had her mother to herself. Eli never wrote. Mitchell sent three postcards from the Virgin Islands, each with the same palm tree and the same message: he was having a wonderful time. For several months Mrs. Coleman waited for him to return from his honeymoon. Then one day she ran into her daughter-in-law on the street and exclaimed, "You're back! Where's Mitchell?" at which her daughter-in-law replied that Mitchell had left her two days after their wedding. She had not seen him since.

Once more appraising Ada's face and figure, Mrs. Coleman felt she understood. For a moment the two women regarded one another abstractly, as strangers might. Then Mrs. Coleman headed back toward home to the china clock, the radiator, the rubber plant, and all the photographs of her lost children.

THE INTRUDER

In the morning Eugene Levcourt, appearing unusually distraught, said to his wife, "I have something to tell you. It isn't easy for me. If only I knew how to begin. Some explanations are terrible. Actually it's not so bad . . . it's a surprise for you. What it is . . ."

But Isabel, uneasy with the way his hair stood on end, said, "I have no time," and reminded herself of all the times he'd fled from listening to her. Now and again, she admitted, he had grasped at ways to cheer her up, but this time there was nothing to suggest cheerfulness in his bearing. "No time," she attacked mildly. "I have to put in three hours at the hospital and then I go to the airport to meet Maxine Barbarelli—she's stopping in Detroit for an hour between planes—and then Aunt Roslyn claims she has to see me and I have to get there before her nap." And Isabel, taking her long, deliberate, blindly even strides, went out the door and embarked on what was, for her, an unusually varied schedule.

After the hospital and before driving to the airport, she stopped at a branch of Levcourt Candy in the Northgate Mall. Here she chose a three-pound box of her husband's finest butter cream liquor-flavored bittersweet chocolates to bring Maxine Barbarelli, and then exchanged the three-pound for a five-pound box since, after all, it was Maxine who had introduced her to Eugene twenty-six years before. In the airport she waited alertly, having lost contact with her classmate, having in fact not laid eyes on her since college graduation. Yet despite her concentration, she failed at first to recognize Maxine in the woman with short gray hair and a sagging chin who emerged from a throng of passengers and took small, quick steps in her direction.

"Isabel?"

Isabel stared. Then realizing that this was Maxine Barbarelli who stood before her, she made up for her rudeness and welcomed her friend with, "You haven't changed," to which Maxine replied, breathlessly and victoriously, "Isabel, I have four children!"

"Four?" Isabel leaned toward the cry of triumph in the woman's voice and presented her with the box of candy. "How very wonderful."

In an instant Maxine had produced a half-dozen snapshots.

"How wonderful they are . . . each of the four," praised Isabel. "I have three," she murmured, letting her glance stray away and thinking it unfair in this instance to mention her oldest child, the brightest, the most rosy-cheeked of them all. Alexander was dead. "Kevin is studying agriculture at Michigan State, Linda's in anthropology at the University of Michigan, and Hillary's captain of her soccer team in high school."

Maxine brought the elegantly boxed candy to her nose. "And what is Eugene doing?" she inquired, sniffing appreciatively at the candy, evidently without noticing the box was labeled "Levcourt." "Yes, tell me all about Eugene," she proposed. "Is he still a bag of bones?"

Isabel frowned. "Was he a bag of bones in college?"

"He was a bag of bones," Maxine nodded happily. "And is he still," she started up again, "so pale and scholarly and absentminded and awkward and naive and bumbling and shy?"

"What did you say?"

"Is he still so naive and bumbling and shy? What I mean is, do you still need to chase after him all the time, or have things changed and now he chases madly after other women?"

Isabel, having begun by breathing eagerly into the visitor's face, now stood several feet away and was sorry she'd chosen the larger box of candy. She also wished she had heard her husband out this morning. With a little more curiosity, she would have learned what terrible explanation he'd had in mind. Was his subject, by any chance, divorce? "Eugene," she enunciated, holding herself upright against this notion, "is very rich." She turned her head aside to let this news travel past her, to give it scope and echo in the high vaults of the airport. "He's very rich and very successful. Of course he never wanted to give up his research into ions, but when his uncle died there was no one else to take the business over. And now . . . well now the American Candy Trade Association," she improvised, inventing the name out of a desire to convince Maxine without putting forth much effort, "keeps honoring him at banquets and," she rounded off, "at banks. No, there's no way you could call him shy. You may never have expected it, but Eugene has put on weight and substance and single-handedly placed Levcourt candy on the map."

Yet out of her own reticence she did not add that ever since a car had struck and killed their eldest son, she and Eugene sat in different rooms at night. The hour passed, the two women leaned forward meaning to kiss goodbye, but at the last they shook hands instead.

Feeling restless and unsettled, Isabel entered the freeway and headed toward her Aunt Roslyn's house. "Oh, you can't tell by looking at me," she spoke out loud, lifting a scuffed walking shoe from the gas pedal and addressing a group of airplanes rising above her, "but I can buy anything at the shops I want. And if you come to my house you will see I have an evening cape in the closet, a three-ply Ping-Pong table on the lanai, a decorator's showplace in the living room, and in the kitchen a third faucet for instant boiling water. On top of that," she threw in wryly, "Eugene's bringing me some kind of surprise."

At Aunt Roslyn's door she inquired, expecting her aunt to make her feel even worse. "Why did you want to see me?"

But Aunt Roslyn was biding her time. "How is Linda?" she sang out.

"Linda's fine."

"How is Kevin?" Roslyn crooned.

"Kevin's fine."

"How is Hillary?" Roslyn warbled.

"Oh Hillary's fine."

"And Eugene?" Her voice plummeted.

"Eugene? He's okay."

Roslyn, pink furry bedroom slippers on her feet, raised herself on tiptoe, the slippers remaining on the ground. She was a little woman. As she rose up, her voice dropped further still. "I have an intuition you're about to lose him. You don't pay him any attention. When I came over for lamb chops last week, the entire time we were eating you didn't speak a single word to him."

"And he didn't speak a single word to me," said Isabel, judging herself generous because she smiled.

"But Isabel," Aunt Roslyn said, "when did Eugene ever speak? And why does he need to? You're the one who always chattered and sang and danced and juggled tennis balls and ran foot races. But now that you never talk, let alone sing or dance, and you keep on wearing the same old clothes and you never change your hair style or buy a lipstick . . . well, I'm afraid our Eugene will simply take a mistress and there you are—you'll lose him."

"Why would he take a mistress?" she asked blandly. "What would he do with her?"

"Still, he would take her."

"Oh, I don't think he would take her."

"He would take her."

"Oh no, I don't think so. She would only interrupt his work."

"He would take her," Aunt Roslyn insisted, "and I wouldn't blame him, I would blame you." A zealous finger shot out of her fist and pointed upward. "Isabel, four, five years of moping around and mourning for Alexander is much too long when two hundred women are employed by Levcourt Candy, out of which how many do you think would stand up and gladly wiggle their behinds for Eugene?"

"Why for Eugene?"

"Why not for Eugene? Well, when you think of it. He's the boss. He owns the candy."

"Oh why for Eugene?" out of a bitter malice Isabel asked, raising her dark, thick handsome brows, her face otherwise expressionless and unyielding like the surface of a clock. Yet as she leaned back on her heels and pretended blitheness and with a single wave of the hand altogether banished Eugene's appeal, there rose unbidden to her eyes the night—had it been nine months ago, ten months, a year?—that Eugene, a man who generally shied away from looking at himself, an intelligent, sensitive man who normally judged his image irrelevant at best—had posted himself for at least seven minutes in front of the hallway mirror. From the dinette where she was poking three quilted place mats and three paper napkins on the dinner table, she had watched the bemusement on his face give way to an expression of mounting fascination and pleasure, as though in the glass he beheld himself in the very process of growing more and more attractive. "Oh why for Eugene?" from low in her throat she muttered and then said loudly toward the sparse halo of dyed honey-colored hair that floated just above Aunt Roslyn's head, "Oh well, let him!" suddenly enraged that Eugene had become sought after and independent without somehow managing to make her more attractive and independent too. Turning on her heels, she shot past her aunt and dove further into the house.

Roslyn quickly shuffled after her. "And let us say," she said, "he singles out a little someone and takes her to lunch and she orders a steak tartar to begin with and a chicken Kiev with two vegetables and a rice pilaf and for dessert a chocolate mousse garnished with a piece of cheesecake and two or three martinis . . . why," they reached the kitchen, the furthest point of the house, "she'll feel singled out, she'll feel convinced she's already accomplished something."

"The toad!" said Isabel as a pang of hunger attacked her. She pulled open all six of Aunt Roslyn's cupboards and shut them, as usual finding each cupboard bare.

"And if in due time," Aunt Roslyn went on, "he gives her twelve full boxes of nougats and twenty-four of bittersweet centers . . . not to mention some of the profits."

"Let him!" Isabel broke away. "Let him!" She strode to the front door, shut it firmly behind her, and cast off all tenderness for her husband, telling herself why should she care if he had a mistress when she and Eugene were so rarely together, when they so rarely shared a bed? Why, after all, should she care when it was she who had wept and mourned and aged and grown sallow and dowdy while he, charting his own way back into life, had too soon escaped his share of their sorrow by opening three new branches of Levcourt Candy and then inventing the now ridiculously popular thin melting Levcourt chocolate drops and the all-day truffle sucker?

Pacing the street, her back to Aunt Roslyn's front door, her eye caught a foursome of young people meandering across the sidewalk. Some earnestness in their demeanor suggested to her that these were socially conscious young men and women willing on the instant to fight for justice. Without thinking she said in a loud whisper, "Boycott Levcourt Candy!"

They did not hear her. When they had passed she moved down the porch stairs away from the smell of Aunt Roslyn's old shingled roof and into the sidewalk's voluptuousness of autumn elms and maples whose colors and shadows she recognized and loved, for she had lived for some ten years among these trees and the long street of stolid, large-porched, stern brick houses. Early in her marriage—before she and Eugene had moved to further and further suburbs—they had rented the yellow house with the high arched windows five doors down. Now she wandered to that house, stopped before its hillock of lawn, contemplated the forsythia bush at the windows and the unfamiliar curtains that hid the rooms upstairs and down and, with a tug of anticipation—an anticipation she kept half-secret from herself—made her way across the street to a vacant lot of rough weeds and zigzagging paths where her children had sometimes played. She thought of her meeting with Maxine Barbarelli at the airport and again heard Maxine's triumphant cry, "Isabel, I have four children!" Then all at once, her hands falling loosely to her sides, she allowed herself—limiting the recollection to this one empty lot—an old memory of Alexander. He was pedaling toward her on a tricycle, his feet in t-strapped sandals, his knees akimbo. Standing on the cool autumn pavement she heard the rasp and squeak of his front wheel like the chords of a calliope in the summer's heavy air before rain. Above his sturdy neck and square chin and above his small tanned nose with its indentation like a thumb print, Alexander's dark eyes—defined and luminous—focused on the sky beyond her until, coming closer, he said almost wonderingly, as if her identity surprised him: "Mama?"

Isabel turned from the empty lot, crossed the street again, and got into her car. Somehow, she thought, she must have deserved his dying or else why would he have stopped existing at age sixteen—unique, noisy, radiant, alive—his bones still singing in her blood? Aunt Roslyn was wrong to ask her to behave as though Alexander had only barely existed. She, along with Eugene, was wrong not to understand that he was her firstborn, her first true gift on earth, and that there could never again be any reason to buy new clothes or juggle tennis balls or style her hair or run foot races.

Twenty minutes later when she pulled up in her driveway, she was relieved and comforted to see that her youngest child, Hillary, who appeared from the side of the house and rolled her bicycle toward her mother, stood once more before her, unharmed. At age fifteen Hillary was tall, the height of her mother, with an olive complexion—smooth as a new bar of soap—on which a look of hopefulness and expectancy alternated with that of a closed and wry resignation, as though each expression kept guard over the other. The burlap bag of Hillary's newspaper route swung from her shoulders—shoulders so broad and athletic that after reminding Isabel of herself, they reminded her that her daughter had just been elected captain of her high school soccer team. Bending forward, she delivered a kiss of approval to Hillary's forehead and volunteered, "I've just been to the airport and spent an hour with the woman who introduced me to your dad."

"Well, Dad just phoned," Hillary announced. "He said to tell you that he's coming home early. Before four o'clock." The girl shrugged and grimaced, both hopefully and cynically, and then, to cancel out the grimace, she smiled.

"Home early? Is he ill?" Isabel said and then regretted the sharp scorn in her voice—for inflicting it on Hillary. To improve on her behavior and yet to keep a certain distance, she directed her gaze just past Hillary, as if Hillary were an audience rather than her daughter. Adopting a pleasant manner, she said, "The woman who introduced us used to be Maxine Barbarelli and now she's Maxine Sklar. I still think of her as Barbarelli. Yes, she was much better as Barbarelli . . . it gave her a certain amount of style. For example, when she introduced your dad and me, I remember she said, 'Isabel, this is Eugene, Eugene, Isabel, neither of you are superficial people.'" Isabel fluttered a gracious hand.

"She said that? She said neither of you are superficial people?" Hillary queried, her mouth a crescent of pleasure that so laid bare her eagerness that Isabel hastily amended, "She didn't mean anything, even then. What I think is, it was just her way of talking. Anyway, that's what I decided today when she asked me if your dad's still a bag of bones."

Hillary flushed. "What did you tell her? I hope you weren't trying to be . . . something."

"I just said that he's fat."

"Mom, you didn't!"

"Oh I did!"

"You didn't—you're just exaggerating," Hillary groaned. She dug the toe of her tennis shoe into a crack in the driveway. "Why do you always exaggerate? Why do you always do that?" She went on trying to plant her foot into the cement. Then abruptly freeing herself, she pushed off on her bike and spun down the street to call back half a block later, "He isn't fat. I think he looks very good these days."

"He is, too, fat," Isabel muttered to herself and proceeded into the house. In the living room she confronted the furniture Eugene had selected for her two years earlier when the idea of redecorating had come to him as an inspiration, almost as a last resort. Before that he had tried to persuade her that a change of scene was bound to raise her spirits. But no matter what vacation, what country he offered—whether New Zealand, China, Italy, Russia, England, or France—she had refused adamantly to travel, and so he'd decided to change the living room furniture instead. "Isabel," he'd murmured gently, "I wish there were some way you wouldn't stay so sad." And because this one time, before flying out the door, he'd uttered the very sentiment she'd wanted to hear him express, she had tried at first to like the new pieces—to enjoy the vistas of sculptured off-white carpet, the tall corner tansu chest with a tall basket on its top, the two low Oriental couches, the pair of matching teak wood coffee tables, and on the walls the six framed prints of Chinese warriors in kimonos, variously unsheathing their swords and snarling. Yet the longer the furniture remained, the more its formality seemed to reflect Eugene's mounting need for order, the more she felt personally challenged by the swords of the Chinese warriors. And as the months went by, she longed to search among the objects in the Salvation Army's warehouse so as to locate and bring back her old multicolored shag rug into whose thick pile her children's pick-up sticks lay buried, her immense overstuffed brown sofa on which Alexander, as a young boy, stood up to make announcements, her round-backed armchairs that Alexander, along with Kevin, Linda, and Hillary, had driven like buses and like trucks.

"He is, too, fat," she muttered again, with a certain envy picturing Eugene and a faceless mistress spooning up their bowls of chocolate mousse. Shutting her eyes, she tried to bring back the afternoon's memory of Alexander riding his tricycle through the high sun-bleached weeds of the vacant lot. But this time Alexander eluded her. When she opened her eyes, through the living room window she caught sight of her husband parking his Oldsmobile by the curb. She went outside, the better to face his confession squarely. She watched as he backed his legs out of the car, then twice bent back into the car before at last emerging to turn around and straighten up. He was a round-faced, stocky man buttoned into a three-piece gray herringbone tweed suit, a rumpled tie lolling over his starched white shirt. Under one arm he balanced two boxes of candy while with the opposite hand he held aloft—and at a certain fastidious distance from him—a large bouquet of russet-colored chrysanthemums. Quickly he marched up the curving path and when he reached his wife he said, "Blossoms for a pretty lady."

"The last time you brought me flowers," she remarked, regarding him coolly and observing that his pale blue almond-shaped eyes held a determination that had not been there in the morning, "was on the day Hillary was born."

He knitted his brows. "So long ago?"

"And before that, on the day Linda was born."

"Did I miss Kevin, by some chance?"

"No. Nor Alexander," she added, after a pause.

"Well, then we have a kind of coincidence," he said, and still holding out the chrysanthemums he repeated, "Blossoms for a pretty lady."

Fascinated by his behavior, Isabel trotted into the kitchen, dropped the bouquet into the sink, and immediately came out. She found Eugene in the den. He was opening a box of Levcourt Candy and at her approach he informed her with a practiced, professional air, "This is our latest Halloween mix. Everyone seems to like it." Carefully he popped a miniature sugared pumpkin and a large green jelly goblin into her mouth and then watched her chew on them with an attention at once solicitous and intense and as though, she now began to worry, he meant to fatten her up for some unknown future purpose.

"Have another." He offered her the box but grew impatient and set it down even before she refused. Back and forth he paced, his hands swinging agitatedly along his sides rather than, as normal, clasped with abstracted preoccupation behind his back. "I have a surprise for you," he began. "Actually it's a surprise for the whole family. It's . . . something of extraordinary value."

For a moment she wondered if it was another suite of living room furniture but abandoned that idea when he went on, "If you want to see, you'll have to come with me to the park. We can take Hillary if you like."

"To what park?"

"The closest one. The one three blocks away."

"Why should we go there?" She eyed him warily.

"So we can see . . ." he broke off. And then the next thing she knew, to her astonishment he was down on one knee, grasping hold of both her hands, perspiration lining his forehead. "Isabel, if it's possible . . . if in some way you can manage to take the broad-minded, the larger view, something extraordinary . . . something wonderful has happened!" He got up from his knees and brushed off his trousers. He brushed them off again, seeming to lose his train of thought. He also seemed to lose his courage, for he sank down into an armchair. A minute later he sprang from the room and stood by the banister, calling up, "Hillary! Hillary!"

"Hillary," she informed him when he returned to the den—her tone and the angle of her head meant to illustrate how little he knew of what went on in the house—"is on her newspaper route."

"Then we'll go alone, the two of us . . . like in the old days." And paying no attention when she claimed that in the old days they had never gone to the park, he took her elbow firmly and propelled her out of the room, down past the lawn, across the sidewalk, the dun-colored flattened strip of grass at the curb, and into the front seat of the Oldsmobile.

From this edge of the suburb they started toward the park, passing a short stretch of billboards and olive-colored meadows and cutting into a brand-new street to glide by four new Tudor-style houses in a row, two Spanish and two French provincial houses under construction, and an unfinished light-brick medical-dental building, sitting on a corner like a hat. Unexpectedly, "Blossoms for a pretty lady" played over in Isabel's mind. The phrase combined in a kind of tune with the novelty of the uncompleted street, the autumn afternoon, the spacious leg room in the car, and Eugene's expertise behind the wheel. Leaning back against the upholstery, Isabel gave her husband a stealthy glance. It was true, she thought, that he was growing heavier, even to the pouches beneath his eyes and that his hair was thinning so that it lay across his head like spread-out pale fingers. But to be honest, she admitted, she was fond of these changes: they stood for a passage of time that joined them.

In the soft, haze of that afternoon, they entered the park. Selecting a bench, Eugene dusted it off and they sat down. In the center of the park slim poplars, set evenly apart, surrounded a grassy oval, while at the far end this trimmed and formal landscape gave way to a tangled, densely wooded piece of land. Eugene checked his watch.

A nervous flitting motion cut across his lips. He stood up, paced to a tree and back, then paced to a further tree and returned, checking his watch again. Isabel, her knees together, her hands on her lap, turned her attention to the autumnal gold and apricot colors that softly lit up the woods. She watched a baby carriage emerge from one of the misty paths and followed its progress. It came closer— a large English carriage pushed slowly by a middle-aged woman who wore a high white nurse's cap and a sour expression on the features of her bunched-up, stocking-colored face. Still closer the carriage rolled and shortly seemed to be bearing in on them—at which instant Eugene leapt up. Then he shouted—every trace of nervousness gone and with a smile that was radiant and full—"Oh here it is, here it is! Here is my surprise! Oh Isabel, if you can find a way . . . if you can find it in your heart to take the broad-minded, the larger view . . . oh Isabel, come look at this baby!"

Isabel got up unsteadily and was about to remind her husband that he had never really cared for babies—that he'd kept a distance from his own small children, even from his favorite, Alexander, until each of the children was old enough to read. She was on the verge, in fact, of delivering a small sermon on this subject when she remembered Aunt Roslyn's warning and sat down in silence to reflect that possibly Aunt Roslyn had given her warning a bit too late.

"Come see the baby," pleaded Eugene, and the nurse discreetly moved away.

"I don't want to see it."

"But this baby's different . . . unusual."

"No, no, no. I don't like babies."

"But you always made a fuss and cooed over them every time we saw one in the supermarket. My God," he implored, "you were always crazy about babies. Come look at this one."

"If you've seen one baby born in the suburbs of Detroit," she said in a gloomy voice, staring at the ground, "you've seen them all."

"Isabel!"

"You've seen them all," she held him off and by riding the same breath was able to ask, "Whose is it?"

Eugene jumped slightly. But then he straightened his tie, pulled down his vest, lifted his head, and looking from the buggy to Isabel, declared with a courageous, stalwart air that fell off slightly as a bit of fussy embarrassment joined his pride, "He's mine."

"Is that so? Well, well, so now you have a baby," she remarked and forced herself to keep from peeking into the carriage to check on whether the infant was really his. What she did allow, however, was a hasty glance at the woman in the white oxford shoes who stood a short distance away, at which Eugene rushed to explain, "That's his nurse."

"I see," she said, reality slipping away from her as she tried to figure out how to extricate herself from this crowd of Eugene, the buggy, and the nurse. If only, she thought, she could set off and run at a dignified, even pace until she had gained the wilderness at the edge of the park and could hide amidst the brambles to take off her shoes and flail her arms and blubber over the fact that Eugene not only had a mistress, he also had a child. How had it happened? Why had he bothered? Why hadn't he stayed in research, safely hidden in a laboratory—that's where she'd meant for him to belong. Then at the notion that her importance to Eugene was lost, that everything between them was over, she clutched her hands to her head.

"Isabel," he objected, "you're pulling your hair."

She shook her head: she had no use for such an observation. Demanding his car keys, she said with a grand air, "I have plenty of hair," and then felt sorry as she set off for the car, the keys clutched in her palm, to have chosen so paltry, so meaningless a rejoinder for her final exit.

Twenty minutes later she was changing into tennis shoes and trying to keep calm when she cast a look out her bedroom window and beheld the buggy bumping along at a good clip—just now passing the Windemeyer's house— with Eugene pushing it, the pale sides of his hair flying behind like coattails, while a bit further behind jogged the nurse. Eugene was pursuing her, she thought; and at the spectacle of her husband attached to the carriage and huffing and puffing up the street she laughed aloud and immediately felt cheered up. She leaned out the window and, safe from this perch, reflected that Eugene, the old devil, the old stodgy devil, had actually taken a little someone to lunch, had ordered chicken breasts and chocolate mousse and had produced a baby inside its buggy. It was only when he started shifting the large pram onto the curving path that led to their house that she realized—why hadn't it occurred to her—that he planned to bring the child inside. "Stop! Stop!" she commanded. With one tennis shoe on her foot, the other still in her hand, she raced down the stairs and scrambled out the door and barred the carriage by threatening it with a size nine-and-a-half Adidas.

"Be reasonable," Eugene said.

"I am reasonable."

"If only you would look beyond convention."

"Take it away. It isn't mine."

"Now there's a matter for interpretation," suggested Eugene, all the while trying to maneuver the pram around her.

"Get it away! Off the premises! Not a step further! And here's Hillary," she warned as Hillary, finished with her newspaper route, coasted up the lawn, hopped off her bike, and said, "Hullo?"

"Hillary," Eugene greeted his daughter, "I have something to show you." He gripped her arm and ushered her forward. "You can be honest. What do you think of this handsome infant?"

Hillary shot a guarded glance from her father to her mother. "Is this a joke?" she asked. Taking a deep breath, she plunged her head into the pram. She scarcely had time to see anything when she removed her head and allowed, "Not too bad."

"What did I tell you? A handsome baby."

But Isabel had already set her jaw like iron, every promontory in the oval of her face as stark and ungiving as the numbers on a clock. With a gesture of despair Eugene waved on the nurse and the carriage. Still, Isabel ignored him. She marched into the house and pulled the door shut behind her. In a minute he, too, had entered the house and was circling after her in the living room, threading his way behind her through the dining room, and ducking between the rubber plants in the dinette until at last he cornered her in the den. Here he imprisoned her in between the desk and the bookcases and said urgently, yet softly enough for Hillary not to hear, "I have to tell you this: the child's mother is already married. She doesn't want him and I, of course, I never want to see her. What's excellent," he gave a brusque, pleased nod, "is that she doesn't want to see me either. But that's neither here nor there. The point is, he belongs to me. He's mine. I brought him from the hospital straight to a new, airy three-room apartment across the street from the park and I hired a sunny, warmhearted nurse—that is," he revealed, a cheek twisting ruefully, "the last nurse was sunny and warmhearted and this one is cranky. The last one was offered a better job and she left for Massachusetts. Still, that's neither here nor there. The point is," he moved closer to his wife, "ever since he was born, I've wanted to bring him to you. Ever since I first laid eyes on him I've thought that maybe some kind of justice actually exists . . . that more than furniture, more than travel, even more than science and books, he can be our consolation, yours and mine. He is our new chance . . . a kind of replacement, so to speak." He stopped and regarded her hopefully. "The point is, every time I pick him up I think . . . yes, I feel . . . I feel very strongly that you and I have a stake in him to-gether . . . that if he belongs to me he also belongs . . ." he paused again and when again she made no response, he appealed to her by extending an arm. "If he belongs to me he also . . ." he seemed unable to finish the statement. After a minute he cried out, "Isabel, don't you understand?" Straining to communicate, his eyes bore fervently into hers. At first she kept herself from comprehending. After some moments, however, she admitted he was trying to declare, either simplemindedly or cunningly, that whatever was his was also hers.

"Aren't you going too far? Isn't that a bit extreme?"

"Extreme?" He shook his head from side to side sorrowfully in a gesture unfamiliar to her. "What hasn't been extreme? Isn't it extreme to be this miserable and lonely? Still, loneliness is only loneliness . . . there's no way to go back and undo what's been done. So I've tried to concentrate on what's important. I've done everything I could think of for the boy . . . laid in a good supply of clothes, bought all the latest toys and the best soft cloth books and I stop in twice, sometimes three times a day. But as soon as I step inside the apartment I'm aware that something's wrong. There's a peculiar emptiness . . . something missing, worse than an echo. The point is, if I brought him home . . ."

"I don't want him," she interrupted.

"How can you know?"

"I don't. Under any circumstances."

"Well, if you don't . . ."

"I don't," she assured him with a shudder, imagining Linda and Kevin arriving home for Thanksgiving and Aunt Roslyn entering the house to point an accusing finger as she exclaimed, "Who is that little boy shaking a rattle in the playpen in the middle of the living room? Where did he come from and why does he look exactly like Eugene?"

". . . and yet I feel . . ." he studied her earnestly.

"Oh what a lot of nerve you have!" she wailed. "Oh how thick-skulled you are! Can't you get it into your head that this is the last place in the entire world that he belongs?"

Eugene's shoulders sagged. "I understand," he said, and he let her go.

That night after she had finished the dishes she went upstairs, sat down by the bedroom window, and opened a book. Toward nine o'clock the moon caught her eye. It glowed brilliantly through a grove of dark oak trees—the only grove of trees on this street—and what it lit up was a high white nurse's cap beneath which, bundled into an overcoat, the nurse steadily pushed the English carriage.

"Everywhere I turn," said Isabel angrily, "I see the same old impossible buggy."

Like some deliberate, slow-moving, mournful ship the carriage sailed over the pavement to the end of the block where the nurse swung it around, retraced her steps, and again passed in front of Isabel's house.

"Go away!" Isabel yelled out, her eyes narrowed. Yet when it had vanished and time passed and it did not reappear, she was left with the sense that still she wanted something. She could not identify what it was. "Go away, go away," she muttered. Eugene's confession of loneliness came back to her. Worn out, she brushed her teeth and took to bed.

Almost immediately, the baby sprang up and joined Isabel's dreams. Unknown, he looked like Hillary and like herself. She heard him crying her own cry, begging to come into her arms. Doggedly she banished him, but after each time he rolled after her in a wheelbarrow, pleading for entrance into the carpeted spaces of her house. Waking, she got out of bed and crept in the dark thickness of the night and felt on top of her dresser for the thin silver-framed photograph of Alexander. She gripped it tightly, carried it out to the wall, switched on the light, and stared hard at Alexander, hoping to block out all images of the intruder. But Alexander, who looked back at her calmly, told her she had frozen herself against his father and reminded her she was responsible for the baby's birth.

"Alexander!" she cried at the photograph, wanting her son back. She moved down the hall, quietly pushed open a door and peered into Alexander's room, where Eugene now slept. She pulled her night clothes around her tightly and lifted her brows in sorrow, regretting her coldness to Eugene and the cruelty, the resentment that had blossomed from her grief. Returning to her own bed, so afraid was she to fall asleep that she lay with her arms and legs stretched down rigidly to guard against the unlocking of any further torments.

But when at last she slept again, this time she dreamt it was she who was Eugene's mistress. It was she who wore new shoes and the latest patterned stockings, who crossed her shimmering ankles under a restaurant table laid with smooth linen, a vase of roses on its top. And as she sat there across from Eugene, gradually she became aware that her breasts were growing larger and filling up and her stomach was expanding and that both she and Eugene were observing this phenomenon with interest and with pride. Then in the dream itself she recalled Maxine Barbarelli's introduction and remembered first falling in love with Eugene—drawn by the integrity she'd sensed in his serious light blue eyes, by his ponderous scholarly tread, and by an intuition that had come to her in the middle of a history exam that, unlike other men she knew, if she pursued Eugene she could have him. She had loved him, she understood, even before knowing the reward of his covert, his absentminded closeness.

In the morning, at the instant of opening her eyes, she awoke confused: was Eugene's baby really hers? Then she forgot her dream altogether. But before going to the hospital she made a detour and circled the park. She put in six hours—a longer stint of work than usual—and after leaving the hospital brought Hillary's winter boots to the shoe repair, bought some light bulbs at the hardware store and a Halloween pumpkin at the supermarket, and, just before four o'clock, drove to the park.

Here she sought out the bench Eugene had dusted off for her, and hovered in front of it. A few yards away, a group of five or six children in costume, boldly issuing orders and commands, jumped on and off a cement block by the water fountain, their wings aglitter and their feathered headdresses, tall as buildings, slipping down around their cheeks. A short elderly couple marched by. In collars and caps from another time, they matched their brisk steps, each one answering the other's chatter. The weather turned colder, and a deep metallic gold had just begun to burnish the dark wintry sky when Isabel spotted the buggy coming up a slight incline. She strode forward and, just before reaching the nurse, exclaimed, "What a beautiful baby!" so as to gain permission to look into the carriage. Fearfully she lowered her head. And there, raised up at her, she saw Eugene's loneliness in the boy's blue, almond-shaped eyes, recognized Alexander's nose with its indentation like a thumb print, and, as if for added mystery and intrigue, was confronted with the delicate lips and mouth of Eugene's unknown mistress. She thought then about Eugene's mistress, speculated, almost with awe, on how she and Eugene—without the advantage of having been introduced by Maxine Barbarelli—had arrived at love.

Isabel bent over and picked up the baby. She gazed at the infant in her arms. She held him tightly and paid particular attention to his nose. After awhile the rest of him also appealed to her as charming, wise, and exceptional; and when presently he began to fret, she settled him in the carriage and pushed the pram up and down the paths, stopping to rock it slightly. Glancing furtively around she sang, "Don't cry, don't cry"—the only words she could remember from Hillary's early time.

Soon the air grew colder still, the sky in its grayness hung lower, and the children in their bright clothes scattered, abandoning the park. With a certain hesitance Isabel made a left turn by the water fountain. She nodded at the nurse who was still sitting on the bench and on an impulse passed her by, turning right at the end of the row of poplar trees. When she reached the street she quickened her pace, walked past her car, smiled shyly at the infant, and thinking that Eugene might already be waiting for them, she straightway wheeled the carriage home.

THE INSULT

Arnold Isaiah Hepplemeyer, for some years comfortable with his name, pleased with his contribution to mankind, and no longer at odds even with the large size of his shoes, swallowed his two slices of unbuttered whole grain toast, savored his mug of half-regular, half-decaffeinated brew, remembered to kiss his wife goodbye, reminded his thirteen-year-old son to put out the empty bottles for recycling, and, satisfied at having gotten all that behind him, went speedily down the cement steps bordered by ivy and brush that led from his front door to his 1986 Volvo parked on the street. When he reached his car he stopped next to its hood, which he fixed with a gaze of pain. Then he got inside the automobile, drove the ten blocks to the Altway Repair Garage, and said to the mechanic, "Four days, are you sure?"

"Four or five at the least."

"Well, I suppose that's all right . . . for an automatic transmission. Six hundred dollars?"

"Seven hundred and fifty," the mechanic replied.

Arnold Hepplemeyer gave a stoic nod. Setting his lips, he handed over his keys and forced himself to leave the garage, twice twisting his head to send his Volvo a few covert signs of reproach and farewell.

Yet out on the pavement, one foot lifting after the other in his suburb north of San Francisco, he felt a sudden sense of liberation and he began to look forward to riding to his office on the bus. He recalled his old fondness for buses—in particular the Dexter #41 bus in the city where he was born, whose yellow and brown presence, two blocks from his mother's apartment, had promised freedom and release from his mother. In his mind's eye he saw that vehicle come barreling toward him like some friendly and overlarge dog, and, lengthening his stride, he gaily carried certain selected happy memories of a distant time and place past this town's splendid deli-liquor store, past the wilting pyramids of shampoo containers in the drab window of its beauty parlor, past his son's junior high school, fog still rising from the pebbles and empty spaces of the playground, past the juniper trees in pots attending the car wash like soldiers, and one block further north, where he crossed the street to the bus kiosk.

Here he found himself at the edge of a flock of nine or ten women, similar in height and somewhat pigeon-like in shape. They were young to middle-aged, flat wool cardigans buttoned over their shoulders and large tote bags at their feet. Because they appeared to Arnold to be Central American in origin, he guessed that they now resided in San Francisco and that on weekdays they transferred from a city bus and rode up the county to get off at various stops and clean houses. Companionably he nodded, took up a position to their right, and soon noted that no chatter, no conversation—not a single word—passed between them. How remarkable, he thought, and he gazed open-eyed at these women who worked in the houses of others, thinking that their stillness was like that of silenced birds and wishing there were some gesture of tribute or reassurance he could offer. Then, anxious lest one of them cleaned house for his wife—one whom he could not distinguish from the others—he devised a general smile. He was on the verge of delivering it around when he discerned in the women's gentle and guarded faces that what they wanted from him was not to be disturbed.

Arnold withdrew as quickly as he could. He moved from the curb where, hunched over, his eye on a discarded popcorn carton, he commended himself for his sensitivity to the feelings of others. He stepped off the curb, tried to praise himself again, craned his head for a glimpse of the bus, caught sight of the bus, stepped back, turned his head, and saw scrawled on the back wall of the kiosk, "Hepplemeyer is an ass."

For an instant he forgot that his name was Hepplemeyer. When that instant ended, it seemed to him that the Hepplemeyer on the kiosk wall must certainly refer to someone other than himself. But then his ears began to burn, his head to pound, his throat to dry, and, swallowing with some difficulty, he confronted the fact that in all the county there was no other Hepplemeyer. Stealthily he looked at the wall again. From the wall he glanced anxiously at his oversized oxblood Cordovans and then at the unchanged faces of the silent women. At least, he thought, none of them knew who he was. Grateful for this bit of anonymity, he circled around, joined the end of a line just now forming, felt in his pocket for the exact change for the bus, and reminded himself that he was a decent, worthwhile citizen—that he had been married to the same woman for eighteen years, even when she bored him, that he had sired and was bringing up a son and owned a house, an excellent Volvo, a vintage Plymouth, a fine stereo system, four walls of books, and seven paintings of the sunset.

As he added the paintings to his list, the bus reached the kiosk. It stood alongside like a dragon, panting and spewing a few plumes of smoke and appearing to Arnold a good deal less friendly than the Dexter #41 bus. Looking up, he observed that at every right-hand window, passenger after passenger stared out idly or with interest, each elevated position offering an unobstructed view of "Hepplemeyer is an ass." Looking down, he tried to guess how many of them had actually registered the statement and were even now connecting it with him, with Arnold Isaiah Hepplemeyer, the orthodontist. Confused, he tried to shrink himself smaller, then to make himself thinner. When the line began to move he hid behind the woman in front of him and inched forward like her shadow, but came to his senses and with dignity boarded the bus on his own, keeping in mind the good character of his wife and the fact that, if not he, then at least his son was handsome, clear-eyed, athletic, and at ease with his peers.

It was his love for Jonah and his knowledge of Jonah's love for him that he then took along with him as he worked his way up the aisle and located a seat in the rear. He thought of Jonah, recently elected president of his eighth-grade class, and though he often disapproved of taking pride or comfort from the accomplishments of others, he now imagined his son applauded and universally acclaimed. From there he remembered Jonah as a child of four or five, walking at his side from one end to the other of the downtown. He remembered that on one occasion they had ambled along for a good number of blocks, silent on a summer's afternoon, Jonah's hand gripped in his father's, when the young boy had piped into the air, "Do you like strawberries?"

Arnold recalled that he had not answered right away—that some unexpected assurance and authority resounding in the child's voice had caused him to pause, had led him to reflect that his son's question went beyond the matter of strawberries, that it involved more than a mutual assessment of the sky or snow or cars or houses and dogs and cats, that indeed it came out of Jonah's assumption that his own and his father's existence on the face of the earth was utterly simultaneous and shared.

Hepplemeyer peered out at the ochre hills dulled by fog and scolded himself for his response to the writing on the wall. "It's simple foolishness. It's utter foolishness," he declared to the hills.

Then he cast a kindly gaze over the heads of the passengers in front of him and considered his accomplishments as an orthodontist. In his mind's eye he arranged his former patients, the Macmillan family, a very tall father, mother, daughter, and son. Over the years he had worked on the teeth of all four, and he now recalled the gaps he'd done away with, visualized the tongues for which he'd made room, reviewed the bites he'd improved, and came at last to their straightened smiles. He had on a recent night run into the family on their way for ice cream at Baskin Robbins. It was they who had spotted him first and had come plunging toward him, enthusiastically baring their teeth. The warmth of their greeting expressed through the high bright splendor of their smiles had dazzled and filled him with pride.

Smiles such as the Macmillans, he reflected, could easily light up half a shopping mall. What did one scurrilous statement on a bus stop wall matter when he'd experienced true success! "Jonah," he considered advising his son, "every person who goes to sleep at night wakes up in the morning in danger of being insulted. That hazard is universal. So what you have to do is square your shoulders, ignore the insult, and march on."

Arnold faced straight ahead, squared his shoulders, squared them again, and was starting to enjoy the bus ride when the bus hit a pothole and reared up in the air to descend in the path of an oncoming truck. The driver swerved widely, the vehicle rocketed out of control, passengers and parcels tumbled together, and Arnold, gripping his seat, thought desperately, "What if I should die today? If that happens, what would be the last my son would know of me—that I was responsible for the Macmillans' wonderful teeth? No," he laughed and shook his head, "not their teeth or anyone else's." And a knife seemed to burrow its way into his chest as he identified his last legacy to Jonah, as he pictured Jonah in the kiosk, alone and then in the company of his mother and after that surrounded by the city council, all of them reading the wall.

Arnold jumped up. He pulled on the cord above him and stood by the exit, lurching with the bus and ready to leap out at the first possible moment—prepared to jog back and erase the graffiti. As the bus righted itself, he was able to block from his mind all other responsibilities. Yet by the time the vehicle had pulled up to a curb and halted and the other passengers had retrieved their possessions and vented their cries of annoyance and giggles of relief, he was sitting down again, furious that his schedule of appointments had returned to his consciousness, equally furious that he attached so much significance to the writing on the wall, and for the first time wondering who had wanted to cause him so much pain.

Was it, he speculated, someone so unlikely as the stubborn, sallow-faced clerk at the dry cleaner's with whom he

had almost come to blows when she refused to acknowledge that the dry cleaning had frayed the cuffs of his
pinstriped suit? Was it a colleague swept away by envy?
Was it a disgruntled or a difficult patient, such as Sally
Lehman who dragged into his office on Thursday afternoons, her fierce face closed like a fist, her muddy eyes
squinting with hatred as she hailed him, "Hullo, torturer!"?
Was it his mother? But his mother was dead.

He had not finished with drawing on possible suspects
when he got off at the stop nearest his office and, a short
distance away, caught sight of Adeline, in his opinion the
region's prettiest prostitute. Adeline, whose territory
started near the kiosk in Arnold's town and extended north
to include a third of the county, stood decoratively on a
curb by the crossroads, her blonde hair streaming down
her shoulders.

Arnold made out the pink bows stuck on the toes of her
high-heeled shoes and thought, "Of course! It's Adeline! It's
obviously Adeline who has defamed my name." And it
seemed to him that she had good reason.

Six days ago when he stopped for a traffic light at the
kiosk corner, she had opened the door of his Volvo, had
stuck in a pointed rose-colored shoe, and leaning in his
direction had whispered something—he'd not been able
to decide exactly what. "I didn't quite hear you, would you
mind repeating that?" he'd asked, extremely flustered.
Then speaking quickly so as to let her know the range of
his good will before the light changed, he declared—his

voice surprising him, almost a shout—that he had long opposed the police harassing her and her friends and that whenever he passed her by he never failed to admire her silhouette outlined against the fields and against the sky.

At this Adeline had quietly removed her toe and turned her back, slamming the door of his car.

Oh why, Arnold now lamented, had he abandoned his quiet ways and his normal reserve when he knew that Adeline and her cohorts sometimes took their coffee breaks in the kiosk. After listening to such a speech, surely it made sense she would be moved to reach up and write "Hepplemeyer is an ass." How he wished he had not been misunderstood by so pretty a girl! Realizing he was about to pass in front of her, he lowered his eyes, twisting his head so that it was bent as far as possible the opposite way. So awkward was the position that something in his neck began to hurt. With this new physical pain topping off Adeline's contempt, other injuries in his past rose up and smote him for the first time in many years: the poverty of his childhood, his mother's taunts, the absence of his father, and his mother's insinuation that it was because of him that his father had abandoned the family. Bitterly he retraced the indignities of his adolescence and took into account the long hard hours he had worked to put himself through college and professional school. He had stepped into adulthood demanding very little and asking for no fanfare. He was a man who had paid his dues conscientiously. Then why, he questioned, was he not exempt from ridicule in public?

Unfair, unjust, he passionately objected and, entering his office, he nodded coolly at his receptionist.

The rest of the morning he was haunted by the graffiti. He had the sense he would never be rid of it. It was as if that heinous judgment had been destined for him from his birth—that his father had left the family knowing what lay ahead. Everything desirable seemed to have forsaken him, even his Volvo.

Then he thought about the cleaning women in the kiosk, realizing with shame that for all his civility and approval he had held himself superior—had not seen himself as one of them. It was all he could do to usher in his new patients, to ask them what grade they were in, and to warn it would loosen their bands if they chewed on ice or on French bread. In between his new and his old patients, he sought out a glass-enclosed case that was mounted on the wall and that displayed two long shelves of dental impressions. He hovered near the shapes of white plaster, hoping to find in these souvenirs of his work some intimation of peace or at least a bit of comfort. When he found neither he went to the window. Glumly he stared into the parking lot at the stand of eucalyptus trees stretching their straggly hungry-looking limbs over two Hondas and three Toyotas. He watched as a Subaru bumped into the lot. The driver, a tanned woman in a denim skirt and a blue work shirt, got out of the car, came around, opened the passenger door, and began yanking and pulling at a teenager's arms and legs. Arnold recognized the teenager, his next patient. He came away from the window and stood by the display case, heartsick and thinking that the time had perhaps come to give up his practice—that the gift of radiance he had meant to bestow on Marin County was no longer viable since these days fewer and fewer people smiled.

By two o'clock he could stand his work no longer. He canceled the rest of his appointments, strode out onto the street, and set forth to restore dignity to his name. What tools, he wondered, were most appropriate for the task? A long knife? A sharp sword? He had only a handkerchief, he reflected, putting his hands through his pockets; and he turned and ran back to his office building and from a hall closet borrowed a scrub brush, a sponge, and a plastic can of 409. He put these in a plastic sack, yet wanted something more. After a moment's thought he dove into his own office and added to the plastic sack the latest offering of a dental supply company—a giant demonstration toothbrush, the size almost of a cane. Armed with these instruments he rode the bus in the opposite direction and got out at the north side of his town. He hung back from crossing to the kiosk until its present occupants, old Mrs. Fowler, the pharmacy cashier, and two construction workers had boarded a bus that trundled toward the highway, leaving the kiosk empty.

Arnold moved toward the wall gingerly. He lifted his eyes. Though it seemed impossible, "Hepplemeyer is an ass" was still there, shocking him anew. Stealthily he took out the 409, the sponge, the scrub brush, and the tooth-brush. But the job was not as easy as he'd expected. Though he used each of the implements, though he doused the wall's rough pebbled surface with 409, little happened. Worriedly he glanced across the street in the direction of Jonah's school. Classes, he knew, would soon let out. He renewed his efforts and the "H" disappeared. He read "epplemeyer is an ass" and consulted his watch. In fifteen minutes his son would leave the classroom. If Jonah stayed on the playground to shoot some baskets or for soccer practice it was conceivable that from one of the higher rises of the field he might spot his father. And if he did and if he wandered over to ask what his father was up to, at what juncture would he arrive? Would part of the "epple" still be there? Would all of the "meyer"? Sweating, Arnold continued to scrub and scour and scrape and scratch until at last, helped out, it seemed to him, by the long handle of the toothbrush, each of the letters vanished.

He finished with some minutes to compose himself. When his hands stopped trembling he angled across the street down toward the junior high school. Here he waited just inside the gate. At three o'clock doors opened and from the complex of buildings, boys and girls of vari-ous heights rushed out, and presently Jonah emerged. The three students who accompanied him peeled away short of reaching Jonah's father. As Jonah approached, a question on his face, Arnold took a step forward and then stepped back, suddenly feeling both shy and truant to have arrived so unexpectedly on territory not his own. "I thought I'd stop by," he explained. "With the Volvo in the garage. . . ."

"Great," said Jonah. "Are you going home? We'll walk together." He carried a book bag in one hand and laid his free hand on his father's shoulder. Together they started up the street but had advanced no more than twenty paces when Jonah stopped and Arnold, following his gaze, saw chalked on the pavement, "Hepplemeyer is a turd."

Arnold flushed, his ears and the back of his neck flaming. He turned away and faced the slow traffic and the twin squat office buildings across the road. If only, he thought, he had never married; if only he had been clever enough to go through life unrelated and alone, then he could easily have withstood any insult.

"'Hepplemeyer is a turd,'" Jonah repeated as though ruminating. He shook his head. "This is the fourth one today. There's a "Hepplemeyer sucks" in the dirt in the playground and there's a "Screw Hepplemeyer" by the back parking lot, and a third one that says . . . I forget the exact words."

"There's a 'Screw Hepplemeyer?'" said Arnold weakly, still facing the traffic.

"It's over by the tennis courts," Jonah confirmed, his voice quite cheerful. "It's written there twice. And it's all the work of that dumb Willy LaBotte. He acts like he's still in second grade."

"Willy LaBotte?"

"He won't leave me alone. Ever since I beat him at—"

"It's you?" Arnold puzzled.

"What do you mean, it's me?" Jonah asked, scuffing out the first few letters with the sole of his Nikes.

"It isn't me?"

Jonah frowned. "Why should it be you?"

"Oh," Arnold began. "Oh no reason," he went on, utterly amazed. He waved a hand in midair, relief coursing through him with the headiness of bliss—bliss of the same order, he recalled, as the time he'd unexpectedly won $525 at the races. Better my son than me, his insides sang out. "Willy LaBotte. Well, well! We'll have to deal with him. Where does he live? Who are his parents? What does his father do?" He paused. At the center of his giddiness a queasy sensation crept in. "We'll have to deal with him all right, we can't let this go on." Gradually his muttering ceased, the notion of his relief—of its base and ignoble nature—filling him with silence.

"Don't worry about it, Dad. It isn't serious."

"It is serious."

"It isn't serious," Jonah laughed. He pointed to the pavement. "That doesn't bother me." He took his father's arm and tried to pull him along.

"It doesn't bother you?" Arnold objected. "Why not?"

Jonah looked at his father and considered the question. He shrugged. "It just doesn't. Sticks and stones. . . ." He let go of his father's arm, threw his book bag into the air, caught it, and laughed again.

"Sticks and stones . . . ?" questioned Arnold, and listening to the sound of his son's laughter—hearing in his soul its easy notes—he seemed to be lifted up into an unfamiliar state of grace. From this high vantage he understood that his worthless childhood and adolescence had long gone by. He joined his son and they strode along, passing the car wash, the beauty parlor, the liquor-deli. "You're right, it's just sticks and stones," Arnold concurred, glancing at Jonah with admiration. For a moment he shuddered to think that what lay ahead was Jonah's departure from home and the aging years of his marriage and of his Volvo. Then, like one more sign of grace, the Macmillan family sprang into his mind and with them the entire bright dream of suffusing Marin County with radiance tooth by tooth. Arnold Isaiah Hepplemeyer continued up the street—in his orthodontist's eye a happy image of the tall Macmillan father, mother, daughter, son—their carriage erect, their perfect, their wide and astonishingly beautiful smiles gleaming in the sunlight and under the stars.

HOSPITALITY

On a Wednesday evening Penelope Eakins, one of my roommates, told us she'd invited a murderer to dinner for Thursday. We were seated at a bench around our oilcloth-covered kitchen table, admiring our new salt and pepper shakers, when Penelope broke away from her end of the table and uncurled herself to her height of six feet one. Penelope, who is full of inward conversations, frequently garbles her words; they tend to stay in her chest. But this evening her speech took on an almost clarion distinctness as she informed us she had known the murderer shortly before he had murdered. They had been in Meredith's Contemporary Civilization seminar and at least once every other week had walked from the seminar into the corridor together. On one occasion he had even borrowed her notes, returning them the next class meeting with the comment he could not read her writing. Soon after the class had ended, his photograph had appeared in all the papers.

"You know who I mean, don't you?" she asked.

But Rowena, spinning out her air of indifference, pretended she had no idea who Penelope meant. "One of your little people," Rowena murmured. "One of your lost and impaired," she said, and went on writing in her notebook.

And then there we were: in the middle of their contest over which of them brought home the more interesting, the more illustrious guest. This evening Penelope appeared to believe she had won. Standing before us, she jumped up, touched the ceiling with the flat of her hand, and declared she had been surprised to see her former classmate going in and out of the bookstores at ten o'clock in the morning in Harvard Square. She had been surprised, she said, until it dawned on her he must be out on bail, at which she'd crossed the street and followed him into Wordsworth's where she asked him to come to dinner.

"You've invited Paxton Eliot?" I exclaimed with surprise.

"Paxton Eliot," she affirmed, and strode to the stove where she rattled an empty fry pan as though she were on her way to becoming the most important person in our flat—the one who showed us what to do and how to act. As there were no more than four of us in the flat— Penelope, Rowena, Ginny, and myself—and therefore only three to rule, any effort to achieve sovereignty seemed to me scarcely worth the trouble. In Penelope's case it was her height, I believe, that lured her on. It was responsibility toward her height and, of course, the presence of Rowena—blonde, full-bodied, competent Rowena, with the suggestion about her of famous, felled, erudite lovers and of purses packed with fellowships to Europe when every one else's purse was empty. Yes, it was Rowena, a rope of hair to her shoulders, a geranium at her ear, her teeth like high bright walls, whom Penelope strove to lead, for when Rowena was not around, Penelope became kind and rather sloppy.

It was Rowena who now inquired, as though she had never before heard his name, "Paxton Eliot?"

"Don't you read the newspapers?!" Penelope demanded.

"The son of David and Erica Eliot," I spelled out.

"Their only child," said Penelope with a certain pride.

"You walked right up to him when he was out on bail," I puzzled, "and said, 'Come to dinner'?"

"I said," Penelope nodded, "'come at seven.' I explained we are four women who share space and duties. I said that there's nothing sexual about the arrangement, that three of us are graduate students, and that our fourth roommate, Ginny Bolinger, works in a warehouse office in Boston."

Ginny Bolinger blushed. She was a skinny, olive-skinned girl with devotion in her hazel eyes and wide mouth. She would have been a graduate student if she could. Penelope and I, realizing her low opinion of herself, often professed admiration for the speed of her typing and word processing. But though we professed it with diligence, and she listened to us with respect, we failed in the end to convince her—failed in fact after so many attempts that I, too, began to wish she were a graduate student. On the other hand, so grateful was Ginny to be included in our household that when the four of us assembled to drink coffee and read the *New York Times*, a smile spread over her cheeks and she gazed around her as though blessed.

And in certain ways Ginny had reason to feel blessed. For ours was an apartment with style—the living room elegant with a pair of end tables we'd sprayed a wondrous shade of lapis lazuli, a couch we'd covered in a Matisse-like, printed cloth, curtains we'd stitched from antique pieces of fabric, and on the walls two watercolors of water lilies which we'd borrowed from Gropius Hall. As if this were not enough, on top of each end table sprouted the head of a cactus while at the far end of the room stood three potted ferns, each plant constantly growing. Yes, ours was a household of dreams and anticipation into whose careful setting Rowena had brought to tea or dinner four of her professors, one by one—two of whom I believe she took to bed. She also brought us the dean of Arts and Sciences, the chairman of Mutual Fund Insurance, the vice-president of Gen-Tech of Massachusetts, and just ten days ago, the president of Harvard.

How could Penelope live up to that?

"Paxton Eliot?" Ginny slowly uttered the name. Glancing at Ginny, I saw her unwillingness to risk betraying an unsophisticated attitude toward crime. "Pen, I'm not sure I understand. You mean, the Paxton Eliot who shot a middle-aged woman he didn't know—who just happened to walk past his window?" Sorrow clouded Ginny's face. She lowered her head, unhappy at showing herself faithless. "Penelope," she apologized, "I like everyone you've brought to dinner. I particularly liked the prostitute who came near Christmas with the flu or was it the measles. I thought it showed real hospitality that you invited her to stay the week. I hardly minded she was still contagious. I didn't even mind the man without legs . . . did I ever mention this to you . . . the man with roller skates on his stumps who goosed me as we carried him up the stairs? And if your friend had, say, robbed a bank or stolen a car, or even if he had had . . . some good reason . . ."

"If it had been a crime of passion," I finished her thought.

"If it had been that," Ginny agreed, her palm forward to acquit Paxton. She turned her palm the other way. "But it wasn't a crime of passion, since he didn't know her."

"Nevertheless," Penelope assured Ginny, "it was a crime of passion. Of deep passion."

"But he didn't even know her."

"It was a symbolic act," Penelope explained, and cast an eye on Rowena who, continuing to write in her notebook, appeared to pay no attention. "That's what it was, he was killing symbolically."

"Who?" I inquired.

"Who?" asked Ginny, her hair standing on end. And at this I glimpsed Rowena's chin lifting slightly from her notebook.

"Why, his parents of course," Penelope replied. "He was killing David and Erica Eliot."

We grew silent then, and I, for one, began thinking about David and Erica Eliot, a couple renowned for their team-teaching at the University, their joint research into genetics and, most recently, for their gallantry toward one another in middle age. On occasion I would glimpse them in the Wursthaus, eating pastrami sandwiches in a booth at noon. Always pleased to recognize them, I would secretly regard their long, ascetic, fine-skinned faces—faces grown alike, their expression a seamless blend of saintliness and self-love. I also saw them in magazines and scientific journals—sampled aspects of their life as portrayed in photographs taken in the classroom or the laboratory, in their library, in their rose garden, in their gourmet kitchen, on the high slopes of the Alps—but never, it now occurred to me, in the company of their son.

"The Eliots as parents," Rowena mused. She shut her notebook. Leaning back, she swept the kitchen with her long-lashed glance that seemed to cleanse the room by fading our presence. "Now let's see, what prizes have they won this year? The Commodore. The Rubenstein. The Terence award."

Penelope frowned. "Their son is a victim."

"The Whitsun," Rowena went on. "No, that was last year. The Centennial McAllister. We mustn't forget the Centennial McAllister, that glorious, that . . . substantial prize."

Penelope's frown deepened. I read the worry in her face—her fear that Paxton had been associated through reasons of birth with too many prizes. Then, of course, I understood her concern, for the fact was, Paxton Eliot had been brought up with privilege while in the past Penelope had always sought out a more obscure and needy specimen of man. I had watched her—her brows drawn in concentration—pluck forth only the trampled and the battered—whichever ones would come with her as she made her way through Harvard Square. Was that compassion, I had sometimes wondered; was it simply guilt because her father owned a building- supply empire? It was both of these, I'd finally decided, but also that she wanted to wrest from each mangled person the special secret of his or her life so as to bank it in herself. But Paxton Eliot's life?

"If only he hadn't killed someone," Ginny sighed.

Penelope considered Ginny's remark. Lifting our glass salt container from the ledge above the stove, she glumly, absently shook salt on her thumb. But then she set down the salt, stood up tall, and with her short-cropped dark hair looked noble as a knight. "He is a victim of his parents' success," she pronounced, striding back toward us from the stove. "He is an outcast. He is," she concluded, checking her shadow on the wall, "among the wretched of the earth. For that reason we'll use our linen napkins."

Penelope, Ginny, and I waited for Rowena's response. At last Rowena murmured, gazing into the scepter of her enameled and jeweled pen, "Well, why not the linen napkins."

"Absolutely," Penelope declared triumphantly, "absolutely the linen napkins!" She returned to her place at the table and, as she did, it struck me she gave these performances in the kitchen as much for Rowena as for herself.

The next morning Penelope summoned me, and we readied ourselves to shop for groceries. It was Penelope's week to cook, Rowena's to clean the bathroom, Ginny's to mop the kitchen, and mine to help with marketing and to wash the dishes. Every Monday Rowena wrote out and posted the schedule, and although Penelope believed she ought to be the one who offered such directives, the sharing of our space and duties never failed to thrill her. She saw us as a handy commune and gladly fulfilled every obligation, often while wearing a rebellious-looking hat. This morning, however, she set out bareheaded, with one hand motioning me onward while with the other she maneuvered our defective grocery cart along the bumpy pavement and under the canopy of trees. Turning onto Massachusetts Avenue, she danced over the cobblestones and breathed in deeply of the air filled with bus fumes. She was thinking, I believe, either of Paxton Eliot or of life's grand though elusive meaning. Then closer to the Commons she abruptly stopped and placed an arm around my shoulder. "It was here," she said, "the woman was walking when Paxton shot her. It was there," she waved up at a row of windows in a four-story red brick apartment house, "Paxton lived and pointed his gun." She leaned down, closer toward me. "I think he's more important than Rowena's president of Harvard. He is the ultimate outsider, the outcast no one knows what to do with. He . . . well, he combines misery and degradation with social and cultural advantage. He has more to say," she said as we left the Commons and threaded our way through the pedestrians and past the craft shops, the flower stands, the yogurt parlors, "he has more to say because he reveals to all of us—and to Rowena as well—the nature of mindless violence and the rise of anomie in the modern world."

"Anomie?"

"The loss of community. You and I," she went on, ignoring my attempt to make some remark, "you and I, we share a kitchen, a living room. We might have our differences, but we also have our common floor space. But Paxton . . . he lives alone. Whenever I saw him, he was by himself. He is the definitive miserable, well-born graduate student who at last combines Rowena's standards with mine. Imagine—not only Rowena's standards but also mine!" She gave our cart a forceful push. "So what do you suppose," she turned toward me, "he would like most of all to eat?"

Her question took me by surprise. "Well, since you're the one cooking tonight," I demurred, pausing to take into account certain difficulties—that for one thing Penelope was a vegetarian. Yet she was the only vegetarian in our flat. Sometimes, to keep her company, Ginny would quietly renounce meat. But I would not; and as for Rowena—in front of Penelope she ate her chops and chickens with a gleaming ostentation, baring the considerable stretches of her giant white teeth. In turn, Penelope would chew her carrots with a self-righteous air of exaltation. Nor did it end at that. For when bank owners or chairmen of boards took Rowena out to dinner, she would return to our kitchen, hint of high-ranking job offers just laid at her feet, and report to Penelope, her smile beatific, "I've had such lovely little lamb chops," or "such choice, sweet kidneys," or "such an outstanding example of New York steak."

"Well, since you're the one cooking," I said again, "how about your zucchini and spinach casserole?"

"No one likes it."

"Or your curry of lentils and apples, with the seven different pieces of grain in it? Or how about . . . what is it . . . your oat and dandelion stew?"

"My oat stew," she echoed from deep in her chest. "I absolutely hear you." But in truth she did not listen, and as we approached the market, she broke into a run, bounded through the automatic doors and cantered to the meat counter where she slipped a standing rib roast into our cart. From there she proceeded to the checkout stand where she took her place in line and stood with shoulders hunched over the cart as if hiding the roast or protecting her shame. "We just might have to feed it to him," she muttered toward me. She began to search her pockets for money. "He just might need it. He just might require a sizeable portion . . . a good-sized hunk of juicy, red, honest meat."

It was then I understood the extent to which the rivalry with Rowena had undermined her. Certainly a few months earlier, she never would have purchased a single ounce of hamburger, let alone a six-pound rib roast. I, too, felt somehow implicated as we quit the store, Penelope's jacket flung over the meat. Soberly we bought bread at the bakery; we bought grapefruit at the fruit stand; we bought candles at the florist's. Then Penelope turned to me and asked, "Is the crime he committed important enough? Does it help us understand the nature of existence? Will it help Rowena understand?"

"It would be easier if he'd robbed a bank," I said.

As it happened, I was the one who answered the door. Penelope was in the kitchen, cooking; Ginny was cleaning the kitchen floor, and Rowena in her bedroom was updating her curriculum vitae. When I heard two gentle knocks, I called out to Penelope. She called back she was finishing the sauce. Reluctant as I was to usher in Paxton Eliot, I nevertheless felt a certain excitement. I pulled open the door, and there in front of me stood an overweight man of medium height with a large, bland head. Looking to the left of him, I reflected that a man who has committed a murder and accepts an invitation to dinner ought at least to be better looking. "Penelope has spoken about you," I said.

He nodded gravely as if accepting this homage, and on second glance I allowed he appeared a good deal more presentable than Penelope's usual guests, clad as he was in a fine tweed suit with a vest, a freshly starched shirt, and a paisley silk tie. And unlike other of Penelope's visitors— such as the leftover member of a disappeared rock band who desperately drummed his fingers on the door frame or the ragged politician unable to stop banging his fist— Paxton Eliot stood as still as could be, his head rising formally from his collar, no message in his bearing of frantic energy or hope.

"Yes, she's spoken quite a bit about you," I said, hoping to act as if nothing in his history had happened. I even pretended I did not notice he'd brought along a suitcase and was sliding it under our hall table, against the wall. "She mentioned the two of you were in Meredith's Contemporary Civilization."

But he made no reply, his eye now on Rowena who had emerged from the back of the hall and was sailing toward us, her hand extended as graciously as if she'd invited him herself.

"How are your parents?" she asked in her queenly fashion. "I'm in genetics as well." She pulled down her green gauze blouse. "My dissertation covers some of the same areas ..." she smiled; and tucking her arm into Paxton's arm, she led him into the living room. When she let go she motioned him into our best but stiffest arm chair, in which he seemed at home, and settled herself on our couch. From there, jingling her silver and ivory bracelets, tugging at her blouse, alternately crossing her ankles briskly and her knees languorously, she sent out signals of efficiency at big business, signals of proficiency at sex.

It was my impression he chose big business. He was sitting bolt upright, his own knees carefully together as though he were protecting himself from unknown dangers in our living room. Or was I wrong? Did I now detect the faintest glimmer in his opaque brown eyes, a swift stirring of desire toward Rowena that made him shift slightly, as if with discomfort, in our hard-backed chair? I frowned with disapproval. "Paxton and Penelope," I reminded the room, "took Meredith's Contemporary Civilization seminar."

As if these words had called her forth, Penelope ran in from the kitchen, carrying with her the smell of scorched green beans and a square tray on which stood a bottle and five glasses. Behind her dragged a pale Ginny, a small wooden bowl of nuts in her hand.

"Sherry, who would like some sherry?" Penelope shouted, her voice cracking. She poured each of us a drink. Paxton gulped his down and said, "This is a fine apartment. It's rare to find rooms so capacious near Harvard Square." His eye roamed briefly, then came to rest on the sherry bottle.

Noting his interest, Rowena grabbed the bottle from Penelope and pressed it to herself. "Another sherry? Some pistachios?" Rowena sang, and turning to Ginny, who stood frozen in the center of the room clutching the bowl of nuts, she said under her breath, "Offer the pistachios, don't just keep standing there!"

"Sorry," Ginny said, "It's just that . . . you see . . ." Her head spun slowly, warily, toward Paxton.

Paxton Eliot winced.

Ginny took a single step forward.

"The pistachios!" Rowena hissed.

Ginny advanced a few more steps and held out her bowl. Paxton accepted two pistachios. "Delicious pistachios," he remarked, nodding at Ginny as if she had made them. He reached for a third glass of sherry.

"Dinner," I said nervously. I signaled to Penelope.

"Yes, time for dinner!" Penelope took up. She plunged toward him, launching a long thin bony arm, which she placed on Paxton's shoulder. "Paxton and I," she said cheerfully, "took Meredith's Contemporary Civilization seminar together." And she led him—the rest of us following—to our table in the kitchen.

The meal began with a small dish of green beans and a bowl of Penelope's gritty cream of spinach soup. Paxton downed his portion manfully, sipping on a glass of our California cabernet. The sherry earlier and now the cabernet seemed to relax him. Turning to Ginny, he inquired in a kindly voice, "Are you from the east coast? I don't detect a Boston accent."

Ginny looked away from Paxton. She kept her lips tightly pursed together. At last she replied, barely opening her mouth, "I'm from Toledo."

"Toledo?" Paxton murmured with interest. "I have a cousin who lives in Toledo." He appeared to accord Toledo a good place on the map. "But certainly you must enjoy living in the east"—he nodded at her encouragingly—"and, of course, living in this fine apartment."

Ginny searched for escape. Her gaze traveled from our orange kalanchoe on the window sill to our Vuillard poster on the opposite wall.

"It's an excellent apartment," he continued, still addressing Ginny alone, "and what you've done to it is wonderful. I like everything about it. I like all your furnishings. I particularly like your place mats . . . your napkins."

Rowena dabbed her mouth and laughed. "Actually I'm responsible for the napkins. I discovered them quite hidden away at an estate sale."

"And we take turns ironing them," Penelope interjected.

Ignoring Penelope, Rowena looked Paxton straight in the eye. "As I mentioned before dinner, your parents and I have specific interests in common. It's unfortunate we've never met."

"My parents?"

"David and Erica Eliot."

"My parents?" His face crumpled. Then, making an effort, he turned once more to Ginny, but this time Ginny's head swiveled boldly away from him. He waited a moment, then directed his attention to me. "This is a wonderful apartment."

I stood up from the table and started clearing the soup bowls. I had no intention of letting him trap me. At the same time I felt in the wrong for turning away. Life had spared me whatever accidents had made Paxton a murderer. If only out of gratitude for my luck—if only to redress that imbalance—it seemed to me I ought to respond with a measure of friendliness. "Yes," I said, it's a great apartment." But I reached too abruptly for his soup plate and the dish slid, crashing to his foot and onto the floor.

"No harm!" he cried, leaping up.

"No harm," I echoed.

"Allow me. Where can I find your broom?" He located our broom behind the kitchen door, removed his jacket, and rolled up his shirt sleeves. "This makes me feel at home," he said as, enthusiastically, he swept up the broken pieces of glass. He took a sponge from our sink, tore off several sheets of paper towel and, bending over, mopped and scrubbed and wiped the floor to an even polish. When he had finished, he sat back down at the table, and sought our attention as if in hopes he had earned it.

"What most impresses me," he said, unrolling his shirt sleeves, "is the comfortable atmosphere the four of you have created. I wager all of you come from different walks of life. Yet you've found each other, pooled your talents, modified your temperaments, and created something warm and special. You're like a family." He paused, but for no more than a few seconds. "You see, I've given up my apartment. Last night I managed to stay with some acquaintances on Trowbridge Street."

With a start, I remembered the suitcase Paxton had left in our hall.

"You're like a special sort of family—one doubtless more satisfying than those of your origins. And so I wonder . . ." he took a deep breath, "if I might stay with you for a few nights? If I might sleep on the couch? I could help with any tasks, any domestic tasks you needed." When no one responded he said, "Just for one night?" He turned to Rowena.

In the silence I heard the rib roast sputtering in the oven. Rowena tapped along her bracelets, her fingers pausing to consult each circle of ivory and silver as if for the measure of Paxton's status. Was he, the son of David and Erica Eliot, worth an extension of his visit, or was his value no more than a single dinner?

"One, maybe two nights?" Penelope considered this prospect. Higher and higher her head ascended, and as I gazed at her wide and noble brow, I thought of her ambition to experience every kind of person—the low born and the high, the conventional and the strange, the sinner and the saint. I thought of her fervor to partake of all knowledge. Then I watched her shoot a quick glance at Rowena as if to determine whether she had or had not brought home the perfect guest. She hesitated. ". . . if you have no other place to go . . ."

"No, no," Ginny whispered.

"If you're temporarily stuck for a bed . . ." Penelope looked at me. I looked back at her and thought about hospitality. I thought about our different visitors in the past— the chairman of Mutual Fund Insurance, the man without legs, the president of Harvard—and I acknowledged that guests had given our apartment an added measure of interest, a certain glamour and panache. I reflected unhappily that because this guest had happened to murder a person, we were trapped in a moral dilemma.

"If you're temporarily stuck for a bed . . . ?" Penelope tried out again.

I glanced at Paxton and considered the virtue of compassion and forgiveness and redemption. He had asked for asylum; would we be wrong to refuse it?

"If there were no place else," Rowena said. "But there is. At this difficult time," she fluffed her hair as if to renew its aura of competence and prizes, "you will want to be with your parents. You can call them from here. You can let them know where you are. Our phone is in the hall. You might even invite them to join us for coffee."

In a desperate voice he cried out, "My parents!"

"Yes," she smiled.

He shook his head. "That isn't possible. Thank you all the same." He rose, put on his jacket, walked from the room, paused in the hall for his suitcase, and proceeded down the stairs without a further word.

And there we were: without a guest. Without a guest and the main course had not yet been served. I expected us to feel relief; after all, it had been his choice to leave our table on his own. Instead, looking around, it seemed to me that something uneasy—something like dishonor—had entered into our kitchen.

"At least we got rid of him," Ginny said.

"Yes," Rowena sighed vaguely.

In the oven the rib roast sizzled louder and louder. The room began to fill with smoke. Finally Penelope hunched over to the stove and removed the dried-out roast. She carved it with a long serrated knife and handed each of us a large portion. For a space of time we stared glumly at our plates. Then one by one we took up our knives and forks and cut and stabbed and chewed the meat, a new vacancy in our eyes, as if the practice of hospitality had betrayed us.

FIRST LOVE

Early one morning an elegant-looking, handsome young man knocked on Regina Brown's door and inquired after her rooms for rent. His head was round and fair, with small, amiable, precise features; he wore his denim shirt with grace, and in that early hour a pleasant aroma surrounded him—of soap, good aftershave lotion and something else—a scent that issued from his well-shaped mouth with every breath and that Regina tentatively identified as sherry wine.

Regina felt surprised. Recently she had bought the house next door—just six months after the death of her parents—and had rented the first floor to three girls in the School of Education and the second floor to two girls in the School of Fine Arts. But she had been keeping her last rooms at the top of the house for someone out of the ordinary. She was middle-aged and sometimes finicky and in her mind's eye she'd visualized a perfect tenant: she'd seen him—tall, near-famous, and academically well endowed—running toward her each month with rent. Could this, she thought, be he?

"How large a place are you looking for?" she asked, and even dared to tilt her head. Attractive living quarters were difficult to find in Cambridge, and for the first time in her life she understood she had something desirable to offer, something to withhold.

"Oh, I'm not inquiring for myself. It's for . . ." the young man spun about. And there, just now starting up the porch steps, was a short, stocky young woman, a pile of brown curls on top of her head and her plump face spread with an amorous, self-loving and self-deprecating smile. "My name," she announced, "is April Shapiro." She offered Regina her hand. "But what's in a name? My parents gave it to me."

"I see," Regina said. "Are you a student?"

"No," replied April, "I'm a secretary. There aren't many of us around these days, we're at a premium. And what's more important, I'm extremely dependable. I might never get married and then I'd live here forever." As she spoke she tossed a spiral notebook into the air, caught the notebook, then threw it up again and missed.

The girl's fidgeting and restlessness in the gray morning made Regina uneasy. She looked at the young man and again felt oddly attracted. Then she looked at April and began to worry that her roof would spring a leak that winter and that all the plumbing would need repair. "I'm sorry," she said, "everything is rented."

"Ah," April returned equably, "I happen to know that's not true. I have lots of feminine intuition and very good sources of information—people tell me things all the time. And I can tell just by looking at you, Miss Brown, that you are a very good landlady. So I'll come back and see you on my lunch hour."

"No, no," Regina objected as the young woman walked away, "I won't be home."

But as she had nowhere to go, she found herself, just before noon, peeking with apprehension through the window. Instead of April she beheld her three School of Education tenants returning home for lunch. School rings glittered on their fingers and the colors of their oilcloth-covered notebooks reflected the blue, autumnal sky. All three girls had spent the preceding summer studying in Florence. They'd returned home, the recipients of fellowships for the fall. Regina, who had once spent two weeks in New Hampshire, adored the idea of foreign travel. She longed to be her tenants' friend. These, she thought, were the sort of girls who moved in the important center of the world: everyone respected them, everyone knew who they were. She ran out onto the porch and called, "Hello! Good morning!"—called out feeling somehow younger than they.

"Good morning," they returned. In the wind their scarves billowed behind them; their shoe buckles gleamed silver in the sun. And Regina decided that if she rented her last rooms to April, her School of Education tenants would see in her a resemblance to April rather than any resemblance to themselves.

At 12:45 April knocked on Regina's door. Next to her stood the handsome young man whom April now introduced. He was, she said, John Galway, a Ph.D. candidate in the English department. She explained his presence by stating she had a need for company at all times, and then went on to complain that John Galway did not live with her, though she had asked him to. After that she asked if they might come in and sit down. John Galway smiled an apology as the landlady reluctantly stepped aside.

Once inside he commented on the restful quality of the surroundings. His accent was southern and pleasant, and he said, "It is nice here—and right. One feels a certain sanctity."

Startled by his remark, Regina scrutinized the room. She beheld the same living room in which she'd grown up—ten blocks from Harvard Square—a small, squat room with yellowed linen doilies on the furniture. Above the sofa, a worn tapestry depicted three weary camels marching across the desert. Next to the sofa and between the pair of chairs stood identical three-legged lamps that seemed dolefully to hang their parchment heads. Regina reflected she had seen other rooms that she liked much better, but this one, after all, had contained her life. For it was here, on an upright piano wedged against the wall, that for the benefit of her stern, her doting and frugal parents, she'd practiced Czerny in the afternoon of every day, improving very little until her parents, worn out by life and the sound of the keyboard, had sickened and finally died.

Now she watched rigidly as John Galway threaded his way between the chairs and the lamps to pause before a pair of gold-framed pictures of her mother and her father. While the young man studied the portraits she noticed that her parents' features looked particularly dyspeptic, particularly sour. Her parents, she remembered with a surge of pride, had always felt prejudiced against most young men.

John Galway then declared that Regina's parents had wonderful eyes. As she did not know what to make of him, she turned her head away and gazed through the window at her property next door. In her youth the Dean of Linnaean College had lived there. He had stood on the small, semicircular balcony—a portly, splendid man who took his ease in a red velvet smoking jacket while he held a glass in his hand. With the other hand he had sometimes waved to her.

"Wave back, wave back," her parents had said, as they had strongly approved of college presidents and deans. They had urged her friendliness even after it was much too late, for one day while she was still in high school, the Dean left off waving. His fingers had stopped in mid-air, an expression of dismay on his face, and Regina became aware that she had not grown up to be beautiful. She had turned and sought a mirror in which she saw that only her eyes appeared vivid, yet too vivid, bright, too alive, and as if in nakedness and unwitting insolence they called out asking for much too much, considering the drabness of the rest of her. But now she owned the Dean's house, and it seemed to her that her circumstances had changed for the best.

"Miss Brown," said April, peering into Regina's face, "I can tell just by looking at you that you're less petty than other landladies. I'm usually not too crazy about landladies. It's my friend John Galway who finds them interesting."

"Less petty!" John Galway strode towards them as if, thought Regina, he rushed to defend her. "Of all your landladies, Miss Brown is the most regal, the most attractively human."

Regina could not decide what that meant. She wanted to be alone to reconstruct his words. Her head spun and her ears rang, and since there seemed no other way to ensure the young man and woman's immediate disappearance, she went into a drawer and gave April the keys to her rooms. Then after they had gone she repeated to herself that John Galway thought her attractively human. Could that mean that he liked her, that he saw her as a sympathetic human being? And who would know the answer? Toward the end of the afternoon she put on her coat, trod to the garden next door, and waited for her School of Education tenants.

When they appeared she said, "Good afternoon, good afternoon!" They answered, "Good afternoon," and told her they were taking a walk to Harvard Square.

She watched them round the bend and decided that she, too, felt like taking a walk. In the nearing twilight she followed a small distance behind them, and as they reached Massachusetts Avenue and entered into the traffic, as they joined the crowds hurrying about their evening errands and the stream of Harvard students crossing from the Yard, she thought of John Galway and noticed for the first time that a large proportion of the people around her were men. She wondered why she had never before observed that men thronged the bookstores, the ice cream parlor, the barber shop, the luncheonettes. Yes, even in the women's shops there were men, buying presents for their women. Men stood in line at the movies, sat in the coffee houses, and rowed on the river—nine or ten to a boat. In their rooms above the trees, other men hung out the windows, whistling Beethoven, whistling Dixie. A wild, unreasonable joy seized Regina Brown. The yellow lights in the shops turned on; the dim pearl of streetlights began to glow. Everything in the narrow thoroughfare seemed rushing, converging, melancholy in its grayness and aspect of abandoned electricity, and yet poignant and intense in a promise for near fulfillment. Catching sight of the girls again and feeling more equal to them than before, Regina placed one foot in front of the other in imitation of their progress toward the very heart of Harvard Square.

The next evening April moved in. Through a window, Regina watched her carting boxes up the garden path. After a short time John Galway joined her. Together they lugged pillows, lamps, a television set. They were carrying armloads of April's clothes when April took a running step, stuck out her leg, and tripped them. The couple, vanishing from sight, landed in the bushes under the veranda.

Regina wanted to dash outside and look into the bushes. At the same time she did not want to see what might be going on. She imagined strewn underwear, her flower beds turbulent, the anger of unknown deans. "Leave my bushes!" she wailed through the window.

April and John Galway reappeared, picked up the fallen clothes, and proceeded up the stairs. Regina, still at the window, stood waiting for the young man to leave. Presently, unable to contain herself, she crossed the garden and climbed to the top of the house. She found April's door wide open and her friend seated cross-legged in a corner on the floor. Perched on a cardboard box with her back to him, April delivered a speech. "I am very sad," she addressed the empty spaces before her, "it always makes me sad to move. I feel unsettled. I wonder what will happen to me." She wheeled about, and catching sight of her landlady in the entrance, she asked, "What do you think, Miss Brown? Will anything good happen? Or will it all be bad and terrible?"

"Leave Miss Brown alone," the young man said. He had a bottle of bourbon and a paper cup at his side. Delicately he poured himself a drink.

April turned to her landlady. She grimaced. "You must forgive him, Miss Brown. He's a dreary man. He drinks all the time and he can't even find a topic for his dissertation and he's much too vain and he'll never marry me. He won't even live with me. You're dreary, John, you're dreary, dreary." She slid off the cardboard box and began to glide about the room, her feet searching for some definite rhythm until all at once she sang out, "Look at me! I'm doing the rumba! Boom boom boom boom! Cha cha cha chaa cha." She planted herself in front of John Galway. Raising her arms and rotating her hips she chanted, "Oh, I'm a girl with good points. Boom boom boom boom. Cha cha cha chaa cha."

Without glancing up at her, John Galway said, "I wish you'd behave, April, because really I'm tired of helping you move."

"Miss Brown," said April, "my friend here tells me that you have a special power of quietness which I ought to study for my own edification. He says that he wants to come and see you." Disparagingly she shook the curls on her head. "When I lived on Trowbridge Street, he kept on taking my dreadful landlady out for coffee. And when I moved around the block, he right away brought my new landlady Alice Pinska half a dozen oranges and a copy of the *New York Times*. He needs to charm every safe and plain and homely woman he meets. Miss Brown, Miss Brown," she wagged a finger, "who knows what he'll do for you?"

Blushing ferociously, the landlady drew her lean bones together and fled down the two flights of stairs. She took a shortcut through the garden, tripped against a rake, and was momentarily blinded by a piece of newspaper traveling through the neighborhood on a swift west wind. Entering her own house from the utility room in back—to calm herself, she tossed a load of clothes into the washing machine. She had always been able to count on the powers of this old machine, its rumblings and mutterings, to soothe her, she'd fancied, like the rolling and deep undertow of the sea. But now as the machine started up, she found she wanted to picture the moon, to imagine her garden disordered, to see before her the heaving forms of violence and love. Quitting her house again, she stood once more in the garden. Through the darkness she saw that the first floor was brightly lit and that her School of Education tenants were entertaining one . . . two . . . three guests; clearly she could make out six figures, male and female, moving between the phonograph, the brick and board bookcases, the canvas chairs. She stood on tiptoe and strained to hear them.

At four o'clock the next day John Galway called on her. He held a small white bakery box in his hand, and he said, "Good afternoon, Miss Brown. I've been visiting in the neighborhood and so I thought I'd stop by and bring you these cakes." But Regina, who was unused to receiving presents, turned her head so as to ignore his outstretched hand.

"I'm very fond of cakes from Rossi's," he continued. "Their flavor is always . . . is always right."

Standing in the daylight, she blinked, thinking his manner gracious, even gallant—he might have charged up the driveway on a tall, white steed. Suspicion tightened her throat; all the same, she invited him in. When he once more offered her the box from Rossi's, she hid the gift behind a lamp. Then she placed herself in the center of the sofa, spread her arms to each side, gripped her lips thoroughly together, and prepared herself to fathom his character. She waited to hear him speak about April. Instead he spoke to her about birds.

He brought up the subject in reference to her garden. Birds, he said, must frequent that place—all kinds of birds—and he supposed that must be particularly true in the spring. He claimed that because his tastes had always been very simple, his favorite bird was the robin. He liked the fact that robins had such little feet and, though it seemed obvious, such red breasts, and he liked the way they skittered about. He also admired cardinals and the woodland thrush, but did not care for blackbirds as they impressed him as greedy. He had noticed that in the park blackbirds would hop right up and try to eat everybody's lunch. Greed had always seemed to him no virtue at all—not even in birds.

After listening to him awhile, Regina searched her mind for how she felt about birds. She had never actually thought about them before. Yet it was obvious from John Galway's hard-working and earnest air that he had chosen this subject in order to evoke some special chord in her, some response. Downward lines formed at his eyes, his lips turned up, his nostrils occasionally quivered, his eyebrows arched and straightened, and now and then he held his round head up and smiled to himself as if, right here in her living room, he were apprehending a full choir of celestial sounds.

Regina felt herself warming toward him. The gentleness of his accent—lingering vowels and liquid l's—cradled the air about her. Shortly she felt with him that the living room was full of birds. They were flying just above her level; they were pecking away at the plaster ceiling; they were destroying the ceiling and aiming to commune with the sky. But then, abruptly, he turned to her—and as if holding in abeyance the image he had created, he detached himself from it, appearing to inquire what did she think about all this: did she feel the same way as he had, a moment before, or differently; and if differently, he was quite willing, he was even eager to hear her views.

The cessation of his talk, his query, and above all the directness of his focus on herself caused her to draw away and become suspicious of him again. She reminded herself that he was merely April Shapiro's friend, and she grew downcast, almost sullen—a change which he appeared to note, for he got up and said, "Please forgive me for going on so endlessly. I thought the subject might interest you."

As soon as he had gone, she remembered the box from Rossi's. She approached and opened it. Two éclairs, a napoleon, and a cream puff met her eye. She bent down and sniffed the pastries. They smelled fresh. Looking up, she encountered the disapproval of her parents in their gold, smooth frames on the wall, but she shook her head, reminding them their influence over her had dwindled. Then she wandered toward a mirror, and when she saw herself she longed to talk to someone, to tell of what had happened. She put on her coat and went next door to wait for her School of Education tenants. In the center of her garden she wheeled to and fro, organizing and rehearsing her facts: a young man had called on her, had brought her a box of French pastry, and had spoken to her about birds.

But instead of the girls in the School of Education, it was April Shapiro who appeared. She was returning home from work, and she said, "Miss Brown, this is a big house and I think you are casting a spell around it. Are you also casting a spell on my friend? If he should come to see you . . . if my good friend should come to see you, don't consider that amounts to anything. The fact is, he drinks too much. He drinks without stopping and he can't make himself work. Who even knows if he wants to live?" Pausing, she moved closer to Regina, and putting out her hand, she gently touched Regina's shoulder. Then almost wistfully she went on, "In a way . . . in a dreary way, the three of us are alike: you, my darling John, myself. We have to settle for less in this world—for lesser kinds of satisfactions, I mean. Otherwise, if he were able, he could have anyone." She took a few steps back. "He could have anyone at all— he wouldn't bother with me or with you." And she walked past Regina into the house.

But Regina had gone beyond pondering April's words. Birds and pastry took up all the space in her mind. That night she placed the pastry on an ivory dish by her bed and allowed herself small bites before falling asleep. Toward five in the morning, a loud knocking awakened her.

"I've come to visit you, my dear Miss Brown. I have something wonderful to tell you."

She dressed and came to the door. John Galway's eyes were bloodshot, his clothes rumpled. She hesitated, but let him in.

"I've been awake all night," he told her. "I actually thought I'd found . . . you'll never guess," he laid his hand on her arm, "the reason for it all. I even thought I'd found a suitable topic for my dissertation. And I kept exulting and thinking to myself, 'This is it! This is it! I must tell Regina Brown!'" He came into the living room and sat down on a chair. "And then . . . a little while ago," he stared before him, "I lost the sense of things again. It disappeared. It went away."

Regina hunched her shoulders but once more found her senses assailed by the drawling music of his voice, mixed with that scent about him of sherry wine. Or this time was it stronger? Was it bourbon? Was it drugs? She wanted to inspect the center of his eyes, but was impelled to gaze elsewhere so as to protect herself from the unsettling, complicated force of him.

"I so much hope," he said, "for life to be beautiful."

Partly in answer and partly to ward him off, she muttered, "I'm sure it will be," at which he turned his bloodshot yet suddenly optimistic eyes on her and said, "You're good! You're good!"

Regina shuddered. A sigh escaped from her throat.

"You're good! Let's go to the beach!"

"In late October?" she objected. "Before six in the morning?"

"Why not before six in the morning? Why not in late October? I've brought my car. It's parked outside."

They drove down Massachusetts Avenue to Harvard Square, across the river, and through the tunnel toward the Shore. On their right they skirted the sea. The weather turned an angry gray, while in its center a pale, white mist spread like the petals of a blossom. Just above the town of Rockport he stopped the car, took hold of her upper arm, and led her through a wood onto the beach. The beach was long and empty. A thick mist blurred the water's edge. For a moment he surveyed the landscape. Then he began silently to lead her up and down. He seemed remote, abstracted, and did not look at her. She lurched beside him as he described a pattern of seemingly endless, aimless arcs the length of the beach. He let go of her arm. She fell; and as he helped her up, she believed with certainty that here in this lone place of rock and cawing birds and dim gray shore he might at any second rapturously embrace her or strike her down.

They continued their walk. Sand filled her shoes and squeezed her feet; she stubbed her toes on pieces of shell and stumbled against the skeletons of fish. Sand lodged in her eyes and tickled her nostrils while the expression on his face remained benign and far away. But he did not loosen his hold on her arm. He directed her toward a cliff of rocks which stood above the sea. Slowly and cautiously they climbed the high terrain, and when they reached the top, he smiled at her, motioned with his head to include the sky above and the sea below them, produced a flask from his pocket, and drank from it at length. "Life," he declared, "has some good moments."

What foolishness, she wondered, had prompted her to join him. As if in answer, she raised herself on the balls of her feet, leaned forward and kissed him—partly on the mouth, partly on the cheek. She kissed him again, tasted whiskey and the sea air, and marveled that her lips had touched this man's tough, rich flesh.

As if from a distance, she noticed that John Galway had not liked it. His face was screwed up with distaste and he rushed to his drink. Through her mind paraded the pride and the disapproval of her parents and of the dean. Shame overwhelmed her. But then she heard the roaring of the sea and determined she must make one more gesture toward love, toward growth, toward liberation. She glanced at John Galway, calculated her distance, lunged toward him, kissed him full on the mouth, and understood she hadn't liked it either. With a cry—using both hands and all her force—she pushed him toward the precipice as he stood on one foot, recovering and sipping from his drink.

John Galway lost his balance. On that October morning he gave Regina a look of faint, of quizzical surprise. Then with a nod as if of gratitude or appreciation, he flailed his arms in a graceful farewell and fell like a gentleman into the sea.

THE THURSDAY MEN'S CLUB

I wake up and I'm a happy man. It's my fortieth birthday. Hey, lots of people I know are already dead. I climb out on my side of the bed, go into the kitchen in my bare feet, and head for the coffee pot. As I take my first sip, I remember my dream in the night. I dreamed I brought Mr. Tom Sharkey, Mr. Edgar Spinoza, and Mr. Gordon Cherniak home for dinner and they sat in their wheelchairs as comfortable as could be.

What is the occasion, I wonder. So far my wife will not extend a dinner invitation to any of the men at the Lyndhurst Home. She does not like my job. She does not believe that in my capacity as an aide at the Lyndhurst Convalescent Home, I am at the forefront of the health care profession. She claims that my work isn't manly—that it's only for women. She says it's a waste of my year at community college. But she's my wife, the person I bring breakfast to every morning, and so I lift the cup from the tray and say, "Hey wife, it's my birthday. Say happy birthday. Forty years old."

My wife opens an eyelid. "Aloysius," she says, "you may be forty, but you never growed up. You are like a child. You are definitely not like a man."

That hurts my feelings. And so I think about my wife's hospitality in my dream. I concentrate on that because I believe that dreams sometimes reveal a future truth.

It is half past six on an October morning in California when I climb on the bus. I transfer to two more buses and get off in Palo Alto. A block and a half beyond the downtown the Lyndhurst Convalescent Home comes into my view. From the outside it resembles a very fine resort hotel, what with its wide driveway for cars and ambulances to pull up on and its broad expanse of green lawn. Two pairs of willow trees stand on the lawn and all the grass is bordered with red and white impatiens that look so vigorous and stalwart that they give the whole area a patriotic air. I am proud of this entrance just as I am proud of the garden at the back of the building and of the fact that this is a democratic institution welcoming rich people, the poor on Medi-Cal, and many middle income people who will soon unfortunately become poor because of the expense.

I enter the lobby, slightly turning my head from the shabby couches—too much of a contrast with the outside —and go past the unmanned reception desk and past the office of Mr. Schaaf, our new administrator. My post is on the fourth floor. Here I study my assignments and debate whether to start right in on them or first visit the men on my floor and see how they've gotten through the night. Mr. Klieg, our former administrator, almost fired me for what he called my unofficial morning rounds. I suspect that Mr. Schaaf might feel more or less the same. But as it's my birthday, I pop quickly into Mr. Cherniak's room.

Mr. Cherniak came to the Lyndhurst Home two years ago. He was at the time a retired rich lawyer and a salesman, I believe. He is ninety years old, but he is a forward-looking man—that is, he is always looking forward to something. As soon as he had accepted he would never leave, he took to devising certain games to entertain himself and me. What he likes is to try and sell me his cashmere scarf, his Bandolini hat in the closet, his monogrammed cuff links. He wants five hundred dollars for each. He wants a thousand dollars for his shoes. Sitting in his wheel chair, he will point down to his shoes. "Never been walked on. Made in Italy. The finest workmanship," he will say. "What am I offered?"

I, too, am a forward-looking man, and so I will say twenty-five dollars and he will laugh and say seven hundred and fifty dollars and I will say twenty-five dollars and fifty cents. He is a man who has traveled widely—stayed at the best hotels, dined in the best restaurants. This morning he indicates the newspaper folded on his tray. Before he can name some exaggerated outlandish sum, I call out, "Fifty cents."

I've called out too fast or else a little too loud and he's stunned, but only for a moment. Then he says with a look of triumph, "It's yours." I give him fifty cents, he hands over the newspaper, and I leave the room.

I go down the corridor and into Mr. Davis' and Mr. Lossy's room. Mr. Davis is the only black man on the floor, and so it always cheers him up to see me. Though I am an exotic mixture of Basque and Filipino and African, that is enough similarity for Mr. Davis, and he likes me to kneel down and pray with him. I kneel by his bed and he sits in a chair in his pajamas leaning on his cane. He is a very spiritual and religious person, and I am therefore happy to join him for six or seven or even eight or nine minutes of prayer. He adds an extra prayer when I tell him it's my birthday. He says, "God bless Aloysius on this special day."

Mr. Lossy is Mr. Davis' roommate. He is watching, bewildered and suspicious, from his bed. I go over and show him the calendar on the wall and have him read what day it is and what month. The calendar is printed with giant letters. It caught my eye in Mrs. Euclid's room, which is on the other side of the nurse's station in the women's wing. Hey, I said to myself, I know someone who could benefit from that calendar. Right then and there I would have taken it, but out of courtesy I waited over a week until it was definitely determined that Mrs. Euclid had passed on.

"October 5th," reads Mr. Lossy, and for good measure he adds the name of our United States president.

Next door Mr. Spinoza tells me his joke about a priest and asks after my wife. I say she's fine. He informs me that his own wife is in the basement ironing and that by and by she will come up and fix us some English breakfast tea. He forgets that she's no longer alive. When he remembers I tell him she's gone to a much better place than even the Lyndhurst Home and I stay around a little longer—adjust his window blinds, trim the wilted leaves from his begonia and his African violet, and fill up his water pitcher. But I have to be careful. Time mounts up and a lot of the aides complain that I get behind in my work and mess up their schedules. Marcella Cage says that I act like I own the facility—she resents that I like my job. And Lawanna Jabbar says I am biased against women, or else why would I have started my Thursday Men's Luncheon Club. Even Jane Creely—the one aide who's my buddy—even she claims that I tend to overstep.

I look at the time: I have spent forty-five minutes. I am late in bringing the laundry up and in giving two showers and three sponge baths. I rush to catch up.

After lunch I return to the fourth floor to find Mr. Cherniak strapped in his wheelchair directly across from the elevator. I figure it's either Marcella or Sonnabend who have abandoned him there. That's how they are, but they ought to know better—no resident should be left to contemplate the elevator on his own. What that does is suggest the possibility of escape to a normal life. Sometimes, first thing in the morning two or three or even four of the women will start out from their wing and wheel themselves with their pocket books in their laps—primed to shop in the mall. As soon as the elevator door opens, they plunge in with such haste, three or four at a time, that the frames of the wheelchairs get tangled together, the elevator door jams and it takes three aides to get the machinery straightened out and everyone back on the floor again.

My men have more dignity than that. They rarely accost the elevator. But to be placed directly facing it— that to my mind amounts to real cruelty. Particularly it is galling today because—while Mr. Cherniak looks on— out of the elevator comes Mrs. Oblenski, her daughter behind her pushing the wheelchair. Mrs. Oblenski is all dressed up with a big circle of rouge on each of her cheeks and a long string of pink pearls over her gray sweat shirt. On her face she has the smug expression of someone with a relative who takes her outside. Her head rises like a superior being as she passes in front of Mr. Cherniak and I flush with anger, remembering that Mr. Cherniak has not had a visitor since his son appeared briefly the first Christmas. I hit the wall with my fist. Then right at that moment I know what's needed for both Mr. Cherniak and for me—whether it's against the rules or not.

"Mr. Cherniak," I say, "it's my birthday," and I go into his room, come out with his hat, and unlock the wheels of his chair.

"Your birthday?" he asks as we ride down the elevator. "What year were you born?"

I tell him I am forty years old.

"Forty years old. Well, Aloysius, many happy returns of the day. And many more," he says as we exit the elevator, go past the reception desk—unmanned as usual—past the coffee and the candy dispenser, and through the thick back doors into the garden. It is a weekday, and with no staff or visitors in sight, the garden is empty.

First we take a leisurely stroll, pausing in front of the various rose bushes. I point out the blooms—pink and red roses, white, yellow, salmon-colored. To my knowledge no one has ever taken him out, and so I wait for his response. He has after all traveled widely—stayed at the best hotels, dined in the finest restaurants. Studying the back of his head with its rim of white hair, I imagine he must be comparing this garden with others he's seen all over the world. But to my surprise, almost immediately after we settle beneath a large oak just beginning to turn a beautiful copper color, he starts to fidget and he says, "When does the band begin to play?"

I look at him, not understanding. "The band?"

"When does the conductor raise his baton?" he asks. And when I still look puzzled he explains, "A garden is fine if there's a concert or a wedding reception or even a performance of Shakespeare. Otherwise it makes sense to continue on."

"Like where?" I decide he's playing a game. "To London? To see the queen?"

He shifts about, his hands gripping the wheels of his chair, and I realize that he is serious. In his voice there's a commanding urgency that makes me feel as though—once having taken him out—I need to come through for him in some real way. "Let's go." he says. "We're all dressed up in our hats and coats, let's not waste our time. There's more happening in front of the nurse's station than there is here." He waves at the roses. "Aloysius, you and I need a livelier scenario."

I nod. He is, I am aware, a man who likes the city. Sometimes while I hold him up in the shower or ease him into his bed, he will describe to me the majesty of Florence, Rome, Madrid, and Paris. So I take a deep breath and roll him out of the garden and onto the sidewalk bordered by old houses and then onto a street of new office buildings, and within five minutes we are in downtown Palo Alto.

The town is bustling. People are entering and leaving restaurants, going in and out of shops, carrying canvases, walking their dogs; people are hand in hand with their children. And I have my reward. For Mr. Cherniak is sitting straight up in his wheelchair like a king, his face eager and rosy. Passersby smile at him—he looks that happy. "A delightful atmosphere," he says, tipping his hat to a young woman. "Cars. Trucks. Buses. Crowds. Lively commerce. Everything as it should be." He removes his feet from the rungs of his wheelchair, places them on the cement, and has me stop before the windows of a men's clothing store, then an oriental rug store, and then a store selling exercise equipment. We cross the street at the light and as we move along, he identifies the make of each car we pass. On the other side he has me read him the menu posted on the French restaurant and the menu on the Italian restaurant. He shows a strong interest in the cost of each entrée. "Prices," he comments, "just keep on going up." Then he says, "Since it's your birthday, let me buy you an ice cream."

I push him to a little outdoor table and bring out two scoops of ice cream—one cherry vanilla, one chocolate—for each of us. "Many happy returns of the day," he says and digs into his ice cream. "Aloysius, now . . . what is the name of this town?"

"Palo Alto."

"Obviously a thriving economy and a good starting place—a good place from which to push off on our travels. Do you own a car?"

"No."

"I'd like to buy you a car. What kind would you like?" He rolls himself away from the table, leans way back, and actually crosses his legs. "A Rolls Royce? A Lincoln Continental? Or would you prefer a Ferrari?"

"A Rolls Royce will do," I say, beginning to feel a little uneasy. I get up and steer him ahead for one more block and then turn around and start on our way back. He doesn't object—he remains silent, but when we get to the Lyndhurst Home he again takes his feet off the rungs of the wheelchair, this time planting his feet so firmly on the ground that I cannot move him. He looks up at the building and declares it is a solid piece of real estate. "Well built. Well maintained. The roof in excellent condition. Obviously a building of substantial value. With travel more and more expensive these days . . . Aloysius, we just might have to sell it."

I glance up and see that from the window of the fourth floor the head nurse is staring down at us.

On Thursdays my men's luncheon club meets. That I am the founder of the men's luncheon club always strikes me as ironic considering that in all my years no one has ever asked me to join their club. Generally people—even strangers walking on the street—tend to like me. Yet an invitation to join has never come my way. I do not know whether this is because club members get a feeling I will not fit in, or whether I myself feel wary and choose not to belong. Whichever—when one morning Mr. Spinoza said to me, "Every man likes to belong to a club," I carefully thought over his statement, located chairs and a large table for the day room, and alerted prospective members. Now every Thursday noon I seek out Jane Creely—she is my buddy on the floor—and we start gathering the men together. Mr. Kramer comes out of his room on his crutches, Mr. Lossy slides forward on his walker, Mr. Gardelli propels himself like he's at the helm of a racing car, Jane and I maneuver Mr. Solitzenisn, Mr. Holbrook, Mr. Pocekay, Mr. Narayan, and Mr. Cherniak; and Mr. Davis inches along using only his cane.

"Welcome, gentlemen," I say, uncovering the first lunch tray. "Today the cook Mr. Estero—who as you all know was formerly the head chef at a three star restaurant in Redwood City—has sent up, especially for us, his special chicken in sherry vinegar sauce, his garlic roasted potatoes, and his peas with sun-dried tomatoes. We are fortunate indeed to have so generous and talented a cook on the staff." Mr. Spinoza applauds my speech, after which I tie on everyone's bib, remove the cover from the rest of the trays, cut up what will be eaten into smaller pieces and—though I do not actually eat—I pull up a chair and join the party.

To be honest, the communication might not be of the highest order. It is hard to figure out who is talking to who or who is listening to who, and what the person who is listening actually hears. But that matters little; it's the atmosphere of sociability and hospitality that counts. I look around—at Mr. Kramer, a retired farm worker, Mr. Gardelli, formerly in the Marines, Mr. Sharkey, a residential architect. I look around and I feel happy to find my-self in the company of this very fine fraternity of men.

At three o'clock my shift is finished. The halls are quiet—I have tucked the people in my rotation into their beds. But before I leave I walk up and down, checking the call lights and glancing into the different rooms. The windows are open today and a breeze blows through the blinds. Like sometimes happens, a sense of timelessness enters me. It's as if—while the men sleep, their souls awaken and start on their journey. It's as if their souls ride out the window and fly a little distance before coming back, then ride out again, each time a few yards further from the Lyndhurst wide lawn and the trees across the street, each time further and higher until they are soaring above the tiled rooftops of the coffee houses in Palo Alto, hovering near the smell of French roast and croissants and Italian roast before returning once more to their bodies and to their dreams.

Connected to their journey, I feel closer to life here than I feel anywhere else.

The Monday after the cook sent up his special chicken in sherry vinegar sauce, Jane Creely brings me this news: the head nurse has reported my outing with Mr. Cherniak and the administrator wants to see me.

"Just don't ask for anything," Jane advises. "You don't need more trouble. Just tell him you're sorry."

So that is what I do; I do not want to be fired. As soon as I step into Mr. Schaaf's office I say that I was wrong—that a foolish impulse prompted my mistake and I will never allow it to happen again.

To my relief he accepts my apology without making a fuss. He is obviously different than his predecessor Mr. Klieg. He is much taller and his smaller mouth is fastened into an expression of ongoing sympathy. He asks about conditions on my floor and about my Thursday Men's Luncheon Club. I am tempted to prolong the interview—to mention the need for salary increases and for a new supply of terry cloth bibs. But I do not want to take any chances. It is only when I get up to leave and he holds out his hand and I take his hand and shake it that, changing my mind, I bring up the subject of Halloween.

"Halloween?" he says with surprise. "Is there a problem?"

I hesitate, not wanting to disturb Mr. Schaaf's equilibrium. "It's this way," I explain. "Halloween is not a holiday that the residents necessarily remember. It doesn't stand out in their minds. It can't help but confuse and frighten them." I think of Mr. Lossy—of the terror in his eyes last Halloween. "Oh, I know Halloween's a favorite holiday for the recreation director—she likes to decorate and make masks and she loves to carve pumpkins."

Concern spreads from Mr. Schaaf's mouth to the thin lines on his forehead. But now I pay no attention. I go on and tell him that it's a simple matter of attitude. And a matter of doing away with some of the costumes and the mobiles of skeletons and maybe some of the recreation director's bulletin board cutouts of hissing cats. I remind him that my men must not be treated like a class of kindergartners—that each of them has led a significant and important life.

This is the strongest statement I have ever made. Satisfied, I leave the office.

That night I mention the meeting to my wife. I tell her I made a valuable suggestion about Halloween that might even advance my future standing.

She sighs and wants to know if I asked about a raise.

"Happy Halloween," the recreation director, the social worker and two volunteers call out on the fourth floor. Each of them carries a carved pumpkin. They line up the jack-o'-lanterns on the counter of the nurses' station and soon there is a parade of residents being escorted past the display. The aides point to the pumpkins, each jack-o'-lantern's face more grotesque than the next. "Happy Halloween," the aides instruct their charges. But the residents, both men and women, look quickly away, as if they have seen nothing, their own faces turning stony. Marcella Page won't let them alone. She stomps back and forth. She is wearing a witch's hat and blackened teeth and she scolds the residents, "Happy Halloween!"

Just then, to my relief Mr. Schaaf emerges from the elevator. Just in time, I think, until I focus on the large black plastic bag hanging from his arm. It is the same bag of masks and disguises that Mr. Klieg always brought up. The recreation director, the social worker, and the two volunteers swarm toward it and lift out various items. One person arranges a Groucho Marx mustache above Mr. Pocekay's mouth, another places a misshapen red nose over Mr. Lossy's nose, and a third fits Mr. Davis with a donkey's ears and snout. The three men submit quietly and—it seems to me—with sadness. Mr. Cherniak alone flails his arms trying to tear off the dunce cap secured with an elastic under his chin. The social worker stands back, regards him, and then regards the others. "They are all so cute," she says. Tears of anger and frustration fill up Mr. Cherniak's eyes, and I rush him into his room, shut the door and talk to him for a time until he's calmed down.

In a fury I head for the administrator's office. I pace back and forth in front of his desk, waiting for his return and planning what I will tell him, among which is that Mr. Arnold was a carpenter who helped build the Golden Gate bridge, Mr. Davis was the head maintenance man at Palo Alto High School for more than fifty years, Mr. Holbrook was the senior partner in his law firm, Mr. Solitzenisn invented a device to tighten facial muscles, and Mr. Narayan served as the jockey for a horse named Pur Sang who once won the Kentucky Derby. I will let him know that it's bad enough the men are already in disguise from their lives. Why festoon them with paper hats like puppets?

On and on I rage, pacing the carpet and expanding on my grievances. Finally I calm down and am ready just to sum things up. "Mr. Schaaf," I say as the administrator enters his office—I say it very simply, "Mr. Schaaf, you have greatly disappointed me."

At first he appears taken aback and surprised—almost as if he cannot fathom how someone like me has the nerve to be disappointed in someone like him. His face reddens and the lines on his forehead deepen. He walks around to the door of his office, which is open, and for a moment I think he is running away, erasing or tossing out my message as he flees. But he closes the door and comes back. He sits down at his desk and, after a minute of clenching his knuckles, he says in a serene voice, "I understand you are a very popular aide in some quarters."

I nod, since this is quite true. At Christmas many of the visiting families press into my hands a flood of hand knitted caps and painted ties.

"You are very popular in some quarters," he repeats. "For that reason, up till now I have chosen to ignore the complaints I hear from several of the aides and some of the nurses."

Somehow he has gone off the subject. I feel a twinge of annoyance and want to remind him I am here to talk about my grievances and not his.

"For example, I hear that no women are allowed in your Thursday luncheon club and that . . ."

I interrupt him. "These are elderly men from a different time . . . they would feel jumbled up . . . uncomfortable if I introduced women."

". . . and that the cook gives your Thursday group preferential treatment . . . he sends up grilled breast of duck and chocolate soufflés and such."

"Mr. Estero is a very talented chef," I say. Then all at once I realize I am in actual trouble. For I now notice that the expression on Mr. Schaaf's face resembles the expression on Mr. Klieg's face when Mr. Klieg wanted to fire me. I recall a conversation with Jane just after my last interview with Mr. Klieg. "Do you think," she had asked, "that if Mr. Kleig had not resigned his post, he would have fired you?" "No," I had said. It was a question that had embarrassed me; I do not like to think of myself as someone who could be fired. "No. Maybe. It's possible. But I don't think so."

"I do not plan to dismiss you at this time," Mr. Schaaf folds his arms, "primarily because I trust you may yet learn you are not the one in charge of this facility. Nor do you have the authority to operate a men's program . . . you are neither a social worker nor the recreation director. What I'd like to suggest, at least for the time, is that you discontinue your men's lunch club. It disrupts the order on the floor."

My head burns and my throat clogs up. I have a hard time getting out any words and when I do they do not make a lot of sense. "There is no order on the floor," I say, after which, without a pause he answers, "You are not cooperating. One more infraction and you're out."

That night I mean to talk with my wife about this meeting, but the subject proves too painful for me to bring up. A week goes by, then a few more weeks. Thanksgiving arrives; then it's after Thanksgiving and still I've failed to confess that I could not keep things together—that I no longer run my Thursday Men's Luncheon Club, and that, no doubt because of the delicacies he sent up on Thursdays, the cook Mr. Estero has been fired.

Meanwhile the days have churned ahead. The halls have darkened with winter, and with no weekly gatherings, each resident's room begins to seem more and more separate. In December Mr. Pocekay passes on suddenly. Everything feels different; yet some things remain the same —that is, the nurses go on looking at their monitors, speaking on the phones, writing in their notebooks, refusing to look at the patients.

Just before Christmas, Mr. Cherniak pushes his call light and I trudge to his room. "The soup at lunch was the worst I've ever tasted," he says. "And dinner . . ." he shakes his head. "Tell me what's going on."

I look away unhappily. An ordinary cook—a cook without talent—has replaced Mr. Estero and a smell of stale bread and bouillon cubes has taken over the floor— stronger, even, than the smell of urine.

"Dinner or lunch, I've never experienced food so bad. Tell me what's happening."

I walk to the window and gaze out guiltily. Since Mr. Estero's dismissal, Mr. Eckhart and Mr. Sharkey have each lost seven pounds. Mr. Arnold has lost thirteen pounds, and polite Mr. Lossy, instead of eating his food, now hides it under his tray. Desperate, last night I finally turned to my wife. I proposed that if she would invite some of the men home for Sunday dinner, I would look for another job.

"A different job?" she said with interest, but then she claimed that the men are senile and would drool at the table and, given her own family, they would not fit in. I pointed out that Mr. Cherniak's son had not visited since the first Christmas and that Mr. Holbrook's daughters visited no more than twice a year. I pressed her till the end of the evening when in a loud and angry voice she declared, "Aloysius, I definitely do not want to hear another word about your men."

Then this morning—as if insult likes to follow defeat—Mr. Schaaf accosted me in the hall. He laid a hand on my shoulder. "A marked improvement," he said in a congratulatory tone. "I'm glad to see that you've settled down and accepted your place in our organization."

As I stand at Mr. Cherniak's window, these words, terrible and undeserved, fester in my head. I think about my wife and about the administrator, and I decide that both of them are wrong.

"Tell me what's happening," Mr. Cherniak insists. "Has the stock market failed? Has there been a major economic downturn? Is it a war?"

I turn toward him and with unexpected satisfaction I say, "Mr. Cherniak, there is no war, no Depression. It's almost Christmas and the downtown is booming."

And so I lift him out of bed and dress him in his coat and Bandolini hat and wind his cashmere scarf around his throat; and as we ride down the elevator he says, "Christmas is the very best time to start on our travels."

In Palo Alto bells are ringing, wreaths are festooned, shoppers are filing in and out of the stores, and the windows are filled with boxed toys and Persian carpets and aerobic bicycles and women's and men's evening clothes and pyramids of flavored vinegar. "Look," I say, "the streets are busy and prosperous and festive . . . exactly as you like."

But after the first five minutes, I find he no longer wants to look in the windows. Nor does he want to look at the passersby, the children, the dogs, the cars. Straining forward he urges, "Let's go! Let's go ahead!" I push his chair and we pass more ringing bells, more wreaths in doorways, one pharmacy and then the next pharmacy. We pass the movie theatre and a sporting shoe outlet. When we are ten blocks or so beyond the Lyndhurst I decide it's only reasonable to turn around. "Mr. Cherniak, this is far enough. It's time to turn back."

"It's time to go ahead."

"It's time to turn back," I insist. But I cannot budge the wheelchair. I try to straighten its tires but with no success. Then all at once the chair acquires a strange and unexpected force of its own, lifting and pulling me and Mr. Cherniak across the street and onto the driveway of the Texaco station. From here I can see the highway, a thickness of trees, and beyond that the rising purple hills. "We're going where?" I ask. "Paris? Rome? San Francisco?"

"Aloysius, just stick with me."

But something holds me back. It clutches at my heart. "What about the others? Oh what about Mr. Sharkey and Mr. Spinoza and Mr. Davis and Mr. Lossy and Mr. Kramer and Mr. Gardelli and Mr. Holbrook? What about all the others?"

From over his shoulder Mr. Cherniak scans the roof tops. "You mustn't worry," he assures me, "they'll soon catch up."

THE MAN WHO LOVED DETROIT

Out of a sense of adventure that was rare in him, Dr. Geffen Levy, a short man in a plaid sport jacket, left his family in Detroit in June of 1943 and went by train to a medical convention in Ohio. He had been troubled for some months by his rejection from the draft and had decided that since doctors his age were setting off daily for England, North Africa, and the South Pacific, he ought at least learn more about medicine. The first three days of the convention he sat through six meetings on the goiter, four on diseases of the pineal gland, and three on abnormalities of the spleen. At the end of the third day he was drinking a whiskey sour in the bar when he began to reflect that each of the lectures he had attended had left him feeling homesick. It then crossed his mind—as it sometimes had in the past—that he lacked the spirit of a true doctor. Perhaps, he thought, he ought never to have become a physician. For proof he considered that after five years in practice with a specialty in internal medicine, he had failed to build up any fondness for the hypodermic needle, the reflex hammer, the tongue depressor, while even worse, he remained too often baffled and uncomfortable in the presence of people who were ill.

Geffen downed his drink. Not knowing what else to do he ordered another. Waiting, he glanced with admiration at the two tall, distinguished-looking colleagues who stood an elbow's distance away, Scotch and soda in hand. He recognized the confidence and the self-satisfaction they exuded, and this, along with the height from which they looked down, produced in him a sense of terrible laxness and of shame. He gave the men another swift, appraising glance and was about to sink more deeply into gloom when he realized his colleagues were talking about Detroit.

All at once the bar's varnished surface seemed to give off a brighter, more festive gleam. The next thing Geffen knew he was advancing toward the two men, deterred neither by his normal reticence nor by his having recognized one of them as the convention's main lecturer on diseases of the spleen.

"I beg your pardon, but I happened to overhear you. By coincidence," he offered, "I'm from Detroit."

"You're from Detroit?"

Geffen nodded happily. His pale blue eyes shone from behind round glasses while his round cheeks formed eager arcs. "I was born," he declared, "and I grew up and I live there."

An expression of pity crossed the taller man's—the lecturer's—face. Then, as if sorry for any rudeness his look of sympathy might have conveyed, he said, "Yes, Detroit, it's near Canada," and looked away. He consulted the near distance and at last intoned with a measured drawl, "Well, it isn't Paris. It isn't London. It isn't San Francisco."

"Still . . ." said Geffen.

"I was in Detroit once," the other man put in brusquely. "I stayed at the Book Cadillac hotel and I rented a car. As it turned out it was pointless to rent a car because there was nothing to do and nothing to see. Some factories . . . a lot of smoke."

The lecturer sent Geffen a guilty glance. "Well, it isn't New York, of course. It isn't Boston. It isn't even Brussels. It certainly isn't Rio de Janeiro."

His companion appeared to lose patience. Slamming his glass on the counter, he summed up, "It's nothing but an ugly, overgrown one-horse town!"

Geffen drew himself up. "It's where the cars come from, it's where the tanks come from, and it's where I come from," he said with an air of dignity. "And if you saw nothing when you were there, why I'm sorry for you." He shook his head back and forth. "You missed a lot." And he thought of how, just a few months earlier, he had placed his newborn son in a car bed in his 1941 dark blue Ford and had driven him about the city. Together they had cruised past the elm, spruce, and maple trees, past the Fisher Building, its spires signaling to the General Motors Building across the street, past the chalk-lime walls of Briggs Baseball Stadium, past the majestic Fox and

Michigan theaters, the Penobscot Building, and the city hall. By the river's edge, near the entrance to Belle Isle, he had parked the car, emerging with the infant in his arms. "Daniel, my son," he sang out, "you have been born in the automobile capital of the world. President Roosevelt has called us the 'Arsenal of Democracy.' When you grow up—no matter where you are—people will treat you with respect." Pressing his lips to Daniel's nose, he had promised to care for him always and to buy him a car.

"What do you know about Detroit?" he now demanded of his colleagues. He grabbed hold of the one's dark-suited arm and the other's rep silk tie. "What do you know?" he shouted, suddenly incensed by their ignorance, their unfairness. "Did you happen to see Belle Isle?" His face turned crimson. "Did you see the statue by Rodin? Where else do you find a statue by Rodin in front of an art museum? What other city can boast of a public park as magnificent as Belle Isle? And think of this: Where would you be, where would the country be, where would the world be without our Fords, our Chevrolets, our Plymouths, our Mercurys, our Buicks, our Cadillacs! Without our tanks and trucks America would lose the war!" And contemptuously letting go of the one man's arm and the other's tie, he turned on his heels, quit the bar, made a detour around the porter vacuuming up a circle of litter, and rode the elevator to his room where he packed his bags and arranged to leave the convention early.

Arriving in Detroit, he learned from the newspaper that two days of unprecedented disorder had taken place. In the dense heat of a summer evening a few isolated skirmishes between Negroes and whites had started up on the crowded bridge out of Belle Isle. Quickly the battling had spread and grown fierce, fueled by the rumor that a colored woman and her infant had been killed and thrown into the water. Whites had attacked Negroes; Negroes had attacked whites. Up and down Hastings Street bands of rioters, after breaking windows, had gone on to smashing human heads. Looters had invaded the shops and snatched up all the goods. An avenging group, armed with stones and rocks and clubs, had crushed automobiles on Woodward Avenue and attacked passengers on streetcars. By the time of Geffen's return nine whites and twenty-seven Negroes lay dead.

Geffen, having grown up in a peaceful part of the city, could scarcely believe this dishonor had fallen upon Detroit. How, he questioned, could such fighting flare up on that calm, beautiful bridge over the seed-green water so near the spot where he'd first kissed his wife and where he'd promised his son to buy him a car? And why would looters smash the shops on Hastings Street when his Uncle David—and no doubt other men as amiable and venerable as his uncle—still owned clothing stores there and gave all youngsters, black and white alike, nickels and whistles for Christmas? He thought of his colleagues in the bar in Ohio and guessed that these new events would strengthen their bad opinion of his town.

Thankful that at least Daniel was still too young to understand, he returned to the newspaper. He read that when the federal troops had been called in to restore order, the brigadier general in charge had accused the police of abetting the riots by their brutal treatment of the Negroes. He set down the newspaper, pushed it aside, and suddenly recalled that, a few months earlier, two colored metal polishers had been transferred to the Packard plant, at which 25,000 white workers—many of them recently up from the South—had walked out on strike, a self-appointed spokesman declaring, "Better let Hitler and Hirohito win than work next to a nigger."

Unhappy, Geffen drove to work. He stood on the cracked pavement outside his office building and uneasily regarded the news vendor, Henry Bothin, his closest, indeed his only Negro acquaintance. He tried to look at the riots through Henry's eyes. Had Henry been part of the packed population on Belle Isle when Negroes and whites competed in the hot day and night for an inadequate number of boats, bicycles, rides, picnic tables? Had the openness of the confrontation, the brutality of the police, and the strike at the Packard plant combined to alter Henry's view of the world? Was he, Geffen, one of the casualties of Henry's new perspective, the warmth between them no longer viable, a matter of the past?

Cautiously Geffen looked at the news vendor and then looked away, fearing signs of aloofness or change. But that day and the next, and the day after that, Henry continued to greet him as always. "How's the Ford, Dr. Levy?" he asked. And when in turn Geffen inquired after the condition of Henry's Chevrolet, the news vendor responded as immediately and eagerly as before. Then gradually Geffen grew reassured that the code they spoke in and the bond between them had not been broken; and from this he soon put from his mind that the riots and the strike had taken place.

For with more and more doctors called away to serve the war and their country, Geffen found that his practice was growing by leaps and bounds. So many patients now visited him in one day that he was forced to buy more chairs for his anteroom. Most frequent among his clients was his high school classmate, Marvin Grossberg, who recommended Geffen to all his relatives and who himself visited Geffen almost every week. Overwhelmed by sheer numbers, Geffen sometimes slid open the door a crack, peered furtively into his jammed waiting room, tried to think of himself as a proper, a dedicated healer, and when he failed, comforted himself by imagining that the war would soon be over, the factories would manufacture automobiles again instead of tanks, and the enlisted doctors would return and claim their clients.

Then one day the fact struck him he had not one Negro among his patients. He made this observation as a family of four colored persons purchased a house on his street, a short five blocks away. They had no sooner finished moving in their table and chairs when Geffen's wife announced that the newcomers would eventually start a riot and destroy all the Jewish butcher shops on Dexter. Gertrude Levy was a thin, sprightly, delicate-complexioned, long-faced, lank-cheeked woman extremely attached to her butcher shops and so enamored of her husband's profession that she had her hair dyed the color of dried blood. Out of what she considered respect for Geffen, she liked to refer to him as "The Doctor." To the butcher she regularly said, "The Doctor likes a nice piece of sirloin steak," and to her cleaning lady, "The Doctor likes a nice spotless kitchen." Yet she paid Geffen no attention when he explained that riots were caused by crowding, by unfairness and fear, and that these conditions did not exist west of Woodward.

"The problem," she summed up, "is that the neighborhood is changing."

"That's what my hope is—that it's changing," was his reply. "The only way to know someone is to live next door." And as he set out with Daniel for their evening's ride, he drove slowly past the dwelling the new family inhabited and imagined they must be people of leadership and courage to have taken up residence here. "What we'll do," he said to his son, "is we'll ask your mother to bake one of her sponge cakes with the powdered sugar. If it happens to rise, the three of us will deliver the cake and introduce ourselves. Or better still, we'll ask our neighbors over."

Yet before he found an opportunity to offer this suggestion, a second Negro family moved to the Levy's street—this time a family of five who laid their claim on a house four blocks away.

"Geffen, the numbers are growing. The distance is lessening," Gertrude accused. And she walked away to let him think things through and then came back and told him that her friends and all of Daniel's friends were moving away, and that the only reason Geffen's friends were staying in place was that he had no friends.

"Daniel will make other friends," Geffen assured her as over the winter a third, fourth, fifth, and sixth Negro family arrived, alighting on houses here and there along the street. "The new people will become part of our community. Not too many more residents will pack up and leave. In a little while, things will settle down."

But in the spring as the last snows melted, hundreds of "For Sale" signs sprang up on front lawns and glinted in the rain. Then Gertrude said, her arms held grimly across her chest, "Think of Daniel. The neighborhood's no longer changing. It's already changed. The value of real estate is down, and before you know it the schools will be down, and the only thing that's going up is the rate of crime."

This last statement Geffen deemed unmannerly and rude. He wanted to tell her there were more white criminals in the world than Negro. Turning from his wife he began to roam the house—from the kitchen into the den, through the hall and the dining room—all the while reflecting on the convenience of this house to the General

Motors Building, the Ford factory, the art institute, the city hall. He trod again through the different rooms, remembering that this was the house in which Daniel had been born, the house that even as a young man he had wanted to own. Indeed, he thought, it was the only house he knew where even in winter the elm trees peered in the windows and the radiators sang like violins.

He stopped by the window and looked into the yard beyond the apple tree where his eight-year-old son was throwing and catching a ball. He tried to clear from his mind that on one of their evening rides Daniel had blurted out, "I don't want to be the only white kid on the block." Backing away from the window, he sat down at the dining room table and forced himself to think about other rides. He recalled how often Daniel had reached out and placed his left hand on his father's right hand on the seat between them. Only nine months before, Daniel had still sat very close, his head resting against the back of the seat as they drove along Second Avenue, the streetlights blue in the dusk of summer and on either side the high dark trees and the porches laden with people. Then into his ears intruded his son's resentful, gravelly, low-pitched voice: "I don't want to be the only white kid on the block." Geffen's stomach turned. For the first time he questioned whether he had the right to impose his preference on two people, on both Gertrude and his son.

In early summer the Levys moved. Four years later they moved again. They moved again three years later and two years after that. Wherever they went the freeway followed them, carrying its citizens further and further from the center of the town. Along with the residents, the merchants moved their shops and the doctors and accountants their offices. And at this Geffen unhappily asked himself, why was everyone he knew fleeing from the colored population as it kept on running after them, wanting no doubt to be friendly? He wished that at the beginning he had stood up to Gertrude, for after the first move the others seemed to him mechanical, automatic, almost without significance.

"If this goes on much longer we'll be living on the Upper Peninsula in Sault St. Marie. Doesn't it disturb you to keep packing the dishes?" he said to his wife as, looking around, he saw that they now inhabited a suburb fifteen miles from downtown on a street that ended in bulldozers and ugly ditches.

Here scarcely any trees existed. The light was hard and harsh and it tore at him with its emptiness. He compared it with the dusty, gentle light of inner Detroit that filtered through the maples and the elms, softening the roofs and the ragged surface of the red brick houses. Here he seemed to have quit the state of Michigan and arrived at some far-off country. Otherwise, how else could he explain that the house in which he now lived appeared to be Japanese, and that next door stood a small Norman castle, and across the street a medium-sized Spanish villa, and next to that a Tudor farmhouse without a farm?

It was on this unfamiliar street that Geffen dreamt in the night he had a black man for a friend—a man as gentle as Henry Bothin, but whose conversation was somewhat broader in scope. He dreamt that they lived next door to each other and in that way came to know one another—to become good friends. Waking up, on impulse he confided to his wife, "I . . . I dreamt I have a close friend."

"You don't need a close friend," Gertrude replied. "What you need is a new location for your office. That way you won't lose so many patients. No one wants to go all the way downtown just to see you. If you really want to attract sick people . . ."

"Who said I'm interested in attracting sick people?" muttered Geffen. Then he left the house and instead of driving directly downtown, he detoured from the freeway to his old neighborhood. His old street was entirely black now. Cruising along, he observed that the lawns and the bushes had been clipped even more carefully than before. He drove past his own house, looked at the roof peaks and the windows, pressed his foot to the gas pedal, and felt exiled and ashamed.

Another year passed, during which Geffen prepared to fulfill his old promise to Daniel. Methodically he read consumer reports, consulted mechanics, visited automobile show rooms, and took along his son. At last, on the day Daniel graduated from high school, Geffen drew his money out of the bank and purchased Daniel's choice: a dark blue Ford Thunderbird convertible with whitewall tires, push button windows, and powder blue vinyl upholstery. And it was in this vehicle that Daniel soon drove off from Detroit forever.

"No one can live here," is what he said. "It isn't worth the gas. There's less and less downtown—the city is doomed. You can visit me out West whenever you like."

"Of course it isn't doomed," insisted Geffen, though in fact he knew that the prosperity which had blessed both Negroes and whites after the second World War had already faded. Packard had closed down; the new Kaiser Company had dissolved; Hudson, merging with Nash, had disappeared into Wisconsin. And where white workers had moved to suburban factories, the Negroes—the least trained, the first to be fired—remained in the inner city, their neighborhoods deteriorating.

"I'm never coming back," Daniel said. "But you can visit me out West whenever you like."

Geffen grasped his son's hand and shook it. He held onto Daniel's fingers for as long as he could. After Daniel left, the farewell disturbed him. It struck him that neither of them had mentioned the hundreds of miles in which they'd steered, their heads lifted to the windshield—the snow thickly falling or the sun shining high—through downtown boulevards, through neighborhoods and parks. Three times in the next week as he passed the newspaper vendor he neglected to ask after Henry's car and instead murmured, "There's something wrong," or, "I have to

hurry." He missed an early appointment in his office with
Marvin Grossberg, who had begun to suffer from arthri-
tis in all his joints. The next day he missed two engage-
ments with other patients, and on the Thursday after,
forgetting that the old Protestant hospital had moved to
the suburbs, he parked in front of the squat brick building
that had housed it. As he mounted the few entrance steps,
he remembered that the hospital was closed. But when the
door opened very easily, as if giving an invitation, he went
into the deserted building.

It was a hospital he had never come to like. Though
he had used it more frequently than any other, he recalled
that he had always placed his hands close to his sides as if
to remain intact or protected from the too-shrill gaiety of
the nurses, the joviality of the other doctors, the jangling
of the buckets and mops, and above all, from his fear that
in each and every room off the corridor a pair of patients,
doubtless his, were dying. Now at random he turned a
corner and entered a convalescent room. He stared at the
broken windows and at a pile of rags that lay on the filthy
floor. Climbing a flight of stairs, he pushed his way
through a double swinging door, then through another
pair of doors to step into the operating room. The arena
was empty of tools and tables, as he had known it would
be, but he was not prepared for the large pack of rats that
skittered away at his approach nor for the corpse-like
stench that seemed, he thought, to rise up from the basement and from the earth. He would write to Daniel, he

decided. He would ask that Daniel come back. He would explain that the mayor had plans for rebuilding the city, that the waterfront was waiting to be restored, that soon there would be jobs for all. He would explain how urgently the inner city needed Daniel's youth and his strength.

But four Christmases and New Years passed; Daniel failed to return; and as Geffen drove to work, he saw that within five miles of the downtown, on either side of the freeway, the red brick houses were falling into disrepair. The tall, beautiful elms were dying of disease, and in the residential side streets, broken roof tiles, old tires, empty cartons lay on the strip of ground beside the curb while islands of black men, wearing damaged hats, hovered in front of the broken wooden steps and cracked porches. Downtown, store after store stood boarded up. Single cars careened wildly through the deserted boulevards. The plan for urban renewal—aborted almost at the time it began—gouged holes in the ground next to abandoned luncheonettes. Each day the talk concerned unemployment, robberies, and unemployment.

Now scarcely more than a dozen and a half patients visited Geffen in any week. They were left over from before: clients grown too poor or too old to move to the newer neighborhoods. Geffen treated each one with respect and at last accepted that they respected him in turn. Yet he was conscious of something erratic in the way they straggled into and perched in his waiting room, as if his office were a temporary way station instead of a long-standing establishment with a respectable worn green carpet and solid glass ashtrays. Once outside the building, he beheld deprivation in the face of any black person he passed. Near corner grocery stores and cut-rate drugstores, he sniffed the acrid odor of joblessness. He imagined suffering each time he glimpsed a child darting out of a passageway into the cold or rain. But as time went by, a sense of helplessness replaced his anguish, and he ended up by dwelling on his own unpaid bills and advancing years.

By June of 1967, three quarters of the tenants in Geffen's building had moved or were in the midst of moving out. Among the latter, an insurance agent with an office on the eighth floor approached Geffen in the lobby. He was carrying a portrait of his mother and a large rolled-up map of France. Leaning towards Geffen, he reported he had heard that a dentist in the next building had had four teeth knocked out and a novelty wholesaler's white secretary had been knifed and robbed.

"Those are just rumors," Geffen said.

"Then how about this? A friend of mine in the steel business told me about a man who got shot for no reason while walking from the public library to Crowley Milner's."

"That's just another rumor," commented Geffen.

"Well, I'm getting out," the insurance agent said. "It's time. If I were you, I'd get out too."

"Not me," Geffen backed hastily in the direction of the elevator. "My practice is here. I'm settled and comfortable

—no reason to leave." For good measure he called from the elevator, "No reason to leave," and pushed the button for his floor.

Stepping out, the hall seemed to him darker than usual. He decided to complain to the management about inadequate lighting. He walked quickly and heard strange footsteps behind him but felt too afraid to turn around and look. Then from out of nowhere a hand clamped down on his shoulder. Spinning about, with all his might Geffen kicked his assailant in the groin—to discover he had lunged at Marvin Grossberg, his first and most faithful arthritic patient who now lay unconscious on the mottled marble floor. Geffen stared from Marvin's ashen face to his formal black shoes and was filled with horror. Kneeling, he took Marvin's pulse, and a great sorrow spread through him that he had knocked Marvin to the ground. He helped him up, apologized for his error, put an arm around his patient's shoulder, and accompanied him to the elevator. While they waited for the elevator, the realization came to Geffen that his son Daniel would never return. He cleared his throat. "Marvin," he said at last, "I'm moving to the suburbs."

Six weeks later, Geffen came downtown for a final visit to his office. It was a Sunday, with no one else around. A few days earlier he had apologized to Henry Bothin. "You and I," he'd said, "we've been here longer than twenty-six years." He had paused, unable to think of anything else to

offer. "We've grown middle-aged together . . . we're getting old. Oh, I know I'm not the most dedicated or talented
doctor . . . still, I need more patients . . ."

He recalled that the news vendor, his eyes gentle as
always, simply nodded to indicate he'd heard. But after a
moment Henry lowered his head, and when he did, Geffen
caught sight of the faintly sardonic and bitter expression
that pulled down the corners of his mouth.

Geffen turned from the window. He sorted through a
sheaf of papers and with one motion dropped the entire
stack into a waste basket, wanting to keep at bay the image
of Henry's mouth. He paced the floor for some minutes.
Then from his walls he removed an aerial view of the first
Ford plant and an etching of how Detroit had looked in
1798. He glanced at the calendar on his desk and flipped
it open to today's date: July 23, 1967. After that he carried
his pictures to the elevator, made his way out of the building, rounded a corner to the parking lot, got into his car,
and entered the freeway.

No more than a few minutes had passed when he first
saw the fires. Ahead of him, columns of flame shot into the
purpling sky like separate edifices rising to peaks. As he
drove on, the blaze surrounded him and he knew, even
before the car radio broadcast the news, that he was witness-
ing the rages of an expanding riot. From the newscaster he
learned that the riots had started in a block of shops and
markets in his old neighborhood and that it was spreading
quickly. The air above him seemed unreal, yet incredibly

momentous and alive. He began to hear the loud clap of gunfire, then from all directions the fire engines endlessly wailing. He kept on driving, flanked by the thick coils of smoke. Then gradually he left the fires behind him and followed an ordinary freeway again.

Arriving at his Japanese-style house, he entered through the shoji screens to find his wife watching the news on television. She was nibbling on slices of meat and crackers and switching channels from battles in Vietnam to fires in Detroit. "It's Mr. Rosenberg's old butcher shop," she greeted him, "and it's burning down! Aren't you glad we moved!" From her excited voice and the way she tilted her head, he understood that the spectacle at least in part entertained her.

"Mr. Rosenberg's store . . ." she went on, and then demanded, "Where are you going?" as he headed out the door and back into his car.

It was already dusk when he reached his old neighborhood. Avoiding the roadblocks that had been set up, he angled circuitously to an area a quarter of a mile from his street. He parked the car, with a mechanical gesture unlocked his medical bag from the trunk, and began to walk. His path at first was almost deserted, and the houses and the trees around him appeared unharmed. Then soon the smell of smoke grew heavier. People sprang into being around him—more and more of them milling about, clustered at intersections and leaning against the trees and cars. Presently he came to his own street and was strolling along, comforted by the terrain, when he discovered that the two houses next to his and his own house had burned into rubble on the ground.

Geffen walked on without stopping. Without quite knowing that he did so, he went in the direction of the fires. The night was warm, noisy with voices, and lit by the glow of the near-distant conflagration. As he passed dwellings, still intact, he remembered his own house whole and despaired that all these years he had never knocked on the door, had never tried to know the man who might have been the friend in his dream, had never stepped inside to ask if the apple tree in the yard had gone on blooming and if the radiators had echoed in the silence of the falling snow.

"Our city is burning," he heard the cry in his heart, while from somewhere in the past, two tall colleagues insisted during a medical meeting in Ohio, "Detroit . . . well it isn't New York . . . it isn't Chicago . . . it isn't San Francisco." But it was still his city, he thought. It was still a grand and powerful city, and if it burst into flames, all other great cities equally bore that danger.

Geffen hurried ahead. In the middle of a beleaguered block of motley stores, he looked up to a cluster of faces at the window above a sign, "Ray's Hardware." He made out both children and adults—a family, he thought—and wondered what had stopped them from evacuating the building. Did they not comprehend that the fires or the smoke might cut them off? Was one of them, whom they were unwilling to leave, wounded or ill? He crossed the street, hovered close to the building, groped for a door handle, then drew his hand away, wanting to climb toward that family, yet questioning how they would respond if he suddenly burst in on them. How could he, a stranger, a short white man with glasses, expect they would heed his warning or accept his help? What could he say to them, what possible credentials could he offer?

At this, Gertrude's words to the butcher rang out in his ears: "The Doctor likes a nice piece of sirloin steak." Ludicrously—instead of hating the statement as he always had—it brought to his mind that he had studied and trained, observed and treated, had wielded a stethoscope, had ministered with pills and injections and had long been equipped to reach out to the victims of his exodus from Detroit. Yes, he thought, he was a bona fide physician; and he felt surprise that after all these years he valued his profession. With a certain light-headedness he entered the building and quickly mounted the stairs. On the second story he identified an entranceway and went toward it, thinking that within lived his neighbors whom he had betrayed and left behind. Wanting—determined—to rejoin them, he took a deep breath and knocked on the door.

But when the door had opened he stood, his hands at his sides, unable to find the words he needed to say.

STAFF OF LIFE

Out of gratitude for her life, Rachel Keppler cooked from
early morning until late at night. For—blessed among
women who resided in Detroit—she possessed a handsome,
virile husband, three growing sons, and a kind, older sister
who lived two blocks away. As if this were not enough,
Rachel's husband was president of the Pinsk-Detroit Soccer and Marching Club, and so it was Rachel who—through
most of the 1930's and well into the 1940's—baked the
Pinsk-Detroit Soccer and Marching Club's official cake.

"Here she comes, my fine fellows!" Joseph would call
to their sons. "Here she comes!" he would announce as the
family prepared to attend the Club's annual festivities.
"Here comes your lovely mother and her unique twelve-
pound hazelnut cake!"

With these words sounding musically in her ears,
Rachel rose each morning as the first light entered through
her windows and went to the kitchen. "Ah yes," she greeted
the stove, the onions, the Crisco, "ah yes, ah yes." Then
she began to peel the apples in their baskets, to slice the

onions, to chop the celery, companionably to beat the eggs and to grate three long bars of yellow cheese. Gradually her wide and milky, pleasant face took on the rich colors and the texture of a stewed fruit compote. Beyond the pots and pans she kept before her the rapt image of her husband and her sons. And while her rust-colored hair fanned about her head, paling to apricot in the heat, she thought about the unknown hungry whom she hoped someday to reach, or about Noah, her sister's only child, who was her friend and helpmate, but who could not learn to read.

As the morning progressed and the small kitchen grew more and more jammed and crowded, to an outsider it might appear that Rachel directed her efforts less to the taste and appearance of her food than to the challenge of producing sheer volume. Strudel issued from her oven in wide sheets resembling muddy acreage. After the strudel, platoons of macaroons advanced as relentlessly as armies, their centers toughened into helmets. Underbaked prune tarts oozed forth next, while off to the sidelines three thousand lima beans bubbled on the stove. A smell of yeast and cinnamon lay everywhere; and Rachel, enraptured by these manifold performances, sang to her cooking, "Deedle deedle."

In the evening she kissed her husband, Joseph, passionately on the mouth and asked who at his work had been fired or taken ill with flu. Then she gave him a carton of strudel to deliver in his car. She gave the Irish mailman— though his pocked complexion frightened her—portions of noodle pudding for his wife. She searched the streets for the ailing and the hungry and slid hunks of soggy sponge cake into pockets wherever she could. And in the early years no one in the neighborhood publicly criticized her strudel. No one mentioned that the weight of her noodle pudding had ruined the mailman's back. No one even hinted that in the evenings the sick grew pale and even sicker at the sight of Joseph bringing Rachel's food.

At the lonely hour—in the middle of the afternoon when her sons were still at school—Rachel set forth to buy groceries. She tied a string of pearls over her house dress; she stepped out through the door. Passing the rows of brick-faced houses behind cement porches sagging toward a tuft of lawn, she trotted along until she met her nephew, Noah, sometimes staring, sometimes intently circling a chalk mark on the street. Together they continued toward the avenue of shops, bought meat, chose horseradish, watercress and lettuce, and then came back with Noah in the lead—his head held high and smirking as though he escorted grand trophies to their rightful home. Together inside the house, gently they unpacked their wares—like lifting out special friends—after which Noah lined up all the cans, put flour into bins, sought out the proper place for cornstarch and then sat down and ate three maca-roons, two prune tarts, some honey cake and half a pan of strudel.

"How Noah eats!" praised Rachel when she visited her sister Torin.

Torin smiled at Rachel, a proud light fighting the sadness in her eyes.

"Ah yes," agreed the overweight Igor, Noah's father, "his appetite is well developed. What's more, no one has a memory as good as Noah's. He's sixteen, almost seventeen, and he can remember every person since his infancy; every name. The problem is . . . if only he could one day learn to read."

"If only . . ." echoed Torin.

"If only . . ." Rachel said.

But as it happened, instead of reading he took to gazing into the panties of the five-year-old girl next door, the three-year-old girl across the street, the four-year-old on the corner porch. Each day he gaped and stared and chuckled and shook his head until at last he was denounced by irate neighbors, interviewed by psychologists and nuns and sent off to a home for the retarded in Quebec.

All three of Rachel's sons warmly embraced Noah or gripped his hand, indignant he was leaving town. Yet soon after he had gone they acted as if his existence now no longer mattered. If Rachel asked, "Please write a note to Noah," at best they pointed out that Noah could not read. If she persisted, "Please ask him how he is, please send off several lines," they dropped their heads between their shoulders and cast their truculent, bushy eyebrows toward the ground. It was then she noticed that they had gradually stopped seeking her out in the kitchen, that they rarely

kissed her when they left for school or work, and in the
summer twilight she saw them picking at her food.

"Come with us to visit Noah," Igor kept inviting.

"Oh Igor, what with all the cooking . . ."

"You should come with us. He always asks about you—
every time we drive up there."

"What does he ask?"

"Why, of course he asks about your strudel."

Rachel flushed with pleasure. "Thank you, Igor. But
what with Joseph and the boys and all the spices wanting
water in the yard . . . it's hard to get away."

Yet as she said this she remembered Noah by her
side—his thick arms folded across her packages, his head
triumphant above the lettuce, his pointed ears like gifts on
either side. A longing to walk with him past broccoli and
oranges assailed her as in a dream. She took a deep breath
and fidgeted, guilty at a desire so strong it tempted her to
leave her family for three long days and travel some place
foreign like Quebec. And yet, the truth was, she had neglected Noah. She said, "I'll come with you next time."

So on a Wednesday morning she brought her suitcase
to the trunk of Igor's old tan Chevrolet and watched him
as he jammed the suitcase in with Torin's and his own.
Then Torin, who normally sat in front with Igor, arranged
herself in back with Rachel. Bolt upright, side by side, the
two women perched behind the driver, their feet in patent
leather pumps, their hats topped with a fuchsia flower.

They rode stiffly and in silence for an hour. Then gradually they took off their hats, their shoes. Carefully they set aside the sack of strudel that rested on their laps and then gazed out with pleasure and with mild surprise at the wide green fields, the vast blue skies, the small farmhouses that took them toward Quebec.

On the second morning when they had almost reached their destination, Igor warned, twisting his head from the wheel toward Rachel, "It's not always pleasant visiting him there, you know. When he first sees us, sometimes he gets angry. But the anger always goes away. The good thing is, it always goes away." He sighed, "Ahh," his head to the wheel again, "if only they would teach him a few letters of the alphabet . . . teach him to add up one or two sums . . . then we could put him in the car and bring him home." Five minutes later Igor said, "We're almost there."

An uneasiness took hold of Rachel. It gripped her even as Igor telephoned from the gate and drove into the stern yet luxuriant park-like grounds that led to a building, reminiscent of a concert hall, which now housed Noah. Rachel, Torin, and Igor emerged from the automobile, righted their clothes and set forth. They struggled up the imposing stairs past banisters and balustrades, and entering the building went here and there before suddenly finding themselves face to face with Noah. He cried out—a yelp of shame and fury—and dodging to one side began running away from them through the lobby and out the massive door. Leaving Igor to straggle behind, the two women

sped off and chased Noah's swift figure down the terraced
stairs to the near garden and the high plains just beyond.
Darting around the hedges, the dark green pine trees, the
stone fountains and the founder's statue astride its bronze
horse, they gained on Noah and grew elated and waved
their paper bags and pleaded, "Strudel, Noah? . . . Noah,
a piece of coffee cake?"

And Noah—forgiving them, it seemed to Rachel—
spun slowly about and stretched out his hand.

Returning home, everything looked strange to Rachel's
eye. Even the overstuffed armchairs in her living room, even
the wide-based lamps appeared less substantial than before,
while Joseph and her sons—Harold, Edward, and Alvin—
looked curiously larger. She had not remembered they took
up so much space. Crowding around her they asked about
Noah's health, Igor's car, the weather in Quebec. But so
identical was their heartiness, each one with the other's, that
in their welcome she detected something forced or hollow.
Embarrassed by their strangeness she made her way past
them to the kitchen. Here she opened the door of the re-
frigerator to discover that the food she'd prepared in advance had not been touched. Not a single pot lid in the
three-day supply had been lifted up; not a piece of wax paper
had been removed or fingered.

"But how is it," she exclaimed, "you haven't eaten?"

The boys at once looked pointedly at Joseph who
stepped forward and, with his manner offhand and cavalier,

confessed that they'd gone to a Chinese restaurant on Wednesday night and on Thursday night, after eating spaghetti at an Italian restaurant, had brought home barbecued chicken.

A presentiment of doom turned Rachel's fingers icy cold—a foreboding that quickly catapulted into truth, for on the weekend her sons suggested that they all go out to dinner.

"Go out to where?" she queried, thinking that this was her punishment for running off to visit Noah.

"To a restaurant," said Alvin.

She bit her tongue, but still the senseless question escaped, "What will you do there?"

"Rachel," Joseph laughed. He put his arm around her waist. But her sons simply laced up their shoes and went out the front door and did not return for dinner.

Two days later, just before mealtime, Harold and Edward disappeared again. Three days after that, Alvin followed their example. After that a week passed with everyone seated uneventfully at the table. Then late one afternoon as Rachel poured farfel into the barley soup, she heard the front door slam. She called her sons. "Harold . . . Edward . . . Alvin?"

"They were here a minute ago," she explained to her husband, feeling a trifle foolish as she watched him stand by the head of the table and gaze with a certain stoicism at the empty places. "They were here," she said, as though this might mitigate their absence, "and now suddenly they're gone." Apologetically she smiled at Joseph, for she knew he looked forward to the evening meal with his sons. She knew he loved performing with his quick, ironic wit and then attending to the boys' guffaws—to their relief that life was not so serious as their mother allowed. Now she berated herself for faulty attention to Joseph's jokes. She scolded herself for forgetting to laugh. Withdrawing to the kitchen, she soon came out again, carrying Joseph a large offering of soup.

"What soup is it?" Joseph asked, his voice a bare whisper as he regarded the large tureen.

"Barley farfel."

At these words he jumped back from the table. He straightened his shoulders, pulling in his stomach until it was flat. "Since the boys are off carousing . . . since they've chosen to eat with us only now and then . . ." backing off, he passed the sideboard, ". . . this is a perfect time to start a diet."

She followed him into the living room. "Where are you going?" she demanded. "Why are you going?"

"To be thin."

"But you're already thin. You're a little too thin. Just compare yourself with Igor."

"I wouldn't want to," Joseph answered; and he grinned at her, declaring as he too left her dinner, "Rachel, I'll be even thinner." He put on his cap and went out.

For a few moments she stood in the center of the room and did nothing. Then she phoned her sister, Torin, who said, "They'll come back. They'll all come back. It isn't possible that anyone who loves you could long forego your prune tarts . . . your carrot tzimis . . . your twelve-pound hazelnut cake."

Rachel, listening very carefully, thought it possible that her sister spoke the truth.

But in the morning Joseph faced her with an air of new determination. "The boys are older now," he lectured. "They're grown-up. Harold even has a steady girlfriend. They're courting . . . branching out . . . spending time with women. These days they have better things to do than eat." And he challenged her by taking only half a piece of toast. "Rachel," he delivered in a friendly fashion, "your passion for cooking is . . . unnatural. It's time for you to change. To stop."

"To change?" She puzzled over his meaning. Did he want her to discard potato kugel? To eschew honey cake? And if she changed, what could she offer that was large or worthy enough? Looking away from him, she envisioned her cupboards bare, her bins and baskets and cake pans empty, her white stove standing with the quiet idleness of death.

"The boys are adults now," he admonished. "There's no need to go on as you have. Now you can stop your cooking and take up a hobby."

A wild terror swept through her. It turned to resentment as she gazed at his worker's hands and his dark hair that grew to a peak on his forehead like a duke's. "What it is," she murmured, disturbed to send such a self-important statement into the air, "What it is . . . I care about you." She uttered these words softly enough to let him choose— as he did—to ignore her. When he had left the house she said to herself, "Perhaps if I cooked a little less . . . if I fixed fewer . . . ," but she could not finish the thought.

Over the next few weeks, Noah began to occupy more and more of her mind. On her way to the market she would pause at the ancient elm and the cracked pavement by the curb where he used to join her. Missing him, she would conjure up his face—his light brown hair, his ears that shot up like an animal's ears, his cheeks that always seemed new-born and furry. Then gradually, as the weather changed, her thoughts shifted and she began instead to imagine the faces of the women her sons would marry. She had always been drawn to the company of women. Sometimes it had even seemed to her a matter of chance she had become so in-tertwined, so dependent on men. She recalled how, as a young child, she had stood on a stool while her mother and eager aunts had taught her how to braid and bake a challah. Now she grieved over their absence, entered the market, and fell deep into a dream of daughters-in-law at her side in the kitchen. Together, she planned, they would walk the neighborhoods in search of all the hungry. Together they would roam past the fallen branches in the vacant lot until they came at last to a host of wandering men and women, perhaps far from home and full of longing, day and night, for prune tarts and for knishes.

Then one afternoon when she had marched past the long rows of grim-faced houses, red and gold leaves on their lawns, she entered her front door to find an unknown young woman seated in the living room. A distance away stood Joseph, looking slim and happy while talking to their eldest son.

"My dear," said Joseph as he came toward her, "I want you to meet Harold's girlfriend. He has brought her home to meet us. This is Harold's future wife, Sheila Ann Levine."

Six months later Harold and Sheila Ann Levine married. Eighteen months later Edward married, and a year after that Alvin married Joanne. To Rachel's mystification, each son wed a woman who did not cook. To her distress each woman, when visiting Rachel's house, sought out the corner most distant from her mother-in-law. At first Rachel did not quite know what to make of her sons' wives. She forgave their unwillingness to work in the kitchen, reasoning that they were young and might wake up any morning, their goals, their perspectives totally transformed. She also forgave them their aloofness, for the fact was, something about them compelled and attracted her: the suspicion that deep within them, within the very same remoteness that rejected her, lay a hidden, constant, burn-

ing hunger. Therefore—as much more for their sakes as
for her sons'—on Fridays she sent Joseph with roast turkey and blintzes to the houses where they lived.

Then one day Joseph flatly refused. "They give it to
the dog," he told her. "Harold has a spotted dog named
Walter who is famous for eating everything." He paused
and spun about, one foot slightly lifted off the ground.
"And if I come to them with noodle pudding and carrot
tzimis in a bag they lock the door or tiptoe to the den in
back, pretending no one's home. But if," he raised an index
finger and planted both feet on the ground, "I come to
them with nothing but my handshake and a hat they treat
me like a hero . . . they take me golfing . . . bowling . . . to
a nightclub with a comedy act." He paused and shook his
head. "Rachel, modern women don't cook as much as you.
If you could only become more modern. How can I persuade you to branch out . . . broaden your horizon . . .
maybe buy a bit of hair dye and put it on your hair?"

She regarded him with sympathy, laying a protective
hand on her graying hair. For almost eight months she had
found him restless and distraught. He had failed to win the
last election of the Pinsk-Detroit Soccer and Marching
Club, and though she knew he could still march all morning and play soccer throughout the afternoon, after all
these years he was stepping down. How could she assure
him that he'd lost nothing—that, most important of
all, he had his family—that his family remained intact?
She said, "Tomorrow it's Alvin's birthday. I've invited

everyone here for dinner and they're coming. I'll bake a honey cake," she nodded and smiled. "And you don't have to bother making deliveries . . . we can give them turkey and blintzes to take home when they leave."

Joseph stared at her in disbelief, a deranged gleam in his eyes. He opened his mouth but no words came out. He walked away to the end of the room and flailed his arms as he came back. "They don't need it," he managed to croak. "They don't want it. They don't want it. Rachel, we could pave the road to North Africa and back with your turkey, your. . . . And no one needs it, no one wants it," he cried out in a voice of pain. "It's a new life . . . a new life!"

At the shrillness of his voice, Rachel's cheeks lost their color. "Well, if they don't want it . . ."

"Why would they want it? Do you think they come here of their own volition? Do you think I don't have to force them? Yes," he shouted, "I have to force them . . . to argue. Beg them. Cajole them. Oh my God, do you think I don't prefer going out with them to staying here!"

She was about to say, "Well, if they don't want to . . ." when the floor beneath her seemed to fly up to the ceiling. As she steadied herself, Joseph moved toward her. But then he stepped back and devised a kind of crooked smile. "Rachel," he said after a moment, "we're man and wife. I only have to force them a little."

She nodded numbly and turned away. She found it difficult to sort through the meaning of his outburst. But the next night when Edward kissed her on the cheek and

Edward's wife loudly proclaimed the gefilte fish delicious, she understood that Joseph had given them orders to humor her. Carrying her platters around the table she then heard her husband reprimand Alvin's wife Joanne who was looking askance at the noodle pudding.

"That's quite enough, don't carry on," Joseph warned the young woman. "You have better things to do."

For a moment her husband's loyalty warmed her heart. At the same time she saw he had taken the young woman's fingers in his hands; he was smiling, playing with her fingers. Was this his new life, she wondered. She remembered that in their youth he had brought her jokes and roses and then had ruefully proposed. Filled with shame, she went into the kitchen, setting down her platters. She leaned over the sink and tried to weep into an onion, but her eyes were too dry. It was then she realized she wanted to stop cooking.

That night after she and Joseph had gone to bed, she lay awake. From the distance of the several rooms between them, she thanked her stove and sent a special farewell to her yeast. One by one she conjured up her wheat, salt, honey, flour, barley, beans, and onions and took separate leave of each. As she finished her last good-byes, a great weight slowly lifted from her. All care, all aching ceased within her bones. To her astonishment, her body seemed to float above the bed. She glimpsed the peaceful realm that lay ahead and folded her arms across her chest.

For two, three minutes she waited patiently. After that she waited for two, three minutes more. Then some ferment inside her bubbled up like gas. It sought to be released. She tried to keep it dormant, holding her arms tight against her chest. She shut her eyes and willed herself to concentrate on utter darkness and the end of disgrace. Instead she pictured that on the other side of the window a silvery moon had risen and the sky was thick with bright stars. Springing up, she filled a suitcase with some clothes, packed a paper bag with macaroons and strudel, slipped past the dense shapes of her living room lamps and armchairs and ran at a gallop the two long blocks to Torin's house.

It was past midnight when Igor opened the door. "Rachel!" he exclaimed and welcomed her in and claimed he knew from her suitcase and paper bag that she wanted to come with them to visit Noah.

Early in the morning Rachel, Torin, and Igor climbed into the tan Chevrolet. They headed north, crossing the bridge to Canada and entering the stretch of open road with Igor pointing out the flat green autumn farmland. On the second day there was a rise in the landscape, a smoky blue aspect to the air and sudden, isolated and melancholy growths of sunflowers. Just before noon they reached their destination, stopping at the high gate to phone to the main building. Solemnly Igor put on a jacket and tie. Torin adjusted her stockings. Rachel smoothed down her hair. Then they started toward the terraced stairs where they caught sight of Noah at the very top. An attendant had just let him out and it seemed to Rachel he was happy to see them, for instead of running away he was scurrying down in their direction.

Rachel called out, "Noah, Noah!" while Torin's soft and Igor's bass voice echoed his name. One after the other they embraced Noah, leading him to a bench in the walled-in autumnal garden. Igor, stepping back, established himself on the ground a small distance away while Rachel and Torin placed Noah between them on the stone bench. Then beneath the shadow of a golden birch tree the two women unrolled their long brown paper bags and brought out cakes, macaroons, green grapes, and strudel. Dividing the cakes into pieces and plucking the grapes from their stems they took turns advancing these into Noah's mouth until at last Rachel comprehended he was no longer hungry, but that he understood and would go on earnestly chewing, his head held at a dignified angle as he accepted their lengthy offerings of love.

HERO

A few days before his thirty-sixth birthday, Jeremy Green received a letter announcing he was the hero of his friend Henry Brustein's third novel. "Why am I the hero?" Jeremy questioned. He began to feel anxious. It occurred to him that since he'd left Cleveland and Henry, he'd felt contented with his life. He reread Henry's letter, thought about Henry and their friendship, and stared at a sentence which declared, "I have blocked out the first half of the book and so far you are a terrific hero."

"A terrific hero?" Jeremy puzzled. As if his surroundings might provide some reason for this label, he gazed out the kitchen window toward the nasturtiums where he saw his young son and daughter busily hitting and kicking one another, then listened to his wife pedaling above him on the exercise bicycle in the guest bedroom.

He asked himself, "What have I done that's good enough or bad enough? What kind of hero does Henry have in mind?" Hastily he culled from his memory whatever he could: the windy July day he had climbed to the top of

Mt. Kiskoe, no matter he was bitten by hornets; the chill March evening when, on a dare, he had stripped, jumped into icy Lake Huron, and emerged with an ear infection; the Italian restaurant to which he'd brought his elegant date and introduced her to his whiskered Aunt Gladys and his bald Uncle Nat when he could have managed to avoid their seeing him.

Jeremy searched for something more. Reason told him he would not find it—that even his acquisition of a small, attractive shopping center with a pharmacy and three other stores would likely count for nothing since Henry—through all the years—remained indifferent to commerce.

Fear edged into Jeremy's throat, terror that he was about to feel discontented with his life. To ward that off, he hid the letter in a basket near the laundry room, then fixed himself a large chicken sandwich.

But the next day he retrieved the letter, read it again, and decided that its meaning might be the one he'd secretly wanted. For the fact was, he had known Henry since the age of nine or ten and almost from the beginning it had seemed clear to him that he esteemed and loved Henry Brustein more than Henry esteemed and loved him. Now, however, it appeared that Henry had uncovered a dimension of Jeremy of which Jeremy himself was unaware and that as a result their regard for one another was about to assume equal proportions. Perhaps, he imagined, the scales had already tipped the other way.

Light-headedly he searched out pen and paper and wrote, attempting a jocular tone, "Dear Henry, I'm delighted to figure so prominently in your new novel. But why me? Why not Billy Mackroyd or Bugs Lipson? Why not one of your colleagues or the dean at your University? Send me a few chapters and I'll tell you what I think. Regards to Margery."

Jeremy posted the letter and waited. After a few weeks with no reply, he debated phoning his friend but decided that under the circumstances his interest might appear unseemly. Instead he took this as a time to consider that the stuff of heroes might actually lay inside him. Walking out under the stars of an evening, he relived his ascent to Mt. Kiskoe and drew up plans for higher mountains. The longer he waited for Henry's response, the more wonderful the feats he imagined. Then one afternoon a note arrived from Margery Brustein in which she informed Jeremy that her husband, having composed a first draft of three-quarters of his third novel, had suffered a heart attack and died.

Jeremy could not believe, particularly at this juncture of their relationship, that his accomplished, handsome friend no longer existed. Wanting to be alone, he sat beneath the palm tree in the court of his shopping center and recalled his youth in Cleveland—remembered gray air he and Henry had traveled through, the high walls of apartment buildings they'd lived in, the basketball, football, baseball games they had shared. He thought of Henry's

Plymouth, the number of miles they'd pushed or run alongside it, Henry authoritatively maintaining that owners ought never abandon their cars. He recalled an autumn night—the look of its moon—when the car had run smoothly, Henry at the wheel, himself in the passenger seat, and in between, Margery Lindquist.

With compassion he thought then about Margery. From there he went on to consider she had likely read Henry's unfinished manuscript. No doubt she had read every chapter, perhaps had read selected chapters more than once. A desire welled up in him to see and talk with her, and on impulse, discounting the number of times he'd questioned why Henry had taken her for his wife, he headed for the public phone in front of the discount shoe store and called her. The next day he kissed his family, departed San Diego, landed in Detroit, and drove in the night to a motel near Ann Arbor. As he passed the dark flat fields that led away from the airport, he wished he had mentioned to Henry that all four discount stores located in his shopping center offered true and worthwhile bargains.

In the morning he phoned Margery from his motel. She told him to come over at ten o'clock. With time to waste, he circled the University and the neighborhoods around it—cruised about, hoping that Henry had modified the strictness of his standards and that one of the gabled houses or rolling lawns, or at least one of the wooded front paths, had belonged to his friend.

But Henry's street, when he turned into it, instantly showed its lack of charm. Lined with squat bungalows and square patches of lawn, its flat terrain reminded Jeremy of his friend's grimness. Halfway up the block he spotted an old, derelict-looking Plymouth. Pulling up behind it, he checked the near house number and approached the automobile. Henry, he thought with amazement, had never abandoned his car. Jeremy touched its bruised door and battered hood and felt an urge to ask for the key, to get inside, to start up the vehicle. Turning away, he climbed a half dozen gray painted steps and pressed the bell to Henry's house. In his mind he saw the young Margery Lindquist; he remembered Henry explaining there was something extraordinary about the way she balanced her head and the great width of her hair on so skinny a neck.

Presently Margery appeared and said matter-of-factly, "Hello, Jeremy."

"Hello, Margery," he greeted, and with a swift glance to check the angle of her head and the circumference of her hair, he bent to enfold her in his arms. When she ducked away from his embrace, he decided there must be some mistake, that surely she must know who he was, must recognize he was the model for the protagonist of Henry's novel. He moved toward her once more, but she dodged him again and said, "You're early," in a bright, abrupt voice that let him know she had no intention of sharing her grief.

"Early? You said ten o'clock."

"It's a quarter to. You're early," she laughed.

The girlishness of the sound—the way it kept him at a distance—brought the blood to his face. He stared at her smooth complexion, at the lack of shadows under her wide eyes, and, most of all, at the unchanged exuberance of her hair. Where were the signs of her suffering, he wondered. Glancing away, he reflected that Henry ought to have married a woman who would appear more mournful when he died. "I would have come earlier," he reproved. "I would have come for the services if you had let me know."

"There were no services. Henry would not have wanted any," she said. She gave a short laugh—this time as though she were being chastised—and led him inside, but only as far as the hall. Here she stood in front of him, arms firmly folded, giving him the impression she was protecting her house.

Cramped in the narrow hall, he wondered if there was something in Henry's manuscript that made her so cautious. He tried to unblock his view—to peer over her head or off to the side—but the healthy spring of her curls seemed to let them uncoil and sprout taller and still wider. How unfortunate, he thought. The next moment Margery broke her stance and moved into the living room. Quickly he followed after her, his gaze taking in a dark Danish couch, a matching armchair, an unadorned coffee table, a bookshelf on either side of the fireplace. He might have expected this spare, ascetic decor from Henry, he thought—might have expected the kind of room a casual observer could mistake for a place where people waited to have a tooth pulled. Yet he, having known Henry for twenty-eight years, could offer something else, could bring to these chaste surroundings a memory of Henry, for example, lavishly supplying thick black cigars on the occasion of Billy Mackroyd's sixteenth birthday. "This is a nice room, " he declared.

"We like it," Margery pronounced. "Henry and I liked it," she reinforced with so exclusive an air Jeremy expected she would lead him out into the passageway again. But instead, as if reminded of her duty, her voice turned small and gracious and she offered him coffee and a bran muffin. "Since you've come all this way, Jeremy . . ." she explained, and disappeared toward the back of the house.

When he realized she was gone, even if for only a short time, an almost celebratory glee seized him. He tried out the couch and the armchair and began to search the ceiling and the walls for Henry's presence. Glancing out the window, he saw Henry's Plymouth parked at the curb. It seemed to signal joyously that Henry belonged to him as much, if not more, than to anyone else. After a moment he felt his gaze pulled in the opposite direction, and he crossed the room, stepping through an archway that he presumed led to the dining room but where, instead of a table and chairs, he made out file cabinets, three walls of books, a massive desk. Henry's study, he thought, and came to stand before Henry's desk.

Just then he noticed that a framed snapshot of Bugs, Billy, Henry, and himself stood in a far corner of the desk.

Bugs and Billy, their features faded, knelt in the foreground wearing white gym shorts still bright as the moon. Henry and Jeremy stood up, poker-faced, in the rear. Jeremy lifted the snapshot, carrying it to the window behind Henry's desk. He held it to the light and peered hard at his past: four young men piling out of Henry's Plymouth and approaching the empty high school track. He saw them racing to be judged in endless tests of skill and strength and endurance. He recalled the unlit track and the combinations of a 220-yard dash, six high hurdles, four cartwheels, twenty chin-ups, fifty sit-ups. He remembered it was always Henry who made the final judgment, whose opinion the others awaited, whose perceptions raised one person and inevitably lowered the next. Jeremy looked at the desk. Which of its drawers, he wondered, contained Henry's attitude towards Jeremy's life? Which of the drawers contained the chapters that added up his final score?

He returned his gaze to the snapshot. Bugs, he recalled, was now the head of a prestigious eye clinic in Phoenix. Billy, recently elected to the Ohio State Senate, was from all accounts about to be elected again. And it was Henry, Jeremy acknowledged, who had sent them on their way—who as early as high school had envisioned eye surgery for Bugs and insisted on politics for Billy. To Jeremy he had awarded a life-long career in nuclear and low temperature physics—had bestowed this calling with such good will and conviction that Jeremy had waited until college to point out he had never been interested in science and that his test scores in science had always been poor.

"Then you'll have to think about public interest law," Henry had pursued. "That is, if you want to reach the top of your field." His dark gaze had seemed to probe, to rummage about in Jeremy's soul, his stern eye fastening on Jeremy's nose. "Yes, I see in you someone who will change the tax structure. No doubt you will also promote the environment and fight with your pen for the rule of law."

"Rule of law?" Jeremy had queried. And almost immediately, keeping other grievances to himself, he had departed college, Cleveland, and Henry, and had made his way across the country where he took a job selling real estate.

With this memory he heard the click of Margery's footsteps and set the photograph down abruptly lest she think he wanted to steal it. He entered the living room from one entrance, Margery—an oblong tray in her hands—from another. On Margery's tray lay a single, shriveled-up muffin and two small cups of coffee. Jeremy stared at this meager offering, and it suddenly seemed clear to him that if in the novel Henry had depicted him as deserving of respect, Margery would have carried in more coffee and a better-looking muffin.

His heart therefore felt unusually heavy as he lowered himself onto the couch and watched Margery set her tray on the coffee table and sit down. She handed him a coffee cup and a spoon, and she said, as if returning to a point in their conversation, "The University wanted to give a memorial service . . . he was a man of importance, you understand. But I decided against it. Whatever would have been said . . . a poem, a speech . . . well, you know, he would have wanted to correct it. He would have wanted to revise it."

Jeremy took a sip of his coffee. He recalled leaving Cleveland and the relief he'd felt at escaping how much trouble it was to be better than himself. Out of curiosity, he tried the muffin. A crumb lodged in his throat like a sharp pebble, and an anger within himself quickened. It occurred to him it was Henry's own fault he had died. "Did Henry still smoke?" he accused.

She regarded him with interest. "What do you mean?"

"Had he given up smoking?"

"He didn't smoke."

"Did he exercise? Did he see his doctor with any regularity?"

She straightened the angle of the tray. Then she reached down and straightened the legs of the coffee table. And then the words burst through her lips in a sound that mixed bitterness with pride, "He did nothing but work. We never went anywhere. We never did anything. We put off having children." As he stared at her with astonishment, her voice softened slightly, "Well, of course he had to work. He needed to work. It made sense. If you intend to be a great teacher, and he was a very great teacher . . . if you intend to be an immortal essayist . . . a significant novelist."

"I'm sure he was a significant novelist," Jeremy murmured.

"With the new book, his reputation would have been assured."

"If I could read. . . ."

"The conception for the main character is so unusual that he would have been lauded."

"The main character?" A new surge of hope rose within him. "If I could just read. . . ."

She shook her head gently, "It's first draft, Jeremy. Henry would never have wanted anyone but me to read his first draft. You have to understand what often happens in first drafts. Botched chapters . . . awkward scenes . . . unresolved plots."

He leaned toward her halfway across the coffee table. "My interest isn't literary."

She went on shaking her head. "You don't understand. I would never do that to my husband."

Jeremy rose up. He put out his hands like a supplicant. "Margery," he said. "The main character is me."

As if she had not heard him, she gathered the tray and its remainders and trod from the room.

In an instant he had plunged through the archway with a single leap. At Henry's desk he seized the snapshot of Henry, Billy, Bugs, and himself and gripped it as if this claim could give him the permission Margery had denied. With his other hand he opened the top right-hand drawer of Henry's desk, inside of which he found a package of rubber bands, a box of paper clips, a nail clipper. He opened a second drawer to discover a thesaurus and a bottle of glue. He was working on a third drawer—so full it had jammed—when Margery's voice sounded at his shoulder. "You can quit looking," she told him coldly. "It isn't there." He wheeled around, heat rising to his scalp. "What do you have in your hand?" she demanded.

"A picture that belongs to my past. A picture from. . . ."

She reached out and took it from him. "It belongs to Henry. It belongs right here."

He wanted to hit her, to shake her by the shoulders. He wanted to argue with her—in some way to insist it was she who trespassed, not he. "Isn't there anything of Henry's you're willing to share? My God, I've never met anyone so ungiving and niggardly . . . you won't even let me share the loss of Henry!"

Her lips quivered and he thought she would give way. Instead—recovering within an instant, she declared equably, "I do want to give you something, Jeremy." She presented him with a gracious nod. "I want to give you Henry's car."

"His car?!"

"I don't actually need it."

"His beat-up 1968 Plymouth?"

"It's parked in front." She strolled into the living room and waved toward the window. "Well, of course it bucks a bit when you first start it up, but often, once it gets going . . . Henry never wanted another car." There was a bowl on the mantelpiece. She removed a set of keys from it and dangled them in front of Jeremy.

He averted his gaze. She'd never liked that automobile, he thought, and now she'd found an easy way to be rid of it. "I'd love to have it, Margery," he said vaguely, "but it could never make it across the country. It's in terrible shape." He glanced out the window. "Terrible," he repeated, shaking his head and envisioning a fouled carburetor and plugged fuel lines in South Bend, Indiana, a cracked radiator and a broken fan belt in Peoria, Illinois, a punctured muffler and a malfunctioning voltage regulator near Amarillo, Texas. "I'd have to spend who knows how many months on the side of the road with the hood up. The rest of the time I'd have to wait in service stations. Why, I'd be waiting in service stations from Jackson, Michigan to Yuma, Arizona."

All the same he kept on looking out the window at Henry's Plymouth, and as he looked, the odd thing was, he saw himself and the Plymouth chugging ahead—pushing and chugging and bucking past the Mississippi and the Ozark Mountains and the Continental Divide to pause briefly at Jeremy's shopping center before coming to rest by the nasturtiums in front of Jeremy's house.

It would be a heroic voyage, a test of his mettle, he fancied. He stopped himself. Such a foolish notion, he thought. Henry, too, would have found such imaginings pointless. "I don't exactly live in the neighborhood," he told her. "I live 2500 miles away. And look at the condition it's in." Abruptly he turned from the window. He noted that Margery still clutched the snapshot in her hand. "Listen, I have to know. I need to know. Why did Henry choose to write about me? Why not Billy Mackroyd or Bugs Lipson? They're both so successful, they've both accomplished a lot. They're both wonderful people."

At first—when she said nothing—he believed she would not answer. It occurred to him she might not even know—might never have read Henry's manuscript. "Why me?" he persisted. "Why not one of his colleagues? Is there some special quality I possess?"

"No. No special quality. Just" . . . she looked down and said almost under her breath, "your ordinariness."

"My. . . ." The snapshot faced away from him. Yet from within the back of its frame, Jeremy saw Bugs, Billy, Henry, and himself hurtle the high school track in workouts of their own devising. He recalled the excitement, the bursts of argument, the laughter, and the way he and Bugs and Billy had bunched together or spilled out onto the street while Henry, as harsh on himself as on the others, decided who among them had shown himself the most inventive, the least imitative, the most accomplished. "Ordinary?" Jeremy drew himself up. "Henry was wrong!"

Margery gave an indifferent shrug. At last she said, "Henry and I, we had come to admire ordinary people. Henry particularly. He had begun to think he'd spent too much time trying to be exceptional. He had decided that the grandeur of Prometheus was overblown and hollow. He admired your lack of ambition."

"My lack of. . . . ?"

She nodded sadly. "He decided that the real hero is the ordinary person."

"Ordinary? Is that what he thought?" The shriveled-up muffin seemed to appear before him, putting him in his place. He backed away. "I have to go." He moved toward the door. "I have things I need to get done." As he reached for the knob—as he prepared to leave Henry's house—he remembered departing Cleveland. After he'd said good-bye to his family, it was Henry who drove him to the bus station. In the depot they'd sat without talking, Jeremy's baggage piled at their feet. They had waited together in silence until presently Jeremy had the sense there was something unfettered and clean in the spaces surrounding them, something grand in their affection, one for the other.

"I have to go," he repeated. She followed him to the door. Just outside he stopped. "Ordinary." He threw open his hands. "Of course. That's what I am. That's what I always was. But at least," he looked away from her, "did he consider me his friend?"

For the first time Margery moved close to him; he could feel the warmth of her breath. Her hair filled the doorway, spreading, it seemed to him, like a crown. "Jeremy," she said, "you were his most important friend."

Stunned, he bowed his head. He wanted to make some appropriate or grateful response, but when he looked up, the door was shut and she was gone. Turning, he descended the gray painted stairs. "Henry's most important friend," he mused. He smiled and for a moment relived his exhilaration at reaching the top of Mt. Kiskoe.

But at the bottom of the stairs he beheld a solitary tree that stood next to Henry's driveway. He regarded the tree's meager growth—studied its sparse leaves dry as paper. Presently he walked on toward his rental car, letting his hand trail the rusted door and the battered hood of Henry Brustein's Plymouth.

THE ROOFERS

Taking his ease high up on the roof he and his coworker Kevin were repairing, Bud Platt downed a can of beer and his tuna fish sandwich. He ate a second tuna fish sandwich and his cheese-flavored crackers. He had just started on his sliced tomatoes and green olives when beneath him—three slopes down the hill that led to town—he happened to spot a man emerging from the back door of a house. The man stepped into a yard that was wide and flat, surrounded on three sides by growths of eucalyptus—growths so dark and thick no passersby, no neighbors could see inside. Yet from above, the yard offered itself as though it were a stage. Looking down on its lone player, Bud saw the hose of a vacuum cleaner wound like the coils of a snake around the man's neck and his arms. He guessed the man's age the same as his own and Kevin's, mid or late twenties. Yet he seemed to Bud a creature altogether unlike them as he moved with the slow and programmed gait of a sleepwalker toward the rear of a red Toyota parked close to the house. Disentangling himself from the vacuum hose, he opened the trunk of the car and removed an object that appeared to be a roll of gaffer's tape. Then he shut the trunk and—his bearing turned suddenly intent—began trying to attach one end of the hose to the automobile's exhaust pipe.

Bud Platt acknowledged the seriousness of the scene he witnessed. But he believed it showed a flaw of character and a lack of manliness if you paid too much attention to what other people were up to. He dug into his lunch pail, pulled out a large container of his wife's pasta salad, and forked up the salad, pleased with the extra thick mayonnaise and the bits of green pepper—content with the knowledge he had a wife too loyal to vary her ingredients. Then he cast a glance at the sky and allowed himself another look into the yard.

"For Chrissakes," he said with annoyance, for the man—despite his air of concentration—kept fumbling and getting his fingers stuck on the tape. Twice the vacuum hose slipped and fell. Twice he unrolled a large quantity of tape which, after adhering to the car, ended up adhering to his arms.

"Clumsy fucker," Bud remarked. He turned to Kevin who, having brought a more modest lunch, had long since finished and was stretched out on the flat roof on top of several rolls of felt paper. "Look down there," Bud said. "Down there." He pointed with his rosy square chin, stretching the ruffle beneath it of firm, cherubic flesh.

Sitting up slowly, Kevin directed his gaze to the area below and nodded but said nothing.

"Never saw a guy that clumsy. Ever seen him before?"

Kevin squinted into the yard a second time. He shook his head.

"Not at Smitty's? The Ploughman's? What about the Hare and the Tortoise? You sure you don't know him . . . you were born in this town." Bud unwrapped a chocolate cupcake. Holding it in the palm of his hand, he waited as if to coordinate the pleasure of eating a cupcake with the reward of hearing Kevin's reply.

"Don't know who he is," said Kevin. After some moments he added, "Never set eyes on him." He spoke in a neutral and unperturbed voice; yet as he continued looking into the yard, two lines of worry gradually etched into the forehead of his smooth, impassive, and handsome face.

Appreciatively, Bud noted these lines of concern. "If you never saw him," he assured Kevin, "you missed nothing." He brought out a second cupcake, tore off a section that he checked for adequate frosting, handed the portion to Kevin, and put the rest in his mouth. "The rate he's going he'll screw the whole day and nothing'll happen." Bud snapped his lunch pail shut. "So let's get back to work."

But neither made a move. Rather they inched forward and stood and watched side by side as, below, the man—having at last succeeded in securing the hose to the exhaust pipe—began hauling the free end to a side window. The window seemed to have been prepared in advance—the glass rolled down, a piece of cardboard affixed to its frame. A hole had been cut into the center of the cardboard and into this opening the man inserted the hose, stretching it to its limits and taping it slowly. When he had finished, he paused for a moment, marched stiffly to the front of the car, wiped his forehead with the back of his hand, fished in his trouser pocket and lifted out a set of keys. Then he pulled the door shut behind him.

Bud groaned. "Right under our eyes."

"Yeah," Kevin said.

"Such clear air, you can see everything." His arm swept from south to north, indicating a wide, blue sky and the sharp outline of fresh cedar shingles on half a dozen new roofs. "Such a beautiful day."

Kevin said nothing.

"You'd think he'd have better manners. Right under our eyes and on such a day."

"Yeah," agreed Kevin, the sweat starting on his brow.

"You'd think . . . well, it's his funeral, it isn't ours. We never saw him before." Bud faced his friend and co-worker. Then he tilted up his cap, folded his arms over the substantial rise of his belly and rocked back forth on his heels. "Kevin," he said at last, offhandedly, "why don't you run down and check the temperature on the kettle. I want the tar up to at least 450 degrees. While you're there you could take another two minutes' break, scoot down the hill and pull off the hose. I'll finish nailing the base while you're gone."

But instead of returning to the job, Bud stood watching at the edge of the roof. Over the past years he'd begun to believe that with his wife, his two young children, his sizeable mortgage and newly burgeoning shape, stature and authority had been conferred on him. It therefore made sense, he reasoned, to stick to his post and send down a second, particularly as he considered that whatever was going on in the yard was none of his business. And what better second than Kevin Jones, just slightly less mature than he, still restless, slim, and unattached, still out in left field running after women. Resting a hand on his hip, Bud followed Kevin's nimble descent down the steep trail of eucalyptus leaves and pebbled dirt.

Inside the red Toyota, the man sat behind his steering wheel. Bud could just make out the upper portion of the stranger's back: narrow shoulders that sloped down like two sides of a triangle below a long, thick neck. A back like that, reflected Bud, was not worth giving other people so much trouble. Even worse there was, he mused, something foolish and too expectant in the stranger's upright posture, as if the man assumed he would be first in line to enter heaven.

"Well, we'll see about that," thought Bud, and waited for Kevin to enter the yard. But Kevin had stopped just before the eucalyptus trees that bordered the yard. Was he changing his mind, Bud wondered, or was he merely deciding how best to proceed? Once more Bud checked on the stranger. He noted the man had not yet keeled over—Bud allowed him credit for that. At last Kevin slipped past the trees and slid along the edge of the yard.

Crouched low—bent almost double—he scurried to the rear of the Toyota, yanked the hose from the exhaust pipe with one sure motion, then, still bent over, sprinted out of the yard and was on his way up.

When he reappeared on the roof, Kevin said, "I got the tar up to 478."

"Pretty good," said Bud. "Took less than five minutes. The whole thing." He clapped Kevin on the back and they returned to their work, neither saying another word, each seeming to pretend that aside from its speediness, the errand in the yard had been routine and everyday. It was only after they'd finished with the base and had started mopping on the tar that something inside Bud—something that made a tune like a little bird—suggested that he and Kevin might be selling themselves short. He peered down the hillside, singling out the man's upright form in the front seat of the car. "Look down," he asked Kevin. And when Kevin looked down, Bud said, "If it weren't for us he'd be dead by now." He threw a glance at Kevin, expecting to behold Kevin's immobile, blank face. Instead he saw that Kevin was smiling.

"Still alive," Kevin said.

Bud echoed, "Still alive," and continued spreading the hot tar. It now seemed unimportant that the stranger was someone toward whom he felt neither sympathy nor interest. "If it weren't for us," he said, and breathed in the wisps of steam, its pungent vapor intensifying the suddenly heady sense of power and well-being he felt atop this roof in touch with the seamless, the brilliant sky. Moving to the opposite end of the roof, he began to lay down the first layer of felt paper, cutting it to fit around the vents and the railing posts. When he had finished, he stood up and stretched his arms and legs and looked up. And then he looked down.

The man was seated upright, exactly as before. "For Chrissakes," Bud complained. "Hasn't budged. Doesn't even know we've saved his life."

Kevin laughed.

"The stupid fucker, still sitting there."

"He's got patience."

"He might as well go get himself a sandwich and a beer. For Chrissakes, does he want us to write him a letter?"

"Maybe," suggested Kevin, "maybe he wants to die."

Bud shook his head. "No one wants to die," he said, glancing toward the Toyota. "Not even him."

Just then, as if Bud had telegraphed this message, the car door opened into the yard and the stranger stepped out.

"Didn't I tell you?" remarked Bud. "Took him a little longer to catch on."

But instead of walking away, as Bud had expected, the man investigated the cardboard in the window and slowly proceeded to the rear of the car where he discovered the source of his problem, retrieved the roll of gaffer's tape from the ground where he'd dropped it, and once again set about taping the vacuum hose to the exhaust pipe. This time—no doubt the reward of practice—his fingers managed the tape with improved facility and control. He kept on until he'd used up the entire roll. Then he hopped back into the front of the car and shut the door.

"Forget him!" Bud groaned. "Jerk's got no gratitude." An instant later, he threw Kevin a warning and sidelong glance.

"Not me," Kevin returned. "I've already been."

"You've already been," Bud allowed. "You've already been once, I can't send you again." He flipped off his cap and tapped it on his arm with a ruminative beat. "So what I'll do," he gave a judicious nod, "is . . . I'll go with you."

The two men climbed off the roof and headed for the trail—Kevin not as quickly as before, Bud plodding behind him, his wide hips disturbing a stand of African daisies and the brush on either side of their path. As they descended, the sweet clean scent of foliage and the cool air lulled Bud into believing that theirs was an outing for pleasure and recreation. But as they came closer to the peeling bark and the tall curtain of eucalyptus, as he noted the leaves swiveling from light to dark, he began to regret what they were doing. He hung back when they entered the yard. "That red Toyota," he remarked to Kevin. "My brother-in-law has the same model, different color. It's given him nothing but trouble."

Then Bud saw that the door of the Toyota was open, that the stranger sat half in, half out, that his face was in his hands and he was crying. The man's despair and lack of dignity took Bud by surprise. "What's the matter?" he called, walking toward the stranger. Just short of reaching him he stopped and took a long step back. "What's the difficulty here?" he asked. "What seems to be your problem?"

The stranger removed his hands but made no attempt to stop the flow of his tears. He had a round, now very red face, a straight freckled nose, a receding chin, and a light brown cowlick at the top of his head. He regarded Bud and Kevin through wet eyes. And as if he were no stranger, he waved a woeful hand at the dashboard and said, "I've run out of gas."

Kevin stared frozenly at the man while Bud—a queasiness at the pit of his stomach—muttered, "You'll be all right," and, placing a hand on Kevin's shoulder, he led Kevin out of the yard. It was only after they'd finished mounting the trail that Bud first grasped the joke. "The damnedest thing. The funniest thing. The hopeless jerk. While the hose was off he used up all his gas." Bud laughed. "Anyway . . . we saved his life."

They cleaned up the roof the next day. Below them, the yard was bare but for a scattering of leaves that lay curled on the ground. Bud thought of the stranger's swollen eyes and the light brown cowlick at the top of his head. He recalled the joy he'd felt after Kevin first freed the vacuum hose, and raising his head he tried by looking up to regain that sensation of buoyancy and access to the infinite bright stretch of the sky. Instead a shiver ran through him, and with an odd sense of fear and of loss, he glanced at the darkness beneath cast by the pine and eucalyptus trees and felt almost certain that the stranger had gone off to fill up his gas tank, and if only out of stubbornness, had already ended his life.

That evening on his way home Bud imagined the gas fumes gathering inside the red Toyota. He switched the dial on his car radio from country music to local news and listened hard. Reaching his house, he unlocked the front door and stood in the small hallway, facing a mound of cardboard building blocks and overturned tricycles from which his son and daughter emerged to race toward him. They shouted "Daddy! Daddy!" and he kissed them absently, forgetting to throw them into the air. When he remembered, he bent toward his children but changed his mind: he had forgotten something else. Trying to identify what that might be, he stared at the large umbrella plant at the back of the hall. Jill began to cry and Daniel, eyeing his older sister, opened his mouth and shrieked; and Robin hastened in from the kitchen. She took in the disarray. "Oh sweetie," she said, "what's wrong?!" Gathering her children, she ferried them into the kitchen. "Daddy's hungry," she explained "He's very very hungry. We'll have to hurry up with dinner."

Bud nodded: Robin was right. Dinner would help things out. He went into the bathroom, scrubbed his hands and nails and washed his face, and with some optimism entered the dining room. The table was set with rainbow-colored place mats and his favorite napkin rings, one side of the yellow plastic oval forming the head and beak of a duck. A familiar, delicious aroma drifted out of the kitchen, and the blue china platter that Robin soon carried in was heaped with handsome and familiar food. Bud blessed the meat loaf, the baked potatoes, the creamed corn, and the blue china platter. But to his confusion as well as to Robin's, he was able to eat only two bites of his meat loaf, one bite of his potatoes, one of his vegetable, and none of his custard. With his thumb tapping the handle of his spoon, he glanced around, noting for the first time how small and narrow the room was—how the walls pressed in almost to the table, the increasingly sour smell of dinner taking up all the air.

"Sweetie," Robin reprimanded. "What's wrong?" She then brought out a second dessert, a chocolate and banana layer cake with a butter cream frosting and chocolate bits on top of the frosting, and when he could not eat that, he staggered up, went through the hall, and retreated to a corner of the living room. Alone—the living room was out of bounds to the children—he unfolded the newspaper. He let it lay on his lap. After awhile he opened the paper, scanned the front page and the sports page, and chiding himself, leafed cautiously through the other sections. A small item wedged between two advertisements caught his eye: an unidentified man had jumped from the Golden Gate bridge at eight-thirty that morning, leaving his car in the center lane and causing a massive traffic jam. It was exactly what he'd expected.

Bud Platt shook his head back and forth. A sharp pain attacked his side. In his mind's eye he saw the cowlick at the top of the man's head—recalled it more vividly than he liked. Oh how like his bungling stranger, he thought, to cause a major traffic jam. How like him to wreak such havoc. But then he paused. Something was amiss: his stranger's cowlick was light brown, maybe even blonde, whereas the person in the news item—he read the article again—was dark-complexioned, dark-haired, and in his mid-fifties. Not his stranger at all, concluded Bud. With relief he murmured, "Still alive."

Yet he knew that danger lay ahead. For the next week, irritably he asked the stranger, "Why do you want to die?" He urged the stranger, "Think how great the 49ers are doing. Think what's ahead for the Warriors. Think of your country."

But why should he care, he asked himself when, after ten days, he still left the dinner table and installed himself in his easy chair in the living room and, alone, tried to summon up reasons for the man to go on living. From the back of the house he could hear the television and the sounds of his wife and children playing a game, and he imagined the satisfaction and the pleasure he would feel if he joined them. Instead, shifting about, he listened to the mournful creaking from his chair's plastic cover and regarded the square of patterned carpet in the center of the floor. The stranger's face appeared before him—its colorless tears streaming beneath an unruly cowlick. The revulsion he felt turned to panic. Angrily he demanded, "What's your problem? A woman? Get rid of her. Worried about money? Times will change. A disease?" He considered that possibility. "You look healthy."

He decided finally that the man lacked basic courage. He thought about courage as he gazed through the living room into the hall, his eye resting on the gigantic umbrella plant, its jagged leaves climbing toward the front of the house like evil hands. What would it take, he pondered, for him to end his own life? What would it take for Kevin? He imagined asking Kevin directly—they had started on a new remodeling and roofing job—but he knew that if he said, "Kevin, given the right circumstances, would you ever commit suicide?" his friend would think he was crazy.

Bud got up and left the living room. He stepped over the tricycles and went out the front door. The air was mild and he noted that the hedge surrounding his house was neatly clipped. Everything in his yard, even in the yard across the street, appeared well tended and in good order. Yet when he looked up all he could see in the sky was grayness and indifference. His heart heavy, it struck him that a man could have what he wanted—he could, like himself, have a good wife, two children, and a decent mortgage— and still he might not be able to find in himself the urge to go on. If he took his life under certain circumstances, would that show cowardice? Or would it, in fact, show courage?

Bud gripped his forehead: all this thinking had given him a headache. It was nothing he wanted to continue. "This isn't like me," he muttered. "Basically, I'm a cheerful person." And he reentered the house, vowing to act like himself.

But the next night, as hard as he tried, he could not eat his pot roast, or crawl on the floor and growl like a bear at his children, or feel desire for his wife. Unhappily he burrowed under the covers and in his sleep he shouted at the stranger, "I have a wife and family and work. You are no one I know! You are nothing! You are less than nothing!" So loud was his voice and so filled with rage that he woke himself up. Robin was still asleep. Climbing out of bed he struggled to the bathroom where he turned on the lights and saw how tired his face appeared, how gaunt. Gazing down, he saw his stomach had dwindled. Hastily he pulled the scale out from behind the clothes hamper and stepped on. "My God," he gasped. "I've lost sixteen pounds!"

"Listen," Bud asked Kevin as they finished a second beer at Smitty's, "do you ever see that guy?"

"What guy?" Kevin asked.

"That guy in the Toyota. You get around more than I do . . ." As Kevin's face remained blank, Bud continued, "Chances are, he's not even from this town. Probably he was just visiting from across the bay or from Los Angeles or from some other damned state clear across the country."

Kevin considered this scenario. "Nope," he finally replied. "Not since he ran out of gas."

"Me neither." Bud sighed. "Want another beer?"

The two men squeezed out of their booth, paid, and stepped into the full afternoon sunlight. And there, lit up by the sunlight and walking along in the middle of the sidewalk with an air of self-possession, was the stranger. He came toward them with no sign of recognition—a much smaller and shorter person than Bud had realized. Bud's pulse quickened. "Where you been?" he demanded. His face flushed. "What you been doing?"

The stranger stopped. "Huh?" he said. "Do I know you?"

"You were sitting in your car," said Kevin.

The man stared hard at Bud and Kevin. He nodded. Bud leaned closer. "We saved your life."

"Oh," remarked the stranger. Stepping around Bud, he walked away.

For a moment Bud and Kevin watched the man go. Then they turned and followed him past the dry cleaners, past the leggy geraniums at the beauty salon and the open doors of the health food store. The man turned into the ice cream parlor and Bud and Kevin followed after.

"I have something to ask you," Bud said as the three men waited in line. "I'm not one to butt into people's affairs—I wouldn't want someone to nose into mine, so I usually don't ask questions." He paused.

"What's the question?" the man asked.

Bud squinted at the floor. He plunged ahead. "Are things all right?"

"All right?"

"Yes. I mean, things aren't hopeless. I mean, you're buying ice cream. . . ." he pointed to the counter. "I'm sure if you're buying ice cream . . ."

But the man—his turn about to come up—had shifted his attention to the day's special flavors. "I'd like a single scoop of strawberry royale on a sugar cone," he said. He paid the clerk, but then, to Bud's surprise—instead of heading out the door and taking this chance to escape, he hovered by the cash register, the wallet he'd removed from his pocket still clasped in his hand.

"A double scoop, chocolate macadamia on a plain cone," Kevin ordered.

"The same for me," said Bud. "No, make one scoop wild raspberry and the other butter pecan." Waiting for his cone, he cast a sideways glance at the stranger who, his wallet still in his free hand, seemed on the verge of making some gesture. Was it possible, Bud wondered, that he intended to offer them a reward? He made a point of noting the man's cowlick. It had been slicked down, yet the man's face still appeared sad. The man hesitated. Then abruptly he put the wallet away, turned, and rushed from the store.

Bud and Kevin leaned against a wall and started eating their ice cream. "Well that's the end of that," Bud said.

"That's the finish," said Kevin. "You'd think that after what we did for him, the least he could do was pay for our ice cream."

They sauntered outside and stood near the curb. A block up the street Bud glimpsed the stranger. Something, Bud reflected, had been left undone. "Come on," he said to Kevin, throwing his cone into a trash bin. "Let's go."

"Go where?"

"Just go," Bud said and set off after the stranger. Kevin finished his ice cream and caught up. Quickening their steps, they broke into a run, skirting the path of shoppers, a dog with a spotted coat, and two infants installed in their strollers. At the edge of the shopping district—just past the framer's and the laundromat—they reached the man. Towering over him, they planted themselves on either side. Stride for stride they accompanied him along the street.

"What do you want?" the man asked, his eyes darting from Bud to Kevin.

"What we want," Bud said, "is . . . it's pretty important."

"It's pretty important," Kevin echoed. "You've been on our minds."

"Nice of you," the stranger murmured. "Thanks."

"It's pretty important," Bud repeated, while around them the sky bloomed a grand and luminous pink and blue. "We want you to be happy."

"To be happy?" the man questioned.

"That's right," said Bud. He nodded at Kevin, and they leaned toward the stranger, pressing close—as if they'd been given exclusive charge of his life.

THEIR MAGICIAN

Minutes after Nora and Madeline's father phoned from his apartment in New York City, Nora and Madeline, who lived with their husbands in San Francisco, got on the phone to each other. Nora reported happily, "He said he's next in line for the job."

"Are you sure? Is anyone else in line? What else did he tell you?" asked Madeline, at which the two women—both school teachers who had taken time out to have children—carefully repeated and examined their father's words. They then discussed which of his attributes would lead to success, which others might lead to failure. On the negative side they placed his age—he was just over sixty; on the positive, that he was tall and slim, the spring of his rubbery gait and the light in his blue eyes still boyish and eager, his head rimmed with a sprightly nest of corn-colored hair that still hadn't grayed.

"I think Mama's brothers were always envious of Papa's looks. Of how young he appeared," Madeline ventured. "Remember," she tried out on Nora, "how after

Uncle Ephraim lost his hair, how after he went bald he always used to say to Papa, 'Jonathan, you never change. You always look the same.' I think deep down they were very envious." And she recalled her rich uncles peering at her father as he arrived for family gatherings and stood in the center of a doorway with no word of greeting on his lips but with three thin silver coins up his sleeve and a pink-eared rabbit in his hat.

Madeline waited for Nora's response. But Nora chose to say, "They were never envious. If they said 'you never change' they meant it as an insult, they didn't mean it as a compliment."

"I think they meant it for a compliment."

"They didn't. And why would they?" said Nora crossly. "Anyway, who cares what Uncle Ephraim or Uncle Louis or Uncle Nat thought of Papa? Who cares what Mama's family ever thought? Who cares . . . he's proving them wrong. Papa's changing now. He's in a brand new ball game. He's almost like a phoenix rising. Since Mama died. . . ."

But neither of them wanted to take this any further. The truth was, they had also loved their mother. They had sculpted, shaped, worked over, and hammered out the kinks in that love during their first three semesters at college. Taking long walks by the river and under the low autumn skies, they'd concluded their mother was not to blame her competence had stood in their father's way. It was after all not her fault she'd been able to throw a buffet supper for one hundred and seventy-five people, chair the Special Contributions Committee of the UJA, fix the plumbing, rewire the electricity, read *War and Peace* in two nights, and at the same time hold down a full-time job as a bookkeeper-accountant. In truth, Nora and Madeline hoped to be like her one day. But what room had she left for their father?

"Anyway, things are different now," Nora went on. "Rivkin's retiring and Papa's the new manager of the Fairmont Furniture Company. Yes, I see him in Rivkin's cozy little office with the water cooler in the corner. He's got a fancy new desk calendar and his own digital clock and telephone and an ebony Mark Cross desk set."

"Are you sure that's how we see him?"

"I see him," Nora assured her sister, "and I also hear him. He's calling the factories in North Carolina. 'Bring more sofas,' he says into his speaker phone. 'Bring more dining room suites, more end tables. More . . .'"

"When did he say this would happen, exactly?"

"He wasn't exact."

Madeline frowned and bit the tip of a nail. Reaching into the drawer of her telephone table, she lifted out a formal family photograph, the bottom row of which showed Nora, herself, and their cousins, a blank dismay on each of their faces. Above them presided Madeline's mother and aunts, self-righteous in their chairs, while at the very top of the photograph stood a grim Uncle Ephraim, a serious Uncle Louis, a resigned-looking Uncle Nat, and off by himself in a right-hand corner, a grinning Jonathan Green-baum, one hand to his ear and in that hand the perfect oval of an egg. Madeline studied her father. How joyous and optimistic he appeared! How proud of the egg newly hatched from the side of his head, and how much more accomplished than her physician Uncle Ephraim, her lawyer Uncle Louis, her Uncle Nat, the real estate tycoon. She stared at the egg in his palm and imagined her father ordering furniture—ordering end tables—for the queen. Bending to the phone she intoned, "'Fifty more Louis XIVth armoires.'"

"Fifty more Louis XIVth armoires!" sang Nora. "Manager at last!"

But three months passed and their father made no further reference to Martin Rivkin's job. Pushing their babies back and forth through Golden Gate park, the sisters alternately speculated and fretted. From time to time Madeline pointed out, "Papa's always been modest," and Nora, slightly modifying this observation, said, "He's always been a little behind, so now it's just taking him a little bit longer."

Then one Sunday, unable to contain themselves, they returned from the park to Nora's house, strung little Timothy in his Jolly Jumper, arranged Jennifer in Timothy's playpen, and rang their father. Three times Madeline inquired if he was eating properly; four times Nora asked what was happening in New York. At last Nora took over the phone. She said, "Papa, what about your

promotion?" at which Jonathan Greenbaum replied that
a relative of the owner, a man with a mustache and a new
MBA, was now also in the running.

"Someone else!" Nora exclaimed. She grimaced,
glared at her sister, and said into the phone, "What are his
chances?"

"Oh I know," said Jonathan Greenbaum, "this is a little
disappointing to . . . to you and to Madeline."

"To us, what about to you!" thundered Nora, and
thrust her face in front of Madeline's face to ensure
Madeline received her full share of their grief. "What
about to you?! It's your life, it isn't ours!"

Cautiously Madeline nudged her sister's foot and
placed a hand on her shoulder. She wanted to pull her from
the phone—to lead her away to a corner table and discuss
with her the nature of failure. "What," she wanted to say—
it was a thought she'd expressed to Nora before—"is failure after all? Perhaps there's no such thing. Perhaps it's
only in the culture. In the long run people are . . . exactly
what they are."

Nora ignored her sister's foot and her sister's hand.
"Listen, Papa, you can't let them walk all over you. You
have to go in and stand up for yourself. You have to demand your rights. Tell them you've been waiting . . .
you've been working there long enough. Otherwise, what's
your plan? Do you mean to go on as you have . . . from
the apartment in the morning to the store and back to the
apartment with nothing in your life changing?"

Madeline shook her head and waved her hands, hoping to remind her sister that their father had never judged them. But Nora, buried in the phone, persisted angrily, "If you don't intend to try, then you might as well give up. You might as well move to San Francisco and get it over with. You might as well retire."

Madeline grabbed the phone. "Papa, what Nora means is you can move to San Francisco if you want to. She means it's nice here and that . . . that we miss you."

She heard a faint, muffled sound, followed a moment later by her father clearing his throat. "Don't worry about me," he said.

"We don't. Not for a minute."

"I'm still in the running for manager."

"I know. You told us . . . that Martin Rivkin inherited a restaurant in Santa Fe, New Mexico."

She heard a dead silence. Then in a voice much lower, much stronger and deeper than she had ever known to issue from him, her father said, "I'm still in the running, and besides, I'm much too busy to move to San Francisco."

"Too busy?" Madeline echoed. She tried to make sense of the difference in his voice; did he have a cold? "Too busy? What did you say?"

The deep resonant voice of a television or radio announcer repeated, "I'm much too busy to move to San Francisco."

Madeline beckoned to Nora. She held the phone between them. "Too busy?" she asked nervously, for quite apart from the strangeness of the voice, she had never before heard her father say he was busy. For a moment she suspected him of play-acting. Then she asked hopefully, "Are you really so busy?"

Jonathan Greenbaum laughed—a modulated and self-contained laugh in which Madeline detected no trace of her father's normal giggle. "Up to my eyeballs," he declared smoothly. "But I'll tell you what. I'll let you know if I can get away for a visit. Maybe the week after next. A short visit, naturally. Anything longer is out of the question." And he hung up.

"A short visit," Madeline puzzled. "Isn't that what he said?" Unsteadily she trod across the room to Timothy's playpen where she gazed at Jennifer who, eyes wide open, continued drinking from her bottle. She then straightened Timothy who was dangling crookedly from his Jolly Jumper. She returned to her sister. "Have you ever heard him sound like that?"

Nora still stood by the phone, a tender smile on her face. "It's exactly what we wanted. Papa's found a new voice. He's coming into his own."

Two weeks later, the women sat in the airport: they had hired a baby sitter and left Timothy and Jennifer behind. Settled into front seats in the waiting area, they watched as passengers of every size and nationality—passengers both arriving and departing—filed before them, singly and in groups. Madeline, who missed her third-grade classroom, gazed into the travelers' faces and dreamt of teaching math and reading and social science—oh how she could change the soul of the world! Then she forgot about the other travelers and zeroed in on her father; she pictured him rushing toward them as he always did, joyously waving and waggling his fingers at them, in his free hand an old brown paper bag containing the props for his magic tricks.

I bet," said Madeline when his flight was announced, "the first thing he does is the snake trick with the balloons."

"No, that was last time," Nora said. "Anyway I hope not. This time I bet it's the stand-up rope."

"Or the birds flying. The birds soaring about from out of nowhere. Yes, Papa likes to do the birds flying for airports."

But after they caught sight of him, they realized that a different sort of man was emerging onto the ramp of American Airlines. Had he become manager? Madeline wondered. For instead of trying to catapult toward them, instead of pushing and tripping over himself with his bouncing, eager, awkward gait, he walked calmly behind the other passengers, a magazine held neatly at his side. Madeline saw that his face was older than their father's, that he carried no brown paper bag, and that in the place of loose polyester trousers and a rumpled polo shirt, he was fitted out in a trim and elegant navy blue suit, a white on white shirt, and a tie with a tie pin.

Jonathan Greenbaum approached, his stride manly, his manner confident. He called out his daughters' names. He kissed them, and despite that he bent and kissed them stiffly, Madeline allowed he possessed a certain appeal. For a minute or so the three of them stood without moving. Then after briefly milling about in search of the right formation, Nora and Madeline took up places on either side of their father. Shyly they walked with him toward the baggage claim, signaling to each other to break away to the ladies' room where, as if they were about to rejoin an attractive stranger, they put on fresh lipstick and combed and fluffed their hair.

That night at Nora's dinner table, it was clear to Madeline that Jonathan Greenbaum was a hit. Over the red onion, sun-dried tomato soup, he discussed fiscal taxation with Nora's husband Kevin. Over the pesto pasta with spinach he talked real estate law with Madeline's husband Robert. During the poached pears he embarked on quantum mechanics and the plight of the snail darter and the longfin smelt. Madeline and Nora exchanged glances; in Nora's face Madeline read, "Papa's done it! He's exceeded all our hopes!" Passing the coffee, Madeline felt true happiness well up in her throat. If only, she wished, her mother were alive to hear him, for she recalled that at gatherings of her mother's family, her father had never opened his mouth. She remembered that she and Nora would take turns keeping an eye on him, and that when they saw his gaze go out of focus and a small smile spread over his lips, they would guess with both discomfort and pride he was thinking how best to saw a person in half. Yet here he was, words pouring from his mouth—whole paragraphs about the tribal enmities in Europe and Africa, whole sentences about the future of the Yankees and the Mets.

"Your father's turned out to be an interesting guy," Madeline's husband remarked; and he invited his father-in-law to a Wednesday night basketball game, after which Nora's husband invited him to lunch at "Stars" on Tuesday. But Jonathan Greenbaum, though clearly moved by their interest, thanked his sons-in-law and said he was leaving after the weekend.

On Monday he was packed and ready to leave. "Papa," Madeline said, "we've hardly gotten to know you. Surely you haven't come all this way just for a weekend, it doesn't make any sense. At least stay until after the game on Wednesday."

"Unfortunately," their father said.

"Why are you going back? Do you have a girl friend?" Nora asked, and went on quickly, "If you stay until after the game. . . ."

"If you stay until Thursday morning. . . . Or has Martin Rivkin retired? Why do you have to return?"

"My job. Martin Rivkin's forthcoming retirement." He backed away from them. "I have my ticket and I have . . . any number of commitments."

"Then come back next month."

"Next month, that's October." He removed a leather-bound date book from the inner pocket of his jacket. He shook his head. "Everything starts up in October. Certain customers require my help. Not to mention my mailbox begins to overflow."

"Overflows with what?" inquired Nora.

"Why, the great variety of magazines I now subscribe to," he replied in his deepest voice.

"Then come at least for Thanksgiving."

Jonathan Greenbaum opened his date book. "Thanksgiving . . . Thanksgiving and Christmas, those are difficult times. My calendar fills up. And also I have . . . something not everyone has." He brought out his self-possessed laugh, "I have my own life." And with these words he looked straight ahead.

Nora and Madeline followed his gaze. And there, just beyond the window blinds, it seemed to Madeline that she and Nora discerned an image—vague though it might be—of their father's separate life. She hoped it was the full, rewarding life they wanted for him. But would it, by any chance, shut them out? Against her better judgment she said, "Can't you leave your . . . what you call your own life . . . at least a little longer?"

"My dears," he laughed, "I'll come back in the spring."

"Why such a long time from now?" she inquired.

But after a pause in which he seemed about to answer, he looked instead at his watch.

It was Madeline who took her father to the airport; Nora needed to take Timothy to the doctor for shots. With Jennifer in an infant seat in back and her father in front, she drove out of her street and past Golden Gate Park and the Stonestown shopping center and, some miles into the highway, past the Serramonte shopping center from where they could see the gay banners of Breuner's furniture store.

"Papa," said Madeline, gazing through the windshield at the smooth azure California sky, "do you remember when Nora and I were about five and six and Mama would leave us for an hour at Fairmont Furniture, and if there weren't any customers we'd play cards? We'd play 'Fish' and 'Hearts.'"

"That was long ago," Jonathan Greenbaum said warily.

"To me it's still clear as day," she insisted. "How you used to take us for a stroll through the furniture. You would say, 'Take your choice, take whichever ones you like. Have a chandelier! Have a chaise lounge! Have a spiffy chair, how about this spiffy chair?'" She paused, and when she got no response she said, "Then you'd leap into the chair and sit on the edge with your chin in your hand like . . . like Rodin's 'The Thinker.'"

He shifted about uneasily. "Oh I don't think so."

She nodded. "Like Rodin's 'The Thinker.'"

"That could've been someone else."

"It was you, Papa. And it was you, remember, when Nora and I kept wanting it to snow and you took us past cabinets and kitchen tables to the back window and pointed, and after a while one snowflake fell, then three more, then a hundred and a hundred thousand. Inside, because of all the furniture it was dark . . . only a dim glow from the chandeliers . . . while outside the air filled up with all that brightness, all those magical glittering lights."

"Winter weather," he said noncommittally.

"Nora and I figured it was you who had commanded the snow."

"Oh I don't think so," he muttered. "Of course I can't be sure I remember. Ancient history. These days I have so many things on my mind . . . so many more important things to keep track of."

"More important?"

"Very important and new responsibilities."

"But I remember."

Jonathan Greenbaum said nothing.

"Ah well," Madeline sighed. She changed the subject. "Tell me, Papa, what magazines do you subscribe to?"

"*Harper's*," he replied on the instant. "*Motor Trend*," he thundered out. "*Scientific American*." "*Sierra Club*." "*Personal Computer World*." "That's just to begin with. By the spring, I'll be subscribed to at least five more."

Madeline watched the road; she let some time go by. "Why can't you be here for Thanksgiving or Christmas?"

Jonathan Greenbaum cleared his throat. In a resonant baritone he once more pronounced he was an exceptionally busy man.

In the spring the sisters again drove to the airport. "Nora," Madeline said, "he seemed so distant last time. Like he was made out of wood."

"He was excellent."

"He wouldn't come visit for Thanksgiving or Christmas or for New Year's."

"All he needs is a little bit of fine tuning. Sometimes it takes people a long time to grow into their potential."

"He was like a stranger."

"Don't be like that," said Nora, her eye on the gate. "He was terrific last time. And this time he's even better," she declared as Jonathan Greenbaum appeared. "Look at that terrific hair cut! Catch the air of self-confidence and the shine on his shoes! Why, he could be the chairman of a major board!" And she was smiling with all her teeth, her arms welcoming and open when he strode up and past his daughters with a nod, looking at his watch and announcing, "I need a newspaper!," a stern and purposeful expression on his face—the expression, Madeline realized, of someone in her mother's family.

Turning, they padded after him and stood outside a kiosk while he went in. "He's beginning to remind me of Uncle Ephraim," Madeline muttered.

Nora raised her head above her younger sister's accusing gaze. "We can't just make him to order. Mama would be proud. The important thing is he's headed in the right direction."

"He's headed in the wrong direction," said Madeline as Jonathan Greenbaum, veering away from them, marched out of the kiosk with an air of importance, three newspapers under his arm.

That night at dinner he delivered a long monologue about osteoporosis after menopause. After dinner he stood in the center of the living room and spoke without pausing about the destruction of the ozone layer by fluorocarbons and, after that, about the future of the information network infrastructure. The next morning he accompanied Nora and Madeline, Timothy and Jennifer to Golden Gate Park where, walking along a wooded path—the children in their strollers—he lectured on the American edge in microchip manufacturing.

For fifteen minutes he continued his oration, declaiming sentences which, it seemed to Madeline, he had committed to memory from magazine or newspaper articles. "Papa," she interrupted as she, her sister, their father, and his grandchildren proceeded across the smooth rise of a bridge to descend beneath a thicket of trees in full bloom, "this is no place to talk about microchip manufacturing. This is the right place for . . ." she waved her hand at their surroundings, at the blossoms white and delicate as snow that now fell around the family, brushing their shoulders, transforming their path. "This is the right setting for . . ." she shot a glance at Nora and without waiting said on her own, "the right setting for one of your magic tricks."

"Magic tricks?" he said with surprise.

Again she glanced at Nora, this time more apprehensively. But Nora, with an expansive gesture, declared, "Well, why not? A magic trick. A magic trick for Timothy."

"It's been a long time," Madeline said. "A very long time."

He frowned. "I'm out of practice." He began pacing ahead.

"If you're out of practice, start with something simple," Nora suggested. "What's the harm? Start with a simple magic trick for Timothy. Make something . . . a handkerchief . . . disappear."

Jonathan Greenbaum lengthened his stride and quickened his step. From a distance away, he glanced back at his grandson. "Timothy's too young. He's too young and besides, he's asleep."

"But Jennifer isn't sleeping," Madeline called out.

"Start with a handkerchief." Nora broke into a run. "Surely you have a handkerchief?"

"Papa," Madeline said, bumping Jennifer's stroller as fast as she could over the path of twigs and tree stumps, "just a simple handkerchief trick."

"Is that what you want? I'm out of practice. It's a senseless waste of time. I've given it up." He clasped his fingers together tightly, pressing them against his chest. "I have my own life," he said. But his voice had already begun to change, its pitch rising—a staccato, nervous, a joyous catch to his laugh.

Then the next thing Madeline knew he had removed a handkerchief from his pocket. It vanished and he retrieved it from Nora's ear. It vanished again and he pulled it from inside Nora's sleeve and then found it in the coiled braid of a young girl passing by. Once more it vanished, this time in the blossoms that floated above them.

"Bravo, bravo!" Nora and Madeline clapped.

At this he reached up and plucked three coins from the bright air.

"Just wonderful!" they laughed.

He turned his wrist and six more coins sprang from his fingers, his eyes, even the planes of his cheeks filling with an eager light. His daughters shouted and applauded.

Jonathan Greenbaum bowed. His smile broadened. Facing his daughters he said with an air of anticipation, "Like old times. What would you think if I left New York and moved to San Francisco?"

Nora's mouth fell open. "But your job!"

"Your job!" Madeline bit her tongue, the words shocking her.

"Papa," said Nora, "you can't leave New York. That makes no sense."

Startled, he looked at them. He looked away. "Foolishness. Pure foolishness," he muttered. And as if confused, as if seeking some neutral place, he scrambled to a nearby picnic table, climbed on top and shuffled and hopped, clicking his heels. He tapped his left toe behind his right leg, his right toe behind his left leg, tapping and jumping and dancing as if some spring inside him had broken, until at last Nora put up her hand. "Enough, Papa. That's enough."

He looked at Madeline. She nodded. "Papa, it's too much."

Two days later when he was scheduled to leave, they took him to the airport. They accompanied him past the ticket counters, through the security check, and onto the moving walkway from where, riding in silence, they stared at a display of Native American pottery. When they reached his gate he said—not looking at either of them, looking, rather, into the distance, "I intend to become manager."

"You'll do it," said Nora, and Madeline whispered, "Come back soon." They kissed him goodbye and watched him disappear up the ramp.

It was only after they reached the terminal's main building that Madeline noticed their father was following them. At first he kept a distance behind, dodging around pillars. Uncertain of what this meant, she pretended she hadn't noticed. She went on toward the elevators, and when he entered the same lift as they, when he inched to the far back as if he, too, had not seen them, she glanced at Nora and caught the alarm on her sister's face. The women stepped into the hall and crossed to the garage where, for a brief space of time, Madeline heard only hers and Nora's footsteps. Then she glimpsed their father over her shoulder, slowly moving toward them as though he were walking in his sleep.

Madeline unlocked her car—the front doors and the back. She got into the driver's seat and Nora got in beside her. They sat motionless until, presently, the back door opened and Jonathan Greenbaum stole inside and slid to the middle of the seat. Madeline started up the car, paid the garage attendant, and entered the freeway. In the rearview mirror she caught sight of her father and saw how suddenly faded and ancient his blue eyes had become. Ahead, fog poured across the road like a winter's white shroud. Madeline peered hard into the rearview mirror. "Nora," she said as they drove into the fog and a darkness gathered around them, "do you remember how Papa used to command the snow?"

HOW LOVELY THY BRANCHES

It was because of the twins that I first sang "God Rest Ye Merry Gentlemen." All through the holiday season I watched them stretch their pale necks to the ceilings, open their mouths, and warble "Silent Night" and "Hark the Herald Angels Sing" with no apparent regard for the fact that their names were Malcolm and Ruthie Bernstein. We were in the fourth grade then and had a teacher, Miss Mackenroe, who stood up from her desk in the mornings just to count our thirty-two heads. Of these at least two-thirds were Christian, every one of whom—no matter the differences in their denominations or ability to spell—came back from Thanksgiving break to fuse into a gay and happy crew cozily singing all together "Fa la la."

Most of the Jewish students also began by following Miss Mackenroe's lead. I thought of them as more modern and of a more carefree persuasion than I. Clad in their new shoes, their latest socks, they, too, raised high their heads and bellowed at the blackboard. Yet after a few bars, the words that issued from them dimmed and blurred.

Casting their eyes to the ground, they geared down to a tuneless hum, to a low croak-like buzzing in the throat that got them through "Christ the Lord" and "Our Savior is Born." I, of course, understood their terror; all the same it disturbed me to see them plunge from grace, to hear them fall, song after song, from enthusiasm or boldness into a feeble droning.

As for the other Jewish students, what was left—apart of course from the twins—was me and another boy across the room whose name was Izzy. For Izzy and me there was no question of starting to sing and stopping, as we had been forbidden by our mothers to utter a single sound. Izzy, who for eleven months of the year contented himself with a state of torpor, roused himself as December approached and then managed to surpass me by far, since not only did he keep his lips stalwartly pressed together, he also covered his ears with his hands. Yet as I beheld his long bony elbows and his chin triumphantly sticking out, it struck me he had chosen the wrong way to defend our faith. The fact was, I had come to believe there was nothing wrong about listening quietly to carols. And so, discounting Izzy's elbows, I paid attention to every word. With my lips glued shut, I listened closely and tried to control my yearning and longed to burst into song and might even have tried for a few of the notes except that at every moment I remembered walking down the wintry street hand in hand with my large-boned, gaunt, and dignified mother who gravely instructed that Christmas was not for us.

But if Christmas was not for us, it was clearly for Ruthie and Malcolm Bernstein, recently come to our school. From the beginning of every carol to its end, their voices pealed and chimed like uninterrupted vesper bells. Was their name, I wondered, a mere disguise? Was their mother Christian and their father therefore converted? Had they once been Jewish and somehow grown out of it upon reaching the fourth grade? I studied their eyes, their mouths, their chins and noses for resemblances, vestiges, for clues. But the more I looked at them, the more they looked only like themselves—pale as leaves that fell at the end of autumn, straight-backed as small generals, and thin as gazelles—Malcolm a bit taller than his sister—both with hair that lay flat on their heads, brown-gold eyes, and gold freckles on their foreheads and small noses. Shutting my eyes I listened with awe to their clear voices, and as I listened, I sometimes imagined their Christmas tree. Opening my eyes I took in their faces, saw their matter-of-fact abandon, and dared to wish that I too might sing out "Christ the Lord," and without changing allegiance, become part of a larger, a more resounding, a richer world than mine.

Then one morning Ruthie caught me staring at her. I concluded she had never noticed me before, for now an expression of outrage sprang into her pale face and turned her nose mauve. She pursed her lips and flared her nostrils at Malcolm who, barely moving his head, stared back at me coolly. Mortified, I resolved never to look at her again—if necessary, to look only at Izzy. Then the next thing I knew—at the beginning of recess Ruthie stood directly in front of me, wearing her fur-trimmed hat and coat and blocking my way.

"You were very rude," she said. "Who taught you manners?"

I flushed, suddenly overcome with shame.

"And what do you think," she went on, hands on her hips, "that you're the only person who stares at us?" I noticed that Malcolm stood by, his presence backing her up.

"I'm sorry," I said. "I'm really sorry. I should have looked the other way." But almost immediately I regretted feeling sorry and I came right back, "If you're so used to it, it shouldn't bother you."

"Of course we're used to it." She folded her arms across her chest.

I glanced at Malcolm. He was shaking his head, his long cheeks full of wisdom. "Well . . ." he drawled, clearing his throat, "the truth is, we're not used to it anymore. Not since Peoria." He put his hands behind his back and rocked back on his heels. "We were used to it in the old days. In Peoria, and before that when we lived in Dayton, and even after Peoria when we lived in Chicago." His voice, unlike his sister's, was so mild and kind and solemn and seemingly so appreciative of what I'd said that, I don't know why, I was filled with compassion for him and enormous respect and, not knowing how to respond, I promised not to look at either of them again.

"That's stupid! That's more than stupid! Why should we care if you look at us or not? Go ahead and look at us. Go ahead," she prompted, lifting her nose to the sky, "just so long as it's not too often."

"About once a week," suggested Malcolm.

I smiled at Malcolm, thinking he had meant this for a joke. But neither he nor his sister smiled back—almost, it seemed to me, as if they had discussed the matter of smiling back and decided they had no need of it.

"Or every other week," Malcolm amended. "That is, if you want to." And with this he abruptly signaled at his sister and they trotted off to the jungle gym where they chinned themselves, hung upside down, and presently returned. Again Ruthie stood in front of me. "Your name's Leonard"?

"Yes."

"It isn't Larry?"

"No."

"It's Leonard," she muttered to her brother. "I told you it was Leonard. We just wanted it to be Larry," she whispered, after which they both simply stood there—not looking at me but with thin furrowed brows down at the ground, as though readying themselves to spend whatever time proved necessary to get over their dislike for my name.

I decided not to wait. Spinning about, I headed toward the school. "Leonard!" they called in unison. I continued on. "Leonard!" they followed after me and when at last I turned around they invited me to play at their house after school.

As resentful as I was, I also felt flattered. Even so, I thought it best for my pleasure not to show. "I'll have to think about it," I told them, pretending the decision was up to me when in fact it had a lot to do with my mother. It would not be easy, I knew, to describe the twins to her—to describe them as I wanted: to relate to my mother that on crisp cold mornings all through December, though they were Jewish, they sang Christmas carols heedlessly and at the top of their lungs. Better to begin, I recognized, by informing her that the twins' last name was Bernstein. I could then establish that they were better than Izzy in spelling. Yet how could I suggest without the cruelty I only half-intended that, unlike us, they were not poor? How could I refer to the glamour that enveloped them or brag that they had dwelt in exotic cities foreign to us—in Peoria, Dayton, in Chicago—or speculate that the rooms they lived in were filled with all the couches and carpets and bed-spreads that my mother and I glimpsed in store windows at night, whose bright hollyhock colors, she insisted, were too brash, too foolish, too obvious and, like Christmas, were not for us?

I went over these questions on my way home that afternoon, and took the only way out. After descending the five cement steps to our basement apartment, I told my mother that during the week I would be playing with Izzy. At the same time I told myself I hadn't really lied. I then envisioned that as I arrived at the Bernstein house, there would stand in the entrance at least three rows of Jewish aunts and uncles and cousins pressed close together and singing, "Oh Come all Ye Faithful," while on the roof above hovered geese a-laying and twelve turtle doves.

The next morning I informed the twins I was free to go home with them. During social studies, with a clear picture of Ruthie and Malcolm's Christmas tree in my mind, I set myself rules of behavior: I would shake hands with the twins' mother and father and ask after their health; I would ask after the health of any brothers, sisters, aunts, uncles, and cousins; and I would act carefree and nonchalant in the presence of the Christmas tree.

At last the school day finished, and Ruthie, Malcolm, and I put on our coats and scarves and gloves, traveled the length of the playground together, and together filed through the open gates. A new sense of privilege loosened my limbs. My legs, of their own accord, seemed to lift higher and higher. As we emerged onto the street, I nodded benignly at the fourth and fifth graders who milled about the curb as though uncertain what to do or where to go next. I had Ruthie Bernstein on one side of me, Malcolm Bernstein on the other, and we were headed for their desirable home.

It was only after the twins had turned in a direction opposite from my own—when the furthest traffic boy had lowered his white flag and allowed us to cross—that I began to feel uneasy. I noticed that Ruthie and Malcolm, so self-contained, even so staid during school, now appeared abnormally buoyant and good-humored—Ruthie more buoyant than her brother. How did I come to be in the company of such strangers? I glanced worriedly at Ruthie as she raced in circles around me, slid on triangles of ice on the pavement, hopped and jumped in front of her brother, and with bursts of shrill glee spilling from her lips, declared that because their parents worked until late she and Malcolm had the house to themselves—to do as they wished.

"We've had," Malcolm added, taking long strides by my side, "the run of three large houses now."

"Three whole houses . . . to yourselves?"

"Well what do you think," said Ruthie, suddenly halting, "what do you think, that only old people have a whole house to themselves?" She went ahead a few paces, approached a stretch of ice shaped like a lizard, and as if to shame me, slid to its tail. "We're perfectly capable of having a house to ourselves. What do you think—that if we have a house to ourselves we always get lonely?"

"No," I hazarded.

"And do you know," she asked as if testing me, "why we never get lonely?"

I thought a moment. "Because there are two of you?"

"Because there are two of us," Ruthie affirmed.

I nodded, glad to have given an acceptable answer. Everything was possible, I thought, if only I managed to behave. Dutifully I wove with Ruthie and Malcolm in and out of small streets and long streets and through neighborhoods I barely recognized, until at last we came up a length of path to a flagstone porch where Malcolm, with a key from his pocket, opened the widest, thickest door I'd ever seen. Through the entrance I glimpsed magical pieces of wall, corners of table legs and of hanging pictures. My heart beat wildly, but then unexpectedly I felt a pang that somehow mixed guilt with pride. I hung back as if protecting my very soul. When finally I stepped forward I promised myself that if I caught sight of some especially beautiful object, some vase, some statue or painting—I exempted only the Christmas tree—I would be careful, for the sake of my mother, not to acknowledge its presence fully, careful to avert my eyes.

A great quiet arched over us as we entered the hall. By way of welcome, a nearby radiator commenced a mild thumping. While Ruthie hung up our coats, tucked our gloves into pockets, and draped our scarves over hangers, Malcolm, his hand on my elbow, guided me through another hall into a long, empty-looking kitchen spaced out with multiple counters. "Four cookies for you and two for each of us," Malcolm counted out, setting the cookies onto plates, pouring out glasses of milk, and inviting me to sit down at the small Formica-topped table that stood in one corner. "What would you like to do today? Ruthie and I have some ideas."

"Those are oatmeal cookies," shouted Ruthie, running in at a gallop. "Do you like them? You're supposed to like them." She sat down next to her brother.

I ate half a cookie and stopped. I looked across the table to pinpoint and then hopefully to bask in what I'd found so appealing in the twins. If only they would begin singing, I thought. I then became aware that, seated side by side, they were also watching me. They were watching me chew—the open gaze of their brown-gold eyes intent and yet somehow detached. Wondering how best to chew from the twins' point of view, I took seven or eight minuscule bites and finished the cookie, and as I did, I had the impression that Malcolm and Ruthie's narrow faces grew fuller and happier. At this I too felt happier. It seemed to me we were on our way to becoming best friends. What I wanted then was to share with them the preferences of my life—to let them know, just to start with, that I preferred chocolate to oatmeal cookies. "You've given me way too many oatmeal cookies," I began, "and not kept enough for yourselves."

"It's because you'll need your strength," Ruthie explained.

"For what?" I asked.

"For something really fun to do on a chilly afternoon."

"Like wrestling?"

"Like moving furniture."

"Moving furniture? Moving it to where?" I puzzled, and, disturbed, pictured our returning the furniture to shop windows.

"Well, if it's living room furniture . . . then to other parts of the living room," Ruthie explained; and when we had finished eating, she led us out of the kitchen and toward the living room.

My heart started to hammer again. I believed that in the living room I would come face to face with the family's Christmas tree. I took a deep breath; then the minute Malcolm opened the double glass doors and motioned us in, I began swinging my arms and legs casually, to show myself unflustered. At the same time I looked straight ahead to an area in front of a window and next to the piano where the tree ought to have been standing; but there was no tree. I peered left and then right and went on through to the dining room where again I encountered no tree. What disappointed me almost as much was that both rooms gave forth no glow, no warmth, no welcoming magic or shimmer—gave forth nothing but a gray dim light—as lonely as the light in my own apartment. Bewildered, I wandered back. "I thought you'd be decorated by now."

"We will be," Malcolm assured me. "Let's start with the couch." And he waved a stick-like arm with such authority that the three of us immediately surrounded the tan chesterfield couch, and huffing and puffing, dragged it to the opposite wall.

"Next, I think, the chairs," murmured Ruthie, at which Malcolm directed me to a pair of stiff green upholstered armchairs which he and I then transported from either side of the fireplace to either side of the couch. After the chairs, we traded the picture of a waterfall that hung over the mantelpiece with the picture of a ship that hung near the piano.

"Now let's stop," I suggested, since if we were not putting up Christmas decorations, what I wanted was to ask the twins if they'd ever been inside a church.

"Let's stop for ten or fifteen minutes," I urged. But Ruthie insisted that we keep on moving furniture. So what with changing the position of the coffee tables, the settee, the end tables, what with pulling the area rugs and taking up ashtrays and carrying around a small floor lamp with a wobbly white shade, it was impossible to claim their attention.

Finally we had moved everything except the piano. Taking advantage of that first free moment I blurted out, "Is your mother Christian and your father Jewish? Where do you keep all the decorations?"

But they never answered—so engrossed were they by the changes they'd wrought in the living room—and so disappointed. "It looks worse than before," Ruthie wailed. "This isn't how I wanted it to look for our celebration." And without another word she slid to the floor where she sat as if on strike—bolt upright, her thin legs stretched before her like scissors.

"I don't mind how it looks," I said, trying to comfort her. When this effort did not work, I turned to Malcolm. But Malcolm, after regarding his sister for some moments, had taken to leaning against a wall.

Then the next thing I knew we were moving back the couch, the chairs, all the tables, the ashtrays, and the lamp with the wobbly shade. "We're finished!" I exclaimed, and wanted to mark this occasion by offering the twins one of my favorite knock-knock jokes. Unluckily it turned out we weren't finished. No, next we polished the coffee table and rubbed silver cream on the tarnished ashtrays, after which Ruthie and Malcolm hurriedly led me to the front door, saying it was almost five o'clock and time for Ruthie to practice the piano.

"Come back tomorrow," Malcolm suggested.

I shook my head without hesitation.

"How about the next day?"

"I'm busy the next day, too," I said, and I walked outside and down the long path to the street. Thrusting my gloved hands deep into my coat pockets, I looked through the twilight at the cold chalk-like pallor of the sky and remembered I had meant to tell Ruthie and Malcolm that I had no brothers or sisters and that I did not remember my father. The impulse toward such confession was rare in me—so rare I wondered if I would ever want to admit those facts again. I went on walking, a peculiar ache in my side.

A week went by, during which I avoided the twins. I even considered placing my hands on my ears, as Izzy did, just so I would not hear them singing. Then on the day school let out for Christmas vacation, Ruthie, wearing a new fur hat and carrying a patent leather purse on a gold chain, cornered me outside our classroom to invite me to her house for a Christmas celebration. "Come on the twenty-third, at three o'clock. That's this coming Tuesday. We'll have such fun."

"Everything's ready," said Malcolm, suddenly appearing at Ruthie's side.

"Everything's ready?"

"Even our tree."

I didn't say yes and I didn't say no. The truth was, having decided not to visit the twins, I felt much happier. I had the sense I belonged to myself. Yet all through that weekend and all through a Monday without any school—whenever I left our apartment, Christmas was in the air; and there seemed nothing I could do to stop from imagining plum pudding, gingerbread cookies, gift wrap unfurling, trumpets sounding, reindeer riding at top speed on the snow. I bit my lip and reminded myself of Izzy, of his strong will. I reminded myself of dreidels at Chanukah, poppy-seed cakes and apples on sticks at Purim, but it did no good. Christmas bells went on ringing and gentle reindeer kept on flying until at last, on Tuesday afternoon, with the scent of snow in the wind, I climbed my outdoor steps and started the long trek past neighborhood after neighborhood, recoiling at the thought I'd once again lied to my mother.

I rang the bell. Ruthie opened the door and hung up my coat. She led me to the kitchen where Malcolm, bent over the sink, was carefully filling a wide low bucket with suds and water. I stared at the bucket, all the while backing away. "No more housework! Maybe for you, but not

for me! I'm not going to wash the walls . . . not the floors
. . . not the ceiling . . ."

Malcolm giggled. The sound, so light, was unexpected. "We're just going to wash you," he said sweetly.

"Me?" I looked down at my clothes.

"And not all of you." He pushed me gently into a chair.
"We're just going to wash your feet."

"My feet," I said, getting up from the chair, "are
clean!" The back of my ears began to burn.

Ruthie eyed my shoes and trousers suspiciously. She
addressed her brother out of the corner of her mouth.
"Malcolm, are you sure we're supposed to wash his feet?
Isn't he supposed to wash our feet? Are you sure that's in
the Christian bible? It isn't as though he's Christ, Malcolm.
He's just Leonard Plotkin."

"I don't think that matters," Malcolm assured her.
"What matters is, he's our guest and we want to show him
respect before we show him our tree."

"My feet are clean!" I insisted.

"It's the right thing to do. Even if they're clean, it's
what we're supposed to do," he went on, his manner so
reasonable, his cheeks so earnest that when he repeated,
"It's the right thing to do," he convinced his sister and
almost convinced me.

Somewhat reluctantly I sat down and let Malcolm
unlace my left shoe and pull off my left sock. I allowed
Ruthie to do the same with my right shoe and sock. Then
they placed my feet in the warm tub where Malcolm pro-

ceeded to soak and to scrub and to pat my sole and my heel, while Ruthie, kneeling, poured handfuls of water over my toes. An odd mixture of emotion flowed through me: humiliation, resentment, anger, curiosity, and at last, a soothing pleasure. I relaxed—relaxed utterly.

It was then that something extraordinary happened: I had the sense that I became Christian. It seemed to me this was what Ruthie and Malcolm wanted. I can't figure out exactly how it happened nor do I know how to describe the experience except to say it was a very agreeable one and that every doubt about my worth, and my mother's worth, vanished. As it vanished, I felt my shoulders, my chest, my hands, and my feet expand and grow valuable. "I'm ready for Christmas carols," I said. "I'm ready for your Christmas tree."

With Ruthie on one side of me and Malcolm on the other, we made our way through the double glass doors to the living room. Ruthie, breaking away, raced to the piano, while I stood at the threshold. I looked straight ahead and peered to the right and to the left, but there was no tree. I turned inquiringly to Malcolm. Pride and anticipation lent a pearl-like gleam to his face as he pointed to the lamp with the wobbly shade that stood by the piano. It was a medium-sized, frail-looking lamp on an unsteady base. A single cord of small lights and a few drooping strands of tinsel wound around the shade. Three giant candy canes, their necks hooked over the top, perched on the shade and stood stalwart and rigid, dominating the lamp. At the piano Ruthie played, "Christmas tree, oh Christmas tree, how lovely are thy branches."

I swallowed hard. I wanted to look away from the lamp—to pretend it did not exist—but I could not. Instead I went on staring at the limp tinsel and the meager lights, their paltriness seeming to stand for my loneliness, my mother's loneliness. Even if my mother's beliefs had allowed her a Christmas tree, I decided, this was the kind she would have chosen.

I shook my head bitterly. "That's not a tree," I said.

Ruthie lifted her hands from the keyboard and glared at her brother. "We should never have washed his feet."

The eagerness on Malcolm's face fell away. "We thought you'd like it."

"It's not a tree, it's a lamp."

"We can't have a pine tree," Malcolm tried to explain. "Our mom and dad won't allow it, they never had a pine tree."

Ruthie stopped glaring at her brother. "Didn't you know we're Jewish?" She turned her disapproval on me. "What do you think—that everyone's only Christian?"

"Almost everyone is," I retorted, and then I felt ashamed. I looked away from Ruthie and gazed about the room, thinking that the twins, despite all their show, lived a life not too different from mine. I kept on gazing around the room, for the first time noting the glow from the ashtrays we'd rubbed and the tables we'd polished. I found it difficult to decide exactly what to do. At last, though I kept my head turned to an opposite wall, though I almost wept before I got out the words, I said, "It's a pretty good Christmas tree. In some ways it's better than most."

Hearing this, Ruthie turned back to the piano and resumed playing. She played and sang, and Malcolm, standing next to the piano bench, sang with her. I would have liked to join them, but as always, my tongue would not allow it. The best I could manage was to hum, and that only now and again. So I hummed irregularly through "The First Noel" and "Little Town of Bethlehem" and "It Came upon a Midnight Clear." After that we removed the candy canes from the lampshade and ate them. We ate oatmeal cookies and drank cider, and I told my two favorite knock-knock jokes. Just as it was getting dark Ruthie and Malcolm led me to the door; they called out as I was setting forth, "Merry Christmas, Leonard, Merry Christmas."

Rather dazed I walked down the long path. "Merry Christmas, Leonard," echoed in my ears. It was exactly what I'd always wanted someone to say to me. I ran my tongue over my lips, tasted the sharp mint of candy cane, and gazed up and down the deserted street. For a moment I paused. And then I opened my mouth, and because I knew that only the sky could hear me, I loudly sang, I trilled, I roared, "God rest ye, Merry Gentlemen."

FOR THE GLORY

On the morning of her fiftieth wedding anniversary, Rosalie Peltz woke up, her ears ringing with the refrain of a poem she had heard on her favorite public-supported radio station: "The boredom, and the horror, and the glory." The words played over and over, as they had for the past three days. Peering at her husband, who was still asleep by her side, she exclaimed in a louder voice than she'd intended, "Fifty years!" and got out of bed and packed a suitcase. "I can't stay a minute longer," she said as, within minutes, she chose a handful of underwear and blouses, dismissed her bracelets as part of a more frivolous time, and gathered up a toothbrush, cold cream, her favorite shampoo.

When she had finished packing, she glanced at her watch and determined she had time to clean the house and fix breakfast for Norman. After all, she bore her husband no grudge: it was not his fault she needed to leave the marriage behind. Since this was the case, she stowed her nylon suitcase behind the raincoats in the front hall closet and removed the vacuum from the back hall closet. She plunged the vacuum over the blue pile carpet, and her ears buzzed "The horror, and the boredom, and the glory." But this time they buzzed exultantly—the words of the poem seeming to her to describe the entire spectrum of human experience. Trying them out aloud, she continued with her work—scrubbing the mantelpiece, watering the plants, and for a grand final gesture polishing the eleven-piece silver coffee and tea service which had been a wedding present from Norman's aunts and uncles.

"Norman, breakfast in ten minutes!" she shouted in the direction of their bedroom, and went into the kitchen where she considered phoning Maida Taranian with the news that she was leaving. Maida Taranian was her good friend. All the same she hesitated, speculating that from Maida's end of the phone she would first hear the annoying silence of astonishment, and then the silence of outrage—no doubt directed at Norman—and at last, for Maida was a supportive friend, a measured summing up, such as, "Well, you've given the marriage a fair chance, Rosalie. And if it hasn't worked, it hasn't worked." How could she convince Maida that the marriage, with four children, trips to Carmel in July, and Sunday night dinners at House of Pancakes, had worked very well but was now behind her? She decided not to phone her friend. "Norman!" she shouted again. "Breakfast!"

Almost instantly, Norman entered the kitchen, still in his slippers but otherwise fully dressed in his gray pin-striped suit, his diagonally striped tie, and his light-weight cotton shirt. As he headed toward her and the table, she admired his clothes. She even admired his slippers, but she discerned in him no trace of interest in the glory. Instead she took in his taut face lined with hard thoughts about his business and his chin as long as a medium-sized beard. She went on studying him both fondly and detachedly. He was certainly short, she noted, and judged it unfortunate that in fifty years of marriage he had not grown a single inch. Then unexpectedly his eyes caught her eyes and lit up, and for a moment she feared he had remembered their anniversary—that he had plans to hand her a new wristwatch or a tall calla lily plant, and that these gifts would make it awkward or difficult for her to leave. Instead he asked, turning to the front door, "Did the newspaper boy remember to deliver the paper?"

"He threw it right to the door," Rosalie hurried to assure him, while just under her breath she recited, "The boredom, and the horror, and the glory," and took these words with her to the breakfast table.

Seated next to her husband, Rosalie analyzed that the boredom lay partly in Norman and partly in the bowl of cereal, the dish of prunes, the salt and pepper shakers, the sugar and the creamer. It covered the pebbly ivory ceiling and lay all over the maroon figured floor tile, and it was so powerful and so intense that all by itself it bridged straight into the next part of the poem and became the horror of how little she'd done with her life. How ordinary her efforts had been, how puny! How terrifying to sum them up! For almost half a century, she had done little more than take care of her family and hold down a three-quarters time job as a handbag buyer for the Emporium while others, all over America, England, Europe, and Africa, in small towns and large towns, were winning the Nobel Prize.

And yet, she reasoned, she had no cause for alarm. Her time and the glory were still to come. Deep within her, a notable talent reposed. All she needed was to pinpoint what it was. And giving her husband a final glance of farewell, she made these last observations: that the term of their relationship had been completed; that they had had quite enough of one another; that there was no way for him to recognize her hidden potential; and that nevertheless, particularly after having just finished breakfast, each one of them was satisfied, each one replete.

It was therefore without a qualm that as soon as her husband had left for work, Rosalie took out the box of ivory stationery which she'd purchased half-price. "My dearest Norman," she penned, her writing large and very legible, "Happy fiftieth anniversary! If you look under the sheet music in the piano bench, you will find a present which I sincerely hope you will like. Save the expensive wrapping for another use. Secondly," she paused to gather her thoughts and then went on without stopping, "you have been a good husband, a good father, and I have no complaints. But it is time for me to lead my own life. I have a responsibility that goes beyond this house and our little neighborhood and I can no longer ignore it. I cannot stay here another minute. Life has been kind to me and I need to express my humble appreciation in a way that is large enough to matter. I am therefore going to take up residence in Boston. I will send you my address when I've settled in a permanent apartment and you can write me there if you like."

Rosalie read the note twice, admired its style, got up, read the note again, and wandered to the mirror above the telephone table. Before she looked at herself, she bent over and touched her toes. She was seventy-one years old; yet she felt thirty-five. The miracle was, nothing hurt her. Not a single limb hurt her. She knocked on the wood on the underside of the telephone table and confronted the glass. Speculating on how old she appeared, she first decided on fifty-six and revised that to fifty-four and with a certain amount of concentration stepped forward and squinted her way to fifty-one. But then she remembered that Gregory, her oldest child, was about to turn forty-nine, and so out of a sense of decorum she turned from the mirror and assigned herself age fifty-nine.

It occurred to her, then, that she ought to write a letter explaining her departure to each of her children—to Gregory who lived with his wife and family in Arkansas, to Betty and Imogene, each twice unhappily divorced—Betty in Chicago, Imogene in Miami—and to Amy, the youngest, who had just gone to Alaska. At the thought of her children, she wanted to hold all four in her arms and cook them dinner. But she did not want to write them. They would not like to know she was leaving their father. They would even be angry to discover she'd chosen Boston simply because she'd never been there. Gregory's allergies would no doubt start up; Betty would likely knock at the door of some overpriced therapist; Imogene would waste her money talking long-distance to Betty; and Amy would come back from Alaska before finding a boyfriend. Rosalie stopped. She reminded herself that the time to worry about her children was over—had long been over. Now she had to be willing to take responsibility only for herself.

Ah the glory, she thought, and locked the back door and the front and set off, acknowledging the front walk of each neighbor, all the while carrying her suitcase past the pink, yellow, nude green, and shaved puce stucco houses on her treeless street. On she went through another barren, rainbow street before turning at the corner to walk alongside a savings and loan bank, a storefront Kung-fu salon, a vegetarian Chinese restaurant, and into her neighborhood travel agency. Here a clerk with a wide smile and a dusting of fair hair on his scalp informed her that no tourist class seat to Boston was available that day, but that because of a special fare that had just appeared on the computer, he would be able to secure a very good and a very inexpensive flight for her the following afternoon.

"Not today?" she objected, pointing to her suitcase and tempted to explain she was about to embark on a life in which she meant to contribute something significant to the world. "I had planned on going today. I still plan on going today." But then she registered his pride in the special fare and took time out to inquire what it was. The figure he quoted was a good deal lower than she'd expected. She drew in her breath and observed he seemed a particularly helpful and pleasant young man.

"Dinner on board and a movie," he encouraged.

"Well, I suppose . . ." she debated, "I suppose one more day doesn't matter." After another moment she presented him with her credit card.

Yet once she was out the door, the nonrefundable ticket in her purse, it struck her that one day mattered a lot. One day stole twenty-four hours from the glory! She trod up the street and into the grocery store where she stood in front of the lettuce and scolded herself for failure to resist a bargain. Then she had an idea, quit the grocery, and strode to the bus stop on the corner, thinking she would spend the day trying out her new life right here in San Francisco; she would spend the night conveniently in a hotel by the airport; she would make up for the cost by occupying the least expensive room.

Just then, from across the street, Rosalie caught sight of a woman who appeared a good deal older than herself—perhaps in her late seventies or even eighty. Wiry, sinewy, the thin line of her mouth set in a small, aware, tough face the brown color of a nut, she sprinted off the #41 bus, pirouetted up the street, and danced onto the platform of an oncoming bus with an élan that Rosalie recognized as akin to her own. Smiling with approval, Rosalie boarded the #41 bus in the opposite direction—the direction of downtown—and soon gave up her seat to a young man who looked very tired.

From the #41 bus she transferred to the #56 and then to the #34, gliding onto its steps with the almost giddy sense that wherever she went she had buses at her fingertips. She had never learned to drive but had known from an early age that she had been born with an instinct for public transportation. In her youth, during visits to cousins and to aunts, she had on intuition alone navigated from one end to the other of Buffalo, Chicago, Milwaukee, St. Louis, and Minneapolis. On her honeymoon—with Norman sound asleep in the morning—she had crisscrossed Seattle and Portland. On hers and Norman's fortieth anniversary, she had led Norman from the Victoria and Albert to the British Museum, to the Tate Museum, to Greenwich Observatory, to Hampstead Heath, to Crystal Palace—had led him on and off buses and into the underground with as much assurance and ease as if she'd previously—as if she'd often—visited London. Yes, her intuition about public transport was one of her favorite talents and she meant to put it to use one day, but it was only a means to her goal and would not do for her primary work. For that she needed something powerful enough to buoy up all existence: she needed music.

"Ah, 'The boredom, and the horror, and the glory,'" sang Rosalie, and thought it unfortunate she had quit her piano lessons upon entering the fifth grade and had not started studying or practicing again until a few years back. Luckily, the sensation of talent—as palpable as the taste of honey or the smell of lilacs—had never abandoned her. She had experienced it whether in the springtime or the winter, the summer or the fall. And primarily because of such faithfulness, she got off the #34 bus at the airport terminal on O'Farrell Street, checked her suitcase in a locker, and marched full of hope to Modesto Pellerini's, the vast music store just off Union Square.

Inside, thirty-two pianos greeted her, their various sizes and shapes shining darkly under the fluorescent lights. Bedazzled, Rosalie stood still. Then, excitedly, she tiptoed about, peering at the label above the keyboards and at last seating herself at a Baldwin upright. With a forthright pounce of her hands she commenced playing the first bars of Beethoven's "Appassionata." She played a few more bars, thinking she sounded pretty good and hoping her opinion was shared by the store's customers who trod the central aisle to and from the elevators. Two salesmen wearing boutonnieres wandered the floor. She glanced at them, trying to gauge their reaction. Why had they not approached to offer their assistance? She glanced at them again. But they had disappeared. Her performance was not perfect yet, she admitted, but it wasn't bad and it would surely soon be better. Unable to advance the "Appassionata" any further, she commenced it again, but this time something in the tone of the piano sounded a little off. Worried now, she got up and moved next door to a Yamaha grand. The tone of the Yamaha was much richer than the Baldwin's and the keyboard's action a good deal easier. Encouraged by this improvement, she pressed her foot to the pedal and played as much as she knew of a Chopin nocturne. She played as much as she knew of a Mozart sonata, the first bars of a Bach two-part invention, the first bars of a waltz by Ravel, and presently it seemed to her that if she purchased a Yamaha in Boston, laid in a large supply of sheet music, located a good light and a comfortable piano bench and practiced ten to twelve hours every day, people who heard her might eventually say, "Hark! Listen! Why was I so sad?"

With a murmur of appreciation, Rosalie brought her repertoire to a close. She was about to try out a third piano, simply for the experience and just to make sure, when through the door appeared a tall, slender woman in her thirties, her dark hair drawn back from her pale, alabaster, beautiful face. Attired in a linen suit, beige stockings, and dainty shoes, she threaded her way among the pianos, stopping at a keyboard here and there as if she, too, were choosing an instrument. She paused before a Steinway grand, and still standing up, ran through a few scales. Then she sat down, gracefully lifted her neck, stretched out her long white delicate hands, and began playing Scarlatti. Sounds at once exquisite and commanding issued from her fingers. Transfixed, Rosalie remained seated at the Yamaha from where she soon observed that all those entering or about to leave the store had stopped to listen, a look of wonder on their faces. Even the pair of salesmen who had taken themselves off during Rosalie's performance were now drawing near. Rosalie shut her eyes and opened her soul to this unexpected and free concert. All the same, as she went on listening, an odd sensation intruded into her pleasure—a baffled annoyance, a reluctant irritability which she at last traced to the fact it was this woman, not herself, who played so magnificently and whose ability—she now clearly realized—she could never attain.

"Well, that's all right," Rosalie said to herself, "there are other things I can do." And when the beautiful woman had risen up from the piano, Rosalie—ignoring the ache in her heart—got up, too, left Modesto Pellerini's, bought a sandwich at a lunch counter, and took the sandwich up the street to the park in Union Square.

Here, choosing an empty bench, she ate her lunch and tried to recover from the dissolution of her musical career. Presently she began to take an interest in the activity around her. Throngs of people—tourists, lawyers, priests, shoppers, researchers, bikers, mothers with their children—traveled the paths. A pair of pretty girls, each with a buff-colored mane of hair, trotted along, their heads bobbing like a pair of pretty horses. An old man with a long, dignified face, his polka dot tie tight to his collar, listened to the ball game, a transistor radio in his hand. In front of the monument to Commodore Dewey, two-year-old twins, ferocious as dogs, bawled in their strollers, while a short distance away a mime in white face stood comically on one knee, offering a rose. Rosalie laughed and looked around for someone to laugh with her. Her gaze took in the buildings and the billboards; it took in men and women young, middle-aged, and old; it took in Asians, blacks, Hispanics, Caucasians. It struck her then that this small, teeming park in the middle of the downtown was as large, as various, and as rich as a canvas by Goya or Delacroix. And then she knew what she was meant to do: she was meant to paint it.

Fortunately, thought Rosalie, she was no stranger to art. While her children were growing up, she had taken a number of painting and drawing lessons and had produced three satisfying charcoal drawings of a watermelon: a whole melon, half a melon, and a quarter melon. One of these— the quarter melon—had gone on display at a fund-raiser for the nursery school. That same year she had been elected president of her local artist's co-op. The year after that, on Amy's fifth birthday, she had sketched all four of her children and all five of Norman's brother's children, and had taken a bus ride and sketched part of the sea. Given this history, it now made sense to her that if she went from San Francisco to Boston and rented a studio with good space and proper light and bought the correct easel and confronted her canvas first thing every morning, those who gazed at her work might find in its bloom an end to despair.

Shutting her eyes, Rosalie let the voluptuousness of this plan merge with the warmth of the sun. When she opened her eyes she saw that a woman encased in rags, with a bandaged leg and a swollen purple and red face, had settled on the bench by her side. Four bulging supermarket bags rested at the woman's feet. Rosalie wished—wished particularly because the day was so beautiful—that the woman had sat down somewhere else. Unwilling to hurt the woman's feelings by getting up and moving away, she decided to wait a minute or two simply to appear companionable. While she waited, a foul smell of unwashed clothes and body blew towards her—grew stronger, grew more and more intimate. Bravely she held her breath and slid stealthily to the end of the bench, at which moment a second woman settled into the space Rosalie had cleared—this person accompanied by a rusted shopping cart. With dismay Rosalie glanced at the supermarket bags and at the shopping cart through whose cage protruded the unraveled hem of a blanket and the toe of an old shoe. Thinking it was time to detach herself, she stood up, smoothed down her skirt, and took a few steps, then thought better of it, turned back, and handed each of her neighbors a five dollar bill. As they accepted the bills, she began to feel ashamed. Why did she believe she was any different from these neighbors? After all, she too no longer had a home. She too carried her belongings in a portable container. She too might soon find she had no place to lay her head. With a sudden loss of strength, she sat back down on her corner of the bench.

One by one Rosalie's neighbors abandoned the bench. She alone remained seated. "On to Boston!" she urged herself. But her thighs and her shoulders weighed her down, and she asked herself, what made her think that if she went to Boston she would not paint the sky wrong? Exactly what persuaded her she could become a fine dancer, a great therapist, a softball coach, a writer, an inventor? What certainty did she have that, at seventy-one years of age, she could accomplish something of note for humankind?

Unhappily her eye roamed about, noting that at either end of the park and in front of the monument to Commodore Dewey, dozens of people milled aimlessly. Even the mime seemed to be getting nowhere: he was still trying to give away his rose. He chased after a red-headed young woman who fled his advances, then hurled himself before a man with a briefcase hurrying by, and then, catching sight of Rosalie watching him, his head shot forward and he pranced toward her. With a flourish and a low bow he offered her his rose.

Why had he chosen her? Rosalie asked herself as the mime raced away. She brought the flower to her nose. Had some special quality she possessed attracted him? What promise had piqued his interest? Rosalie laughed at the foolishness of these notions; yet she got up and started for the airport terminal.

Every few yards she then encountered men or women slouched in doorways or propped against buildings. They drooped over the sidewalks or rummaged in garbage containers. Treading past them gingerly, her rose in one hand, she soon quickened her steps, seized once more with the fear she was about to become homeless. At last she reached the terminal where she retrieved her suitcase and thought of Norman, of their blue pile carpet and four walls. She even thought of her friend Maida Tartarian. Then all at once it struck her that she was too old to go off searching for honor and prizes; she was too old and she had never exhibited a relevant talent.

Rosalie lay her rose on a counter next to a pile of bus schedules. Wandering out into O'Farrell Street she peered into the traffic and headed for the bus that would start her toward home. From the #34 bus she transferred to the #56 and from the #56 to the #41. She got off the bus, walked up one street and up the next street and presently stood in front of her gate. She admired her house—the pale pink of the stucco, the deeper pink of the wood trim, the wrought iron railings in front of the windows. It was a comfortable house, she thought, and the life she'd lived in it had often given her pleasure.

At this the refrain of the poem came back to her: "the horror, and the boredom, and the glory." Along with the refrain there then sprang into her mind an image of the wiry woman, a good deal older than herself, whom she had glimpsed earlier in the day soaring and vaulting between buses, her ancient mouth obstinate, her motion free of the ground. She had recognized their kinship from the first—had recognized that what they shared was a love for public transportation.

The refrain played over and over—each time more insistent, louder and louder: "the horror, and the boredom, and the glory." She tried to escape, but the words first hammered at her and then began a steady tolling until at last she understood that though she was no candidate for the Pulitzer or the Nobel Prize, there was something else she needed to achieve. Reaching down, she took hold of her suitcase. Then lifting one foot after the other, she set forth for Boston where she might find the way to express her still undimmed gratitude toward life.